Sundown, Inc: She Who Dares

"I can't say how much I loved Sundown Inc.: She Who Dares. There are only a handful of short stories that have had characters that I connected to so quickly that I felt immediately teary-eyed with emotion over their pain and successes…"
-- *Dani Jacquel, Just Erotic Romance Reviews*

Sundown, Inc: Blue Moon

"If you are a werewolf romance lover like myself, you can't go wrong with Blue Moon. It's a steamy addition to anyone's library!"
-- *Shelley, Fallen Angel Reviews*

Sundown, Inc: What Wizards Want

"Con's internal dialogue was entertaining, swerving from sexually distracted, to wry, to sweet in the blink of an eye. Lily is strong, confident, sassy, and bold. Their chemistry is steamy."
-- *Gretchen, Fallen Angel Reviews*

Sundown, Inc: Baby Sham Faery Love

"Readers will find themselves caught up in the hilarity of the situation. As the story progresses, one is drawn in even more deeply with some steamy sex scenes and some suspense in the form of a murder plot. So what are you waiting for?"
-- *Athena, Realms of Love*

www.ChangelingPress.com

Sundown, Inc.

Cat Marsters

Publisher:
Changeling Press LLC
PO Box 1046
Martinsburg WV 25402-1046
www.ChangelingPress.com

Printed in the U.S.A.
Lightning Source, Inc.
1246 Heil Quaker Blvd
La Vergne TN 37086
www.lightningsource.com

Anthology Editor: Sheri Ross Fogarty
Cover Artist: Sahara Kelly
Cover Layout: Bryan Keller

The individual stories in this anthology have been previously
released in E-Book format.

This book contains sexually explicit scenes and adult language
which some may find offensive and which is not appropriate for a
young audience. Changeling Press books are for sale to adults,
only, as defined by the laws of the country in which you made
your purchase.

Sundown, Inc.: She Who Dares

Cat Marsters

Chapter One

There are nights when I seriously wish I'd never risen from the grave.

I mean, you roll out of bed (because seriously, who sleeps in a coffin these days?), go and take a shower, and five minutes later someone crashes through the window with a stake, screaming death at you.

Whatever. I'd prefer to do my slaying wearing a little more, but a girl's gotta protect herself even when she's naked.

Mostly I was annoyed that he'd broken into my house. He was a teenybopper with a stake and a nervous expression. I gave him an ultimatum: either run away and never came back, or I crush your throat.

He ran.

It's not that I don't like humans. I do. Sometimes I can even eat a whole one.

Joke.

Some of my best friends are human. I've had human lovers, plenty of them. Although the thing with human lovers is they tend to be vampire groupies. They're in it for the thrill of the bite. It's all rather shallow.

I locked my door and added "Update alarm system" to my mental to-do list. Honestly, you spend fucking millions on a system and it still lets humans in. I wonder if the Queen has this problem.

I showered and dressed. Leather, 'cos I was feeling kickass. Yeah, it's a cliché, but for good reason. Strutting around in heels and leather makes a girl feel damn sexy. And when your face and body have been ruined for twenty-three centuries, sexy is hard to come by.

A couple of holsters and I was good to go. The British police frown on civilians carrying weapons, but I learned how to mind-bend policemen years ago. And weapons are *de rigueur* in my kind of job. Yeah, superhuman speed, strength, stamina -- plus a vicious set of fangs -- make mincemeat of humans. But I don't hunt humans.

I hunt scarier things than that.

I double-checked my alarm as I left, and went out to play.

Chapter Two

London is a great place to be a vampire. Bram Stoker actually did us a favor, you know: now everyone's quite sure vampires only live in spooky old castles and bathe in the blood of the innocent. I've lived in cities all my life, I don't give a flying fuck whose blood I drink, and I sure as hell don't bathe in it. In the interests of staying below the radar I just take blood bank stock. They chuck it out after a couple of months, but it still tastes good to me.

There are vamps who drink animal blood. But blood makes me horny, and I've never been into bestiality.

I dropped into Willie's Bar on my way to the office. It's low, dark, and a bit of a dive to be honest, but he mixes a mean Cosmo and rarely comments if I have blood on my clothes. Willie is a short, balding guy who always has sweat patches under his arms. He waved when he saw me come in.

"Hey, Mas," he said as I fought through the crowds to the bar. He was already pouring Citron vodka into the shaker. "How's it going?"

"I've been awake an hour and already someone's tried to kill me."

"Could be worse."

"How?"

"They could have succeeded."

I snorted as he handed over my drink, and turned to survey the bar as I sipped it. Mmm, lovely. "Cheers, Willie. Put it on my tab."

"You want me to keep my ears open for anything?"

"Sure. If anyone comes in asking after me…"

"Funny you should say that," he said.

"What?"

He nodded over to the far side of the bar. It was dark over there. Makeout corner. But you don't lose out on eternal sunshine without getting a few benefits. My night vision was superb, and I noticed one man leaning against the railing of the mezzanine, a woman draped across his chest. He had his back to me, but that just made the view better. Mmmm. Yummy Butt.

Then he turned, and I lost my breath.

He wore dark shades even indoors, and his hair was blond. Long, although it was an expensive cut. He had soft, full, sensual lips and a rather adorable dimple in his chin, but the rest of his face was hard, square, firm. His clothes were dark, leather jeans and a tight T-shirt. Biker boots.

He was what my friend Magda would have called a fucking horny bloke.

Certainly his companion seemed to think so. She was rubbing his chest and smooching his neck, and he was paying her the sort of vague attention one might give a pet when there's a good film on TV.

His gaze rested on me. I didn't need to see his eyes to feel it. I felt it like a warm beam.

"See you've found him, then." Willie's voice sounded far away, and I nodded vaguely. My feet were already taking me toward Mr. Yummy Butt.

The bar was full of people and they were all human. I could feel them, smell them. Their sweat and their blood and their sex. At least two people had been having sex in here. A lot more were thinking hard about it. Their lust filled the air like heavy perfume.

But there was someone here who wasn't human. The sharp scent of another vampire penetrated the fog, and it didn't distract me from the path I was already on.

Mr. Yummy Butt was a vampire.

He pushed his girlie friend away from him as I got near. He must have mind-bent her because she didn't protest, and hell -- if you lost that body, you would protest.

"Masika."

A shudder ran through me at the sound of my name. No; at the sound of his voice saying my name. Great Bast, a woman could orgasm from that kind of sound. His voice was so deep, rough and smooth at the same time, like sand on silk. I felt my nipples rise and my pussy dampen.

"And you are?"

He gave me a lethal smile. "Sekani."

He Who Laughs. That made my eyebrows rise -- I didn't hear my own language often these days. "You're not Egyptian."

"Greek."

"Ah." I tried to keep the sneer from my face. The greatest civilisation in the world -- fuck that, the only civilisation in the world -- and they rode in and stole it from us. Thank you very much, Alexander the Not-So-Great.

His hand reached out, traced the scars on my arm. I didn't flinch; I've had plenty of practice. The skin was sensitive, and the brush of his fingertips was a caress.

"Holy water?"

"Good guess."

"Lucky it didn't blind you."

"That's one way of looking at it." Luck wasn't the first word that came to mind when I thought about it.

"How long ago?"

"That's a very personal question."

He grinned, and it was dazzling. Golden flecks of light seemed to dance around him. I could see where he'd got his name.

"You're Egyptian."

"Prize for the Greek."

"It's your skin." He slid the backs of his fingers up my throat, and I couldn't repress a small shudder. "Like polished bronze. I haven't seen skin like that in two thousand years."

"Ran away back to Greece?"

He ignored that. "Those cheekbones are royal."

I nodded, a touch of pride straightening my back. "My family was high-born."

"Hmm." That voice of his, oh, his voice. It was an audible caress, like dark chocolate, like silk, like hot, deep, breathtaking sex. His voice promised filthy things, and my body wanted very much to take him up on them.

I debated whether or not I agreed with said body. I mean, I'd gotten all fired up this evening with the little slayer-boy. Fighting always made me either hungry or horny, and since I'd downed a bag of blood and a plate of cold pizza, I figured I'd be set for the night.

But I hadn't figured on Mr. Yummy Butt.

His fingertips had arrived at my cheek now. The edge of the scar reached there, a smear of puckered, pink, acid-melted skin. The holy water had missed my eye by a fraction. Sometimes it itched. Sometimes it stung. All of the time it reminded me of what I was.

I was an undead nightmare, a walking corpse, and I'd never asked for it.

My eyes met his. I couldn't call him Sekani. That wasn't his real name, I was sure of it. I could smell a lie from fifty feet. But it seemed reasonably appropriate now. Close enough.

Close enough.

I wasn't close enough.

But I'd hardly moved an inch closer when his fingers tensed. His whole body just went still, like a big cat sensing prey.

"What?" I breathed.

"Woman's just walked in with a stake -- don't look -- under her coat."

"If it's under --"

"She held the door open, her coat gaped. Shit."

"I can handle her."

"You want to cause a scene in here?"

"If the alternative is getting that stake between the shoulder blades, then yes."

His hand slid down my back to rest in just that place. His fingers touched the tattoo I had there, exposed completely by the low back of my halter-top. It was a cat's head, honoring Bast, the goddess I'd most often prayed to as a human. She was a goddess of the sun, and maybe in a small part of me, I hoped she'd see my tribute to her and let me see the sun again.

So far, she didn't seem to be interested.

Mr. Yummy Butt pulled me closer to him and I inhaled his hot, clean scent. He'd fed recently, or he wouldn't be so warm. He felt almost human.

I tried to resist the urge to lay my head against his lovely hard chest and snuggle. You've no idea how difficult it was.

"What's she doing?" I asked.

He caressed my back and side, making me shiver. "Looking around. Don't turn your head."

"I can't see her."

"It's okay. I can." His fingers dipped under the edge of my leather top. Half a centimeter more and he'd be touching my breast.

I ought to have minded, but -- well. You should see this guy. Especially from behind.

"Put your head on my chest," he said.

"What?" My voice sounded unflatteringly high.

"Put your head on my chest. Make her think we're lovers."

"For what possible purpose?"

"She might not notice us."

"Oh, that's such a load of --"

His hand closed around my breast, and the words got stuck in my throat.

"She's looking at us," he murmured urgently. "Kiss me."

"Wh-mmph!"

I didn't get chance to say any more because his mouth suddenly locked with mine, his lips hot and clever and every bit as soft as they'd looked the first time I set eyes on them. His tongue flickered over my teeth and I felt my fangs flex. Whoa. Long time since I'd kissed anyone who could make my teeth come out like that. The noise of the bar faded and my arms slid around his hard, warm body, feeling rather wonderful muscles flexing under his shirt.

Through the press of leather, I felt something stirring in his groin. And it was a pretty impressive something, too.

My eyes flickered closed, open, and I was about to let my lids sink downwards for a while longer when I saw a flash of movement reflected in his dark shades. The woman was behind us, stake raised, and before I'd even had time to think I'd whirled on her, arm raised to knock the stake away.

I guess I was a little overenthusiastic. My head was still buzzing from that kiss, and as I flew around I, er, accidentally hit the wrong person.

Mr. Yummy Butt's girlfriend from earlier in the evening.

I heard her arm snap.

Instantly she started screaming, her arm hanging loose, and I winced. More at the noise than the damage I'd done to her. The woman with the stake, a tall brunette, vanished into the crowds, and I hesitated for just a second.

"Masika!" came Willie's voice. "Stop beating up my patrons!"

Crap. I glanced at the girl, then at the man who'd distracted me into hurting her, and figured she was his responsibility. I shoved through the crowd of gawkers who'd all turned toward us, and tried to get a sense lock on the brunette.

She was up ahead, outside, on her way down the street.

I hurtled after her, and vaguely became aware of someone following me. A certain someone in black leather and shades -- shades in the middle of the night, for Bast's sake -- erupted from the bar and chased alongside me.

"Shouldn't you be looking after your girlfriend?" I snapped.

"Willie's got her. Need to catch that --" His pretty head swung north. "She's up here."

He didn't need to tell me. I was already turning up the little alley, the kind that London is full of, and ducking under the low beams of the building above. Stupid Londoners. I was here when these buildings were built, and people weren't any shorter.

She was in the courtyard beyond, just about to turn a corner and disappear again. I sprinted faster, grabbed a knife as I ran, and spun it toward her.

She saw it, or heard it -- either way she ducked, went into a roll, and came up facing us. I was running too fast, had too much momentum going to stop, and I hit her with a force that toppled us both.

I had a second knife in my hand. She had a stake.

I slashed at her, bringing blood to her cheek. She stabbed at me, but she missed. Ripped my leather, though.

"Bitch!" I cried, and flung her to her back.

The stake pierced the leather a second time, but this time it was right against my heart.

I stopped dead with about half a centimeter between me and eternal death. For a long second my eyes met hers. My heart was pumping, her stake was between my breasts, her blood welled hot and sweet on her face. I could have licked it, could have drunk it, could have drained her dry and she'd never be able to hurt me.

Then something grabbed me by the shoulders and yanked me upright, and the brunette flipped to her feet.

She hissed at me like a cat, twirled the stake in her hands, and vanished into the darkness.

I stood there panting, the smell of her blood still sharp and sweet in my nostrils, and quickly became aware that there was a hot, hard male body pressed against my back. A very hard male body.

"Could have had her," I said, breathing hard.

I heard him swallow. "She nearly had you."

"I've come closer than that." All this tension. I was pumped full of adrenaline. I'd been ready for a fight, a kill, some blood -- and now I was standing here in a pretty little private courtyard with moonlight dappling the cobbles, and a really hot, hard, sexy man behind me. My fangs were out. I needed release.

I swung around and felt the press of his body against my breasts.

"You know, fighting always does two things to me," I said, worming my arms around his neck.

"Makes me hungry," he murmured, his hand sliding over my bare back again, making me shiver.

"Me too." I nipped at his throat, tasted the salt on his skin. His pulse thudded in his throat.

"And horny."

I licked his neck, pressed my body against his. "Me too."

His other hand slid down to mold the leather against my buttocks. The movement brought me closer to him, ground me against the hard bulge in his own leathers.

"My place isn't far from here," I breathed.

"Mine is closer."

My eyes met his, and then in a heartbeat we were falling against each other, mouths meeting in another hot, dark kiss, fangs scraping, tongues plunging.

"How far?" I breathed hard.

"Too far," he said, and then we were falling, stumbling, and it was only by chance we hit the nearest wall. The cold stone against my back made me hiss; the heat burning through the leather to my breasts made me moan.

"Your name," I said against his mouth as we fell. "I still need to hear it."

His hands tugged at the buckles holding my top in place. "You have heard it."

"Your real name."

He gave me a brief grin as the leather fell from my skin, and my breasts filled his hands. Heat and promise spread through me with each movement of his long fingers against my flesh. In the cool darkness of this deserted square, this stranger held my breasts in his hands and stroked them until I lost my breath.

"My friends call me Dare."

"And what do I call you?"

He grinned. "Call me a wanton sex god, anything you like. Just get those leathers off."

I swung him against the railing of a townhouse stoop and licked into his mouth, sliding one leg around his waist, feeling the heat of him burn me through my clothes.

I drew back for breath -- yes, I breathe, get used to it -- looking down at the sprawl of muscle and grace between my thighs. Hmm. He was lacking a little something.

Nudity. That was it.

His T-shirt came off in pieces. I hardly noticed it. I was working on the fly of his leathers when he bent me back and sucked my nipple into his mouth. That gave me pause while I reeled my mind back in, and then Dare had me back against the wall, covering me entirely with his big body, his bare chest rubbing me in delightful places as he kissed me again, his fangs pressing mine, his tongue plunging into my mouth in ferocious mimicry of what I really wanted.

I reached for his fly again but didn't get that far. He pressed my hands above my head and put his mouth to my breast again and I decided I wasn't so bothered about his cock if this was what he really wanted to do. Fine by me. I could let him suckle me for hours.

He held my wrists with one hand and slid the other down my body, flicking open my pants with annoying ease. I was naked beneath them and he groaned softly as his fingers found my bare skin.

I'd shaved my pussy as an Egyptian concubine. It never grew back. Hell, it saves on waxing.

I shivered as his fingertips found my labia and stroked gently, but I didn't want gentle. I wanted hot and hard and endless, and I wanted it now. I thrust my hips against him, and his finger slipped inside my folds, nudged my clit. A flood of wetness spread over both of us as he stroked me.

"Harder," I whispered, and he slipped a finger inside me as his thumb stroked my clit. I stifled a gasp, then thought *what the hell*, and moaned.

"You like that?" Dare asked around my nipple.

"Yes."

"Want another finger?"

"Yes."

He obliged -- good boy -- by slipping another finger inside my slippery cunt and rubbing me from the inside as well as out. My breath quickened. I looked down at the blond head on my chest, my nipple vanishing between succulent wet lips, and felt a tremor run through my pussy.

"That's it," Dare murmured, licking my nipple with long, hot strokes. He added a third finger to my cunt without even asking, and I moaned. "Gods, you feel good."

I was beyond words now. I made a sort of affirmative grunt and Dare gave a soft chuckle as he swapped one nipple for the other. The cool night air whispered against my wet, bare breast, making me shudder delightfully. Dare closed his hot dark mouth over my tight, aching flesh and drew a cry from me.

"More!"

"As my lady commands."

His fingers curved inside me, hitting a sweet spot, thrusting faster. I spread my legs wide and thrust back against him, against his hand which was soaked with my juices, and bucked against his fingers which still held my wrists above my head.

"You taste so good," he murmured. "I can't wait to be inside you."

"Then don't," I panted.

Another soft chuckle. It vibrated through my breast, making me shiver and moan against the wall.

"I want to see you come first," he said, his eyes meeting mine although his mouth never left my breast. "I want to feel it. Want to feel your cunt tightening around my hand. I want to taste it, Masika. When I'm done like this I'm going to lick your pussy until you scream."

I was nearly there. Ten seconds more and I'd be screaming as much as he wanted.

"And then I'm going to fuck you. Over and over. Your pussy is so tight, it's going to be so good…"

"Going to be?" I choked, and then came so hard I heard bells. And a delicious vibration at my waist. Hey, he was good.

No, wait. That was my phone.

Dare raised his head, his lips red and wet, and looked at me with unfocused eyes as the tune rattled on.

"Buffy the Vampire Slayer?"

I licked my lips and pulled my phone from its holster on my belt. I didn't answer him. My brain wasn't working well enough to defend my choice of ring tones. Instead I flipped open the phone and mumbled, "Yeah?"

"Mas. Where the fuck are you?"

Coming my brains out in Westminster. I swallowed and tried to remember why the voice on the other end of the phone sounded so familiar. Oh yeah. He was my boss.

"I -- Johann. Johann?"

"Yes. It's me. As you well know because my name appears on your phone screen when I call you."

"Oh. Yeah. Miracles of technology, eh?"

Johann made a growling noise. He's human -- well, at least officially he is. Magda and I have a bet going that he's really the spawn of Satan. He's our boss and the proprietor of Sundown, Inc., a detective firm that only operates within the law about ten percent of the time. In our defense, though, that's because ninety percent of our cases exist outside of what officially exists. Hard to police vampires and dark magi when you don't believe in them. We're known throughout the country -- and beyond too, we've had calls from Europe and America -- as the firm of choice when dealing with the paranormal.

I've been with Sundown since the start. Two hundred years ago. Johann is just the latest in charge, although I kinda like him.

"You were supposed to be in here half an hour ago."

"Was I?" I looked at my watch. It was getting pretty late for office work, and I felt a pang of guilt for keeping the human team waiting. Well, not just the human team. It was only vampires who needed to work at night. Most of the staff went home at five, like normal people.

"What the fuck is wrong with you tonight, Mas? You drain some stoner or something?"

I couldn't help my eyes twitching down at that point. Just couldn't help it. Yep, there was something stone-like there in Dare's leathers.

Something really big and stone-like.

"I'm all right," I said. "Had a spot of trouble at Willie's."

"Look, fuck Willie. I left you a message at home to meet us here at nine."

"Oh," I said. "Well, look, I have an excuse for missing that one. Some kid broke into my house and tried to make a coat-rack out of me."

"I don't care," Johann said, but some of the fire had left his voice.

Dare was watching me carefully.

"You okay?" Johann asked me.

"I'm a vampire, Johann, of course I'm okay." As I spoke I zipped up my pants and reached for my leather halter, which had ended up on the cobblestones. Dare was leaning back against the stoop now, looking rather pissed off. Unfairly, it suited him. His arms were folded over his beautiful chest, affording me a pretty decent view of his perfectly formed abs. I'm a sucker for great abs.

"Well. Listen. Got something really important for you. Big case. Big bucks."

"Because money is such a concern of mine."

"Not all of us are lucky enough to have had twenty-three centuries to accumulate wealth, Mas," Johann said sourly.

"It's just wise investing. Anyone could see the Internet was going to make a fortune."

"I don't care about the fucking Internet. I've got a vamp for you to kill."

"Is that so?" I finished fastening my halter one-handed, which wasn't easy, but Dare didn't seem to be up for helping me.

"Yes. And I need you here now. Tomorrow's the full moon and my secretary has left her one-year-old with a babysitter."

I winced at the image that gave me. "Okay, all right, I'm going."

I snapped the phone shut and tucked it back in its holster, still very aware of the weight of Dare's eyes on me.

"I have to go," I told him. He stayed utterly still, but something in his face darkened.

"What could possibly be more important than this?"

"Than fucking a stranger I've never met before? You'd be surprised." I turned to go, and he caught my wrist.

For an eternity the memory seared through me of someone else doing the same, someone who had changed my life forever. By ending it.

Dark brown eyes, a heavy brow, an intense power so vivid it made me scream…

Dare saw my face and abruptly let go.

"Two thousand years and you still work," he said.

"Custom leather tailoring isn't cheap." It wasn't my wittiest comeback, but I was shaken.

"So you're just going to go?"

"Looks like." I strode away from him, out of the courtyard.

"I'll see you again," Dare called after me, and I waved a hand, quite sure he hadn't meant that as a question.

Chapter Three

Sundown has its offices in Marylebone, and I jogged all the way there. Doesn't hurt to practice running in heels. Well, actually it does, but it is handy.

Magda was waiting for me as I let myself in. She rolled her eyes and tapped her watch. I rolled my eyes right back.

"Yo, bitch."

"Hey, fang-face. Did I tell you Lucy is teething?"

"Look, I'm sorry, okay? If she's bitten the babysitter I'll mind-bend her for you."

"Don't think it works on babies."

"Haha."

In case you hadn't guessed, Magda is a werewolf. She can control her beast pretty well and only has to change on the night of the full moon, but her kids have extremely unpredictable cycles. Needless to say, she didn't breastfeed.

"So who is he?" Magda asked as we went up the stairs to Johann's office.

"Who?"

She rolled her eyes, and flicked her finger at the rip in my halter. Dammit.

"Mas, what am I?"

"A pain in the neck. Literally, if you don't stop annoying me," I added.

"I can smell him on you."

"That's kind of disgusting."

"You drink blood and you think I'm disgusting. Mas. I'm your friend. Tell me who you've been fucking!"

Of course, Johann chose that moment to appear in his doorway. He raised his eyebrows at us.

"Thought you said it was the other kind of impaling," he said, and if I could have blushed, I would have.

"Can we get on with this? I don't want Magda's babysitter suing us."

"Suing you," Johann said, taking a seat in his swivel chair. "You're the one who made her late."

"Does she have to be here?"

"Yes. It's her job."

Sometimes Johann could be really old-fashioned. And I should know.

Magda swung into one of the other chairs with lupine grace and grabbed the keyboard to herself, delicate fingers flying over it. Magda is quite tiny, with shiny dark hair, and she looks completely harmless in her cute suit and her pearls. But I've seen her rip out someone's intestines for trying to attack her and her kids. Werewolves are not civilized creatures.

"Case falls to you, Mas," Johann said. "The client was quite insistent we get it done soon."

I frowned. "Who is the client?"

"Don't know," Magda said. "Whoever it is isn't in the city. Case was brought to us by a Renfield. Living in a hotel, can't trace the payment for it."

I nodded in understanding. A Renfield was a Master vampire's devoted servant. And I mean totally devoted -- these guys had no minds of their own. The Master could communicate with his or her Renfield telepathically, without needing to be even remotely physically close.

"Okay," I said. "So who's the mark?"

Magda swung the flat screen monitor to face me, and for maybe the third or fourth time since I woke up dead, I was speechless.

"Currently goes by the name of Sekani," Johann said, as I stared at the image of the man who'd been sucking on my nipples about twenty minutes ago. "Real name Darien, known to friends and flunkies as --"

"Dare," I said, my voice hoarse.

"You know him?"

I swallowed. "We've met."

"Conflict of interest?"

I stared at him. Damn, he even photographed well. He wore a business suit, complete with tie. His body was turned away from me as he opened a door, but he was looking back over his shoulder, eyes meeting the camera dead on. Blue eyes, deep and dreadful, full of cruelty and knowledge. He was old; as old as me, maybe.

"Hello? Earth to Mas? Come in, Mas? Bloody hell, you looked like I'd just offered you a gallon of fresh blood."

I smiled tightly. "I haven't fed tonight," I told him, and watched him go a little paler.

"Mas, can you do it?" Magda asked me. Her pale eyes were watching me carefully.

I nodded, because the truth was that I could. I just didn't know if I would.

Chapter Four

I went home, which is a warehouse that looks more or less deserted from the outside. Inside it's not what you might call cozy, but it has electricity and soft furnishings and a basement bedroom where no light ever penetrates. I'm old enough that I can walk about during the day if I stay out of full sunlight, but it's damn tiring. Vampires need to sleep too, you know.

I was thinking about Dare, and not just his incredible hotness. I was trying to figure out who the hell would be trying to kill him. A Master vampire, that much we knew. Surely there couldn't be many Masters older than Dare?

I wondered if he was a Master himself. And then I wondered, if he was, whose Childe he'd been.

An awful thought occurred to me. What if it was Dare's Master who had commissioned me? A Master had absolute power over every vampire he or she created -- except for those vampires who were born the Master's Childer. A strong, almost parental bond formed between the sire and the new vampire. Only the Childe of a Master could become a Master himself. A Master couldn't hurt his own Childer -- because a Childe is the only vampire strong enough to overthrow a Master. It's a bond of trust.

Usually, anyway.

What if Dare's Master, unable to do the deed himself, had commissioned me to kill him?

The idea made my head hurt. I wasn't born a Childe, so I'd never known the love of a Master. My own Master hadn't seemed to like me at all. But still, for a Master to want his Childe dead was like a mother hiring someone to shoot her kids. It was just wrong.

I needed some time to think. Or more accurately, to not think.

I snagged some O Neg from the fridge -- rare treat, they don't throw this stuff away often, you know -- and flopped in front of the TV to see what dreck was on in the middle of the night.

And then I heard a noise.

Some of the old stories are true. The ones about holy objects -- to which I bear witness -- and stakes, and fire, and the ones about movement, sight, hearing. The garlic thing is a load of bollocks though. I love garlic. Especially on Italian food.

And I mean the kind that you eat, not the human kind... although that's nice, too.

Anyway. A noise. A small one, almost undetectable. I tuned out the noise of the TV and listened again. Sweet Bast, two in one day? I really need a new alarm system.

Now I could hear him, and I was sure it was a him, unless it was a really big woman. He moved almost soundlessly, but when I thought hard I could hear the air moving around him.

I breathed in, and there it was. Vampire.

I frowned, and took another breath.

Then I vaulted over the back of the sofa in a movement so fast I couldn't even see myself, and had him pinned against the industrial steel kitchen worktops before I'd even thought about it. A crossbow came to hand, and I had the tip of the bolt pressed against his chest.

"Hey, lover," I said, and Dare gave me a crooked smile as I ripped his shades away. His eyes were the color of the desert sky. "What the fuck are you doing in my house?"

"Bet you say that to all the guys."

"Just the ones who've broken in." Without realizing it my hand had crept to his throat, and I felt his pulse beating there. Despite what the movies say, we're not really dead -- our hearts beat, our blood flows, our lungs work. Paleness comes from never seeing the sun, not from death. Although a vamp who hasn't fed in a while will be a bit chilly to the touch.

Not Dare. He was hot. His skin burned feverish. His pulse throbbed against my palm. His gaze burned into me. He was still shirtless, and I felt him through my clothes. The crossbow faltered.

"What do you want?"

He shifted, only a small movement, but it brought our hips into alignment, and I felt exactly what he wanted. Felt it against my groin. Felt it swell as I brushed against it.

"You ran off," he whispered, his voice like hot silk against my skin, "and we never finished what we started."

I didn't mean to shiver, but his voice really was good. It was the closest to sex I'd ever heard in a voice. I wondered if Dare had ever made a woman come just by talking to her.

I'd be willing to find out.

"I had work to do," I said, and my voice came out all breathy. "How did you find me?"

"I followed you."

I started to say that was impossible, but I'd been really pretty preoccupied tonight. Thoughts of the man who'd made me come my brains out in a public place, thoughts of how to kill him.

His eyes bored into mine, and I knew he knew. After all, he'd followed me to Sundown's offices.

"How much?" he whispered.

"Excuse me?"

He broke into a smile, but it didn't reach his eyes. "My head," he said. "How much is she paying for it?"

"You know who it is?"

"I've known for two thousand years."

Well, there was a conversation stopper. I couldn't think of anything to say, and Dare took advantage of this by tilting his head, just a little, and brushing his lips over mine.

Well, whatever I might have been planning on doing I completely forgot about when he did that. His lips touched mine and my brain just melted. I attacked him, fangs out, feeding on his mouth, drinking in his taste. My canine nipped his tongue, drew blood, and as the rich fullness of it flooded my mouth I felt my nipples contract, my pussy dampen, my beast rise. Told you blood makes me horny.

Dare's hands were on my arms, gripping tight, his fingers digging into the scar tissue on my right side. It didn't hurt. It felt good. It felt right. The crossbow clattered to the floor, forgotten.

We kissed so hard, so fierce, and it felt damn good. Humans don't kiss like this, and vampires are usually too full of agenda to kiss with abandon. Dare kissed like most vampires feed; as if it was sustaining him, as if it might be his last.

My top was off again before I really thought about it, and my bare breasts pressed deliciously against his chest. Someone moaned, and I think it was me.

This time I wasn't going to be satisfied until he was inside me.

I reached for his fly and found him hot and hard under the leather. Found him even harder in my hand. His cock was long and elegant, dark with blood and pulsing in my grip.

I looked up at Dare, and found his eyes closed. I stroked his cock gently, and he exhaled.

"Masika," he breathed.

"I want you inside me," I said.

His eyes opened, warm blue pools in his cool face. "I thought you'd never ask."

I smiled and wrapped my arm around his neck to kiss him again as I stroked him. His mouth really was a miracle, so hot and wet, his tongue stroking all the sensitive places in my own mouth.

I started unfastening my own pants, but Dare stopped me with a hand on my wrist.

"Not here," he said, his voice ragged. Tattered silk. "Not like this."

"Bed," I said, and he nodded gratefully.

I grabbed his hand in mine and we flew across the floor to the stairs, into my bedroom with its reinforced steel door, and I slammed it shut, the bolt falling closed as we tumbled to the bed together. My mind was totally gone by now, and all I wanted was him inside me, his cock sliding deep, that glorious friction, his skin against mine, his lips and his hands on my body. I couldn't breathe with wanting him.

The rest of our clothes vanished. Maybe we took them off, or maybe they were just ripped away. I don't remember. I was halfway to orgasm before I was even naked. I don't know why I wanted him so much but I did, I craved him, I was wet and swollen and needy for him.

Dare held back for a second as he saw me naked, skin glistening, nipples standing up proud, naked pussy beckoning him.

His fingers traced the lines of dots and dashes tattooed on my lower abdomen.

"Priestess marks," he said in wonder.

"Fertility marks," I corrected. Back in the days when a child might have been possible, and the pharaoh's child would have secured my future forever.

Forever. Who remembers the pharaohs now?

He kissed them, kissed the line of dots that curved between my hipbones, sweeping half an inch from my dampened pussy.

Then his lips moved lower, he was between my legs, sucking my clit into his mouth. I writhed and panted and shook as he licked me slowly all the way along my cunt, dipped his tongue inside and tasted me.

"Dare," I cried, my voice breaking, drawing him to me. I was so hot, melting, burning for him. I'd never felt like this before with anyone, vampire or human. Was it love? I didn't know. All I wanted was his cock inside me, moving, never stopping. I never wanted this to end.

His hand cupped my face, fingers traced my scars, and then his lips brushed mine in the tenderest of kisses before he slid inside me, slowly, stretching me, and a gasp escaped me at the pure beauty of it.

"Masika." My name was a whisper of silk on his lips, and I was undone at the sound of it.

"It's never been like this," I choked out, and then Dare was pushed fully inside me and I lost all capability for speech.

He moved, slowly at first, testing me, then faster, harder, as my body urged him on. He filled me completely, not just his cock thrusting into my cunt, but something more, something deeper. I felt him inside me like a fist in a glove, and as he flexed and thrust ever deeper into me I convulsed and cried out, coming. Lights flashed, heat flared, and somewhere in my brain I knew he was coming too, but I was too far gone to really feel it.

I felt sand under my back, the burning heat of it, desert sand, and the smell of it. The hot dry smell of the desert. I opened my eyes to the flickering stars, stars I hadn't seen in two thousand years, and the hot kiss of the desert wind caressed my naked skin.

I felt Dare still inside me, and like a zoetrope of images I saw his thoughts. I was in his thoughts. Reclining naked upon a chaise while the pharaoh licked cream from my body. I was his woman, his concubine, jeweled and perfumed, pampered, kept.

The loss of my humanity hit me like a fist, but in Dare's memory I was still perfect. Still that gorgeous creature with no concerns but how to please herself that day. I saw Djoser, forgotten lover. Though how I forgot him I have no idea. It was Djoser who brought me to this.

Such a lover, the pharaoh's guard. Such a liar, denying all knowledge of the love bite on my breast. Such disgust in his eyes as I was led away to die. Adultery, treachery, betrayal of my god-king.

I felt Dare's despair at my fate. Who was he? How did he even know? But know he did. He knew everything, even about the woman who had come to me the night before my death. The small, strange woman who had filled my mind with peace, then left. I didn't know what she was or what she'd done until I awoke in some shallow grave, spitting sand, still alive even after my body had been held under the waters of the Nile and left for the crocodiles. Left without proper burial, without a chance at after-life. The ultimate insult.

I came back to myself choking and spluttering, sweat-soaked silk under my back, Dare's arms holding me. His voice called me, anchored me, his soft voice caressing me.

"Masika. Masika. It's all right... come back now... it's all right."

I stared at him, breathing hard, panicking. "She t-turned me, didn't she? She sired me and I -- I don't remember. I woke and I didn't know, Dare, I didn't know what I was."

He cradled me in his arms, moved back against the headboard and gathered me in his lap like a child. His touch soothed me, calmed my heartbeat, and I pressed up against him, needing his heat and his solidity.

"It's all right now," he said, stroking my hair. "It's all right."

I calmed enough to relax, and when I felt a little better I realized I was being held by the most delicious naked vampire I'd ever seen. Dare's skin was hot to touch, his body firm with muscle. He wasn't hugely muscled, which doesn't do a lot for me, and he had beautiful curved pecs and the most delightful abs I'd ever seen.

I dipped my head and kissed his nipple, and his body tensed.

"You recover quickly," he said.

"It's a skill of mine," I replied, and tried not to make a face. But I failed, and Dare saw it, and lifted my head.

"Was it really so bad?" he asked. "With the pharaoh?"

I drew back a little. "You know about that?"

"I know."

I let out a shaky breath. No, it hadn't been that bad with the pharaoh. It was after that when things got bad. After I woke, the weakest vampire in a pack of hundreds, needing protection. All my life, human and vampire, I'd traded sex for safety. Sharing the pharaoh's bed meant security for my whole family. Finding a strong vampire protector meant I wasn't meat for the whole pack.

"It wasn't that bad," I said.

"But it's still made a definite impression on you."

I shrugged. "What we are in life shapes us in death. My soul was never weighed against a feather, but who I was made me who I am now."

"You're no one's slave."

I closed my eyes, because it had taken me a long time to realize I was strong on my own. Djoser had cured me of sex for love, and as I became stronger I didn't need to use my body as collateral anymore.

Which did leave me sort of nowhere on the sex front.

Dare was cuddling me to him, stroking my hair, and even though I knew I should have been thinking about the contract Johann had more or less obliged me to fulfill, I didn't. I should have been thinking about the memories Dare had shared with me -- who was he, and why did he know so much about me when I didn't know him? -- but I didn't. I breathed in his scent, and slept, his words in my ear.

Chapter Five

I dreamt of my music box. It was a treasure back then, a treasured toy when I was a child. The tune it made was haunting, beautiful. I still remembered it now, could hear it now, as I dreamed myself turning the handle, playing the tune and dancing to it, skipping across the precious green lawn in the royal gardens. I was naked, a child again, running free just for the joy of it, the sun warming my bare scalp as I ran, dry grass under my feet.

The smell of sand, the heat of the desert…

I tripped and fell, but there were warm hands to catch me. And although I didn't care, because all I saw was my music box smashed and broken on the grass, I knew now who'd caught me.

A Greek boy, a soldier, blond hair curling about his shoulders, blue eyes deeper than the sky.

"Are you all right?"

"I broke it," I said, and we both looked at the sad remains of my cherished toy. A tear rolled down my cheek.

"It can be mended. Are you hurt?"

"I'm fine." Aware he was holding me, sure I shouldn't be letting him see me cry, I shook myself away from him. "You shouldn't be here."

His eyes were so blue. "I saw you fall."

"You should go now." My voice became stronger. He was older than me, but he was just a soldier, and I was to be married to the pharaoh.

"But your toy…"

I tried not to look at it, tried not to let him see how upset I was. "I don't care about that."

He looked at me, and I knew he wasn't fooled. But he bowed his head to me, and he retreated, but although I knew he was gone I felt his eyes on me all the way back into the palace.

Darkness, the stars above me, stars I haven't seen since I left my homeland, and as I entered my chamber I saw the light from the lamp falling over my music box.

It was whole again, and when I turned the handle, the music spilled out.

The air was heavy with perfumed oil as I listened to the tune, perplexed but not unhappy, wondering why he'd done it. I hadn't even been nice to him.

He stood under an archway in the pharaoh's throne room, watching the candlelight on my bare body. If my father hadn't got me into court I'd have been a dancing girl, bare but for a belt of beads, twining my body to music for the pleasure of men. Here I did the same, but it was for the pharaoh and his court, and it was an idle entertainment, just some fun for the bearded men. I was younger than their daughters. Older now, but so young still.

The soldier watched me. I'd never seen him then, but I saw him now, in my dream, his eyes burning blue fire. The heat of his gaze seared my skin, tightened my nipples, and I danced closer, hotter, lifted my arms and grazed my breasts across his chest.

He was naked, and so was I. I felt the hardness of his cock against my hip and writhed against it, the music pounding a beat in my veins, hot and dark, everything fading but for this one man, his eyes burning and his teeth sharpening.

"Will you hurt me?" I asked, running my tongue over his fangs.

"Never," he swore. I ran my hands over his biceps, felt the rock hard strength that went down to his core.

"You could break me like a reed," I said.

"Am I strong enough?"

"I think you are."

"Strong enough for you," he said urgently. "How can I be what you need?"

"Touch me," I said, and he did, touched my hips and my breasts, pulled me to him and kissed me, deep and wonderful, that kiss I loved so much from the first time I tasted it in Willie's bar.

If only I'd kissed him then. If only I'd known. But after the music box, I never saw that boy again. Never saw him grow, never saw him watching me, never saw his desperate search to be better than he was, to do what he should never have done, to be better for me, to be what I needed.

His arms went around me and I felt the total safety of his strength. No harm could come to me while I was here. I didn't fear the court, the politics, I didn't fear anything. His sharp teeth nipped my lip and I tasted blood.

He made a growling sound that vibrated straight through me to my cunt, and my body shuddered with the pleasure of it.

"Please," I whispered.

"What do you want, meu?"

Meu. It meant kitten in Egyptian. My father used to call me that as a child.

"I want you," I said, looking up at his drowning blue eyes, and he pulled me closer, pressing my body against his, soft against hard, weak against strong. His hot cock pressed into me, my nipples rubbed against his chest, and the temperature rose as he kissed me, long and deep, and turned me against the wall so that it was supporting me as he lifted my legs around his waist.

"I have always wanted you," he said, his eyes on mine as his cock rubbed against me. "Always loved you. I wanted you to see me."

"I see you," I said, writhing, desperate to have him inside me.

"There's nobody but you," he breathed as he slid into me, filling me, completing me. I let out a cry: he was so hot inside me, so thick, stretching me. Tears came to my eyes at the beauty of it, and he kissed them away, my Greek soldier, the boy who loved me, touching me and stroking me and building the fires higher inside me until I couldn't breathe with the perfection of it, the rightness of it, and as I came I knew there was nobody for me but him.

I dreamed of my Greek making love to me all night, I dreamed I was loved, and I loved him for it.

Chapter Six

When I woke the sun was rising -- I could feel it, even if I couldn't see it -- and I was alone. Where Dare had lain next to me, keeping me warm as I slept, there was now a bronze mask, and a note, written in the most beautiful script. It contained an address in Paris, and the message "She holds an annual masquerade ball. Wear this."

I picked up the mask, which would cover half my face, and had a cat's eyes and nose. One side fell lower on the cheek than the other, like the Phantom of the Opera's mask, and I realized it would completely cover the scars on my face.

On my dresser was a pile of shimmering things, and when I padded over to them I saw that it was a collection of heavy bracelets for my upper arm, a golden belt, and a jeweled collar. It was the sort of thing I might have worn when I was human. And it too would almost cover my scars.

I looked at my scars in the mirror, remembered the zealot who'd caused them. He was long dead, but I'd survived, fed on the blood of my Master, strengthened until all that remained of my near fatality were these bumps and lines of rigid tissue. It had made me realize my own strength; realize that although I wasn't the Childe of my Master, neither was I beholden to her. I'd left her court, and made my own life. Or death, whichever way you want to look at it.

I looked again at Dare's brief note. Who was "she"? His Master? The vampire who'd commissioned his death?

I showered, ripped open a bag of blood, and booted up my computer. Some vampires, who seem to think the march of time stopped dead when they did, absolutely hate technology. Me, I love it. I sent out feelers to all the vampires I'm in contact with, as well as a few occultists, Wiccans, demons, and the odd human, like Willie, who always knew what was going on.

They all replied with the same thing: the masked ball was given by the oldest vampire Master in Europe for all her own vampires, of which there were thousands, if not millions; and for her friends and guests. This year it was in Paris. Guest invites were scarce, but no one seemed to doubt that I'd get in.

I guess I had a ticket with the whole Sundown thing. Whatever.

I booked my flights and carefully wrapped up against the sun. Travelling can be a bitch when you're extremely photosensitive. Direct sunlight burns vampires to a crisp, even strong ones. Indirect light leaves me weak and lethargic, but I can live through it.

I packed the jewelry and some choice anti-vampire weapons of the sort that wouldn't get picked up by customs. Wood for stakes, holy water (kept in a locked box, of course), crosses and the like. Although I wear a holy symbol on my skin, it doesn't trouble me. I don't know why. Maybe because it's a symbol of something I still believe in.

I told the airline staff I was allergic to sunlight, and made it to Paris just as dusk was falling. Paris is a beautiful city, and I spent a lot of time here before the Revolution. I came back during the Belle Époque and hung around in nightclubs, drinking absinthe, but then all those stupid world wars started, and I moved to America. Isolationism can be handy.

It took a long while to prepare myself, because I was remembering rituals I hadn't used in over two thousand years. Oiled, painted, and jeweled, I walked unseen to the venue, and was admitted by an expressionless Renfield.

He never questioned my right to be there. He simply ushered me into the ballroom, where I stood for a moment, staring.

The palace was one of the rare places that had escaped both the Revolution and the world wars. Or perhaps the Master's presence had scared both of them away. Every surface glittered and shone as if it wasn't just veneered with gold, but with jewels and sequins too. Even the floor shone a highly polished gold, reflecting the glow of hundreds of candles. Vampires of every age and color whirled across the floor in a beautifully choreographed waltz, like puppets or dolls, beautiful but hardly real.

But it was the music that unnerved me. It was just this side of discordant, like a merry-go-round broken down. It had no source -- there were no wires, no speakers, not even any electric lights, and no orchestra either -- but it twinkled on, warped and sinister, leaking from the walls.

It was the music from my music box, and it chilled me.

I lifted my head and stepped into the room, and every vampire stopped and turned a masked face toward me. I felt the weight of thousands of years watching me as I walked through the parting crowd wearing my cat mask, belt, jeweled collar and armlets. The rest of me was naked but for a coat of bronze paint, my scars covered by the mask and jewelry, the tattoos on my back and belly left bare and visible. I had dressed as Bast, a silent plea for her protection as I walked into this nest of potential enemies.

I was the disowned vampire of a distant Master. I could be killed on sight.

I walked on bare feet, and as the crowd parted silently ahead of me I saw Dare standing at the far end of the ballroom. He was dressed in the Greek style, his face covered by a traditional helmet, his arms bare but for leather vambraces. His beautiful torso was covered by leather and straps, original armour, I was betting. The short leather kilt showed his strong legs, his handsome feet in their leather sandals. He carried a sword and a shield on his back. Nice touch.

I felt a prickle of awareness, and saw a human couple standing together. The boy who'd broken into my flat, and the brunette who'd attacked me in the bar. Human followers of a hostile Master. Fabulous.

I walked toward my Greek warrior, and he held out his arm as I approached. Without missing a step, we continued through the curtain at the far end, and as soon as it was closed Dare kissed me so violently I was sure my bronze paint would be smudged.

"I wasn't sure you'd come," he said as he drew back from me.

"How could I resist?" I pulled off his helmet, smiling as his beauty came into view. We kissed again, no metal in the way this time, and as his hands hovered over my bronze-painted body I became aware that only our mouths were touching. Somehow that made it more intense, more erotic, and my breath came faster as his tongue thrust into my mouth, taking charge of me.

"You are so beautiful," he breathed, his gaze burning into me. His hands touched my wig, a thick New Kingdom style, heavy with real gold. "I daren't touch you."

Again I felt the heat of an Egyptian night, and saw myself through Dare's eyes again. The pharaoh's woman. Not to be touched.

"I have spare paint," I told him, and watched a smile curve his mouth. We kissed again, and while his hands skimmed a hair's breadth over my arms, my back, my bare buttocks, he still never touched me. My nipples tightened. My pussy felt swollen, tender, needy, and still he hadn't touched me.

I skimmed my hands up under his kilt and found him bare. Smiling against his mouth, I caressed his tight buttocks, his hips. The soft hair covering his thighs gave way to coarser hair at his groin, and then I felt his cock, already hard, thick, long. Hot, so hot.

I ran my thumb over the tip of it and felt a drop of moisture there. Dare trembled slightly as I spread it over his cock, gently learning him with my hands.

"Masika," he breathed. I loved the way he said my name. Accented, the way it should be; and that voice of his, that deep rich voice that wrapped around me, soft and hot like a glove. Like a cunt.

"I want you inside me," I said, and punctuated it by fondling his balls.

"I -- we can't, I'll smudge your" -- I squeezed gently, and his breath caught -- "your costume…"

"Then we'll have to be very," I caressed his length, feeling him swell to what must have been painful proportions, "very careful."

I glanced around the room, spying a chaise a few feet away. I pushed Dare onto it, lifted the panes of his leather kilt and just looked at his cock for a long while, thinking about feeling it driving into me. Thinking about the heat of it inside me, the slide and the friction and the fullness and the glory of it, and for a moment I couldn't breathe.

"Masika?"

My eyes flickered up to Dare's, and then in one of those lightning moves I could only do without thinking about it, I'd straddled the chaise, straddled his cock, and taken him inside me.

Dare groaned. I held my breath at the feeling of him filling me, stretching me, warming me. Carefully I lowered myself until his cock filled me as far as it would go without my thighs touching him. His cock was buried inside me, and we weren't touching anywhere else.

Dare's hands came up and smoothed over my body, so very nearly touching me, and I felt the heat from his skin as he skimmed his palms over my aching, bronze-tipped nipples. I lifted myself up, my feet braced on the floor, and slid back down again.

Dare's fingers flexed over my breasts.

"When this is over," he said, his voice a low growl, "I'm going to wash that paint off you with my tongue."

My cunt tightened involuntarily. "Oh, yes."

"Until then…"

He thrust up into me, and I met him, barely missing the flat of his hips between my thighs. My hands fisted in midair. There was no paint on my palms, but if he couldn't touch me then it wasn't fair for me to touch him.

Faster and faster we moved, eyes locked, perfectly in time, the grace and beauty you only get from a vampire who's been around a really, really long time. I felt my orgasm building, tightening inside me like a spring. Heat rushed through me. My skin burned.

"I'm coming," I gasped, and then I suited action to words, and felt my body convulse around him. Dare came too, an explosion of power inside me, and it took all my strength to keep from collapsing on his chest.

But he didn't let me. Scooting down under me until his mouth was level with my pussy, he whispered, "You're all wet," and proceeded to clean me up with his tongue. He circled my clit, licked the length of my labia, then plunged his tongue deep inside my cunt. I came again, violently, my hands fisted in his hair, and when I came back to earth I heard someone clapping.

We both snapped to toward the sound, and when I saw who it was, my tenuous control evaporated and I fell to the floor in a disgracefully ungainly heap.

My Master stood on the far side of the room, away from the ballroom, so that we were trapped between her and hundreds of unfriendly vamps. She looked just as I remembered her the last time I saw her, two thousand years ago. Like myself and Dare, and a lot of the vampires at the party, she'd dressed in the style of the time when she died.

Thick stripes of paint on her face and body, and a wrap of fur around her waist. Her body was covered with fine dark hair all over, her legs were bowed, her brow was heavy and her dark eyes were full of intelligence. I didn't know, but based on archaeological research my guess was that she'd last seen the sun thirty thousand years ago.

I sprawled gracelessly on the floor, smudging bronze paint everywhere, and stared at her. Dimly, I was aware of Dare pulling me to my feet, but I didn't take my eyes from her. Nor she from me.

"Masika," she said, and a chill went through me. "You look surprised, child."

"Can't imagine why," someone said, and I realized in horror that it was me.

My Master smiled, that baring of teeth that looked feral if you didn't know what it meant.

"You remember my name," I covered.

"Of course, child. Do you remember mine?"

I nodded, hating the way she called me "child." It was a reminder of what I wasn't. "Uda."

Her gaze moved to Dare. She had to look up a long way to see him; she was less than four feet tall and he was way over six.

"Sekani." She spoke with a strange guttural accent that made you remember her vocal cords hadn't been designed for vowels. I guess Sekani was easier for her to say than Darien.

What he said in reply to her scared the shit out of me. If he hadn't been holding me up I was sure I'd have slithered to the floor.

He bowed his head and said, "Master."

I stared at him. Then at her. Then back at him again. "You're -- she's -- you're --"

"She still does not know?" Uda made it a question. Dare shook his head. "Sekani is my Childe."

I gaped at both of them. I know I'd come in dressed as a cat goddess, but I was now doing a pretty good imitation of a bloody goldfish.

"Does your edict still stand after twenty-three centuries?" Dare asked her.

She looked at us both for a long while, and I used the time to wonder what the fuck was going on. When Uda spoke again, it was not with words, but with the sign language she had used with her vampires so long ago. Human speech was always difficult for her.

"A Master vampire cannot control what becomes of any fledgling she sires," she said. "Until the vampire wakes for the first time and feeds, I can never know if it will be just another drone, or something more special. A Childe. In all my years I have only created two."

"Dare," I said, and she nodded.

"And you, Masika."

I stared at her. I really couldn't think of anything else to do.

"When Dare arose, I was as pleased as any mother with my Childe. Look on him. A lieutenant to be proud of. But I knew... I always knew that he would not be mine for eternity. Only a Childe has the power to become a Master."

I cleared my throat. "You commissioned Sundown to kill him."

She nodded. "How did you know?"

"I knew it was a vampire because of the Renfield who came to us. A subordinate vampire wouldn't have a Renfield, and a stronger Master would have done it himself. The only person in the whole world who would have to get someone else to do the job would be Dare's own Master. I just didn't know who that was."

His hand tightened on my arm.

"Did you really need to have him killed?" I asked.

Her big dark eyes looked sad. "He was less than five years out of the grave when I realized his potential," she said. "I could never harm him myself."

"I've always wondered," I said, "is that a rule between Sire and Childe, or is it actually impossible?"

"Impossible," Dare said. It was about the second word he'd said since Uda appeared in the room.

"Yet I could not allow him to overthrow me. When he made his request of me to save you, I took a promise from him in return that he would leave, and never return to the same lands as me and my court."

It was an information overload. I felt like my computer when faced with a huge download. I just couldn't process it all.

"You -- save -- what?"

Dare cleared his throat, and the silk of his voice sounded a little rusty. "I saw how Djoser dropped you when the pharaoh discovered your infidelity. I killed him but I couldn't save you from the death he'd brought you to. I wasn't strong enough by myself to bring you over, but I knew Uda could do it." He looked right at her. "And I knew she'd demand something for it, too."

"But why?" I asked. "Why did you do it? You didn't even know me."

"Know you?" Dare choked. "I spent my life watching you. I was a boy of twelve when you came to the court."

"I was eight." Raised with the pharaoh's children, and taken as his lesser wife when I was thirteen. "You were tall for your age."

He gave the faintest smile at that. "I knew even then you were special. Knew the pharaoh would never marry you to anyone else. I watched you grow and every day I fell a little more in love with you. Masika..." his blue eyes hit mine, "...I knew you could never be mine. But I couldn't let you die like that. Better eternal life away from you than knowing your light was darkened forever."

"Light?" I said. "I'm a vampire. Light is a distant memory."

"Not for you," he said fiercely. "You glow, Masika. I look at you and I see the sun, I smell the desert, I remember what it was to be alive. You make me feel alive," he said, and for a long moment we just gazed at each other.

Then Uda spoke, with words this time, to get our attention. "His loyalty to you was always greater than it was to me. When you awoke as my Childe, I knew I had to send him away, before he grew too strong to resist me. Before you learned from him what you really were, and eventually betrayed me."

It was all too much. My legs gave way and Dare kept me from falling to the floor. He lowered me to the chaise where we'd just made love, and knelt before me, his hands in mine. Uda had commanded his death because she feared his rebellion. A Childe was the only vampire who could defy his Master. And all this time I'd been a Childe, I could have been a Master if I'd only known.

"How do you think you lived through those scars, child?" Uda said softly, and I realized what she was really saying. Not child, but Childe.

And through it all the persistent knowledge that it was Dare who'd begun all this. Dare who'd loved me as a child, a human child. Dare who'd traded his own family -- for a Master's pack was that, a family -- for my life. For my safety. Dare who was kneeling before me, telling me he'd loved me since before the Bible began.

And it seemed to me I was being offered a choice. Either I could go back to my Master, be her Childe, and eventually the target of another assassin -- just as Dare would be -- or I could be with Dare, this strong man who loved me. And who I loved, truth be told.

My choice?

I drew Dare's sword, stood, and faced Uda. She watched me with those intelligent eyes.

"I could never control you, Childe," she said, and I swung the sword.

* * *

The ball sort of lost its swing after I'd beheaded the Master of everyone there. A lot of them pledged allegiance to me and Dare, the only Childer of their old Master, but I don't think either of us were really paying attention. Dare picked me up in his arms, lifted me into the air, and flew me into the flickering stars over Paris, where he made good on his promise to lick all the paint from my body. Every last inch of it. I wasn't sure there was such an excess of paint on my mouth, my breasts, and my pussy, but hey, I wasn't complaining.

Sundown, Inc.: Blue Moon

Cat Marsters

Chapter One

Magda liked to think she was a reasonably stable person who didn't often go around licking strangers' balls, but today was really testing her theory.

Although to be fair, it was less "today" than "tonight." And he wasn't a complete stranger. Granted, she didn't know his name and they hadn't exchanged any conversation, but at least she knew his species.

Or she thought she did, anyway.

She nudged his cock out of the way and licked some more. It was a nice cock, anyway. Starting to stiffen, because apparently unconsciousness came second to arousal. Nice and straight, long, and enticingly thick. It made Magda want to see what it was like when it was fully erect, and what it could do for her...

She shoved that thought out of her mind. She couldn't possibly have anything to do with this man. Even if he was normal, she didn't need -- or want, want, she didn't *want* -- a man right now. And especially not this one, because despite his incredibly beautiful eyes, which she'd only seen for a second before he passed out, he was a vicious killer.

Even if he didn't intend to be.

She sighed, and lifted her head. The light in the back of her car wasn't very good -- it wasn't quite dawn yet -- and she didn't dare put the interior light on for fear of running down her battery. Or attracting attention. Parked on the edge of the road in the middle of nowhere, French nowhere, she didn't expect anyone would come by, but she still didn't want to take the chance. After all, here she was in her underwear, licking the scrotum of a man who'd recently had his throat ripped out.

She glanced at the wound on his neck. Didn't look so fatal any more. Not that it would kill him. To Magda's knowledge the only thing that would actually take out a werewolf was silver piercing his heart. Or -- well, she supposed cutting off his head might work, too. It killed most things.

She regarded the other cuts on his naked body. Most of them were quite small, on his arms and his legs, and she supposed she should have done those first. But she'd rather get the ball-sucking out of the way first, while he was still unconscious. She might be able to bring herself to lick away a cut on his arm when he was awake, but not on his balls. Magda had only ever licked one man's balls before, and he'd been her husband at the time.

A nudge against her cheek brought her back to the balls in question. His cock was still growing -- good grief, it was enormous! -- and seemed quite eager for her further attention. Magda wondered if she'd even know what to do with one anymore. She rubbed her cheek against it, against the hot velvet skin and tensile steel strength, and she found herself licking her lips. What would it be like to just slip that big cock inside her mouth, to lick it and suck it? To reach down and fondle his balls, to lick the delicate skin behind them, to feel his fists in her hair as she swallowed down his orgasm...

Down, girl, she told herself. *Don't be ridiculous. If you're going to use his cock for anything, get it inside you and give yourself an orgasm in the bargain. How long's it been since you had one of those, eh?*

Shocked at her inner voice, Magda refused to contemplate the answer.

Too long, the voice said anyway.

"Shut up!"

"What?" said the man, and Magda nearly hit her head on the roof of the car.

"You're awake!" Her face got hotter. As he regarded her with those heartbreakingly pretty brown eyes, she felt other places get hotter, too.

"Have been for some time," he said, and his voice was soft, slightly husky with sleep. Just as beautiful as the rest of him. She'd found him in France, but he didn't sound French. Maybe he was English. His voice was too beautiful to worry about accents.

Magda thought her face might melt. She'd never been so embarrassed in her whole life. "This isn't what it looks like," she said desperately.

"Isn't it?" He looked a little disappointed. His chocolate-drop eyes took on the look of a puppy no one wants to play with.

"No, I, er --"

But she didn't get any further, because right then a light flashed outside the car, and someone tapped on the window. "Oh fuck," Magda said, looking out and seeing a police car parked behind hers on the grass verge. "Oh holy fuck."

"What is it?"

"Police. Do you speak French?" Magda asked, because the only thing she could remember from French lessons at school was how to label the contents of her pencil case, and how to ask for a large ice cream. Why couldn't she have picked him up in Germany? *That* language she spoke!

The werewolf nodded and sat up, carefully, holding her against him. Magda realized he was using her to shield the wound on his neck, which would have been pretty difficult to explain.

He buzzed down the window. "*Bonjour.*"

The gendarme asked something in rapid French, and the werewolf answered with a slight chuckle, stroking her back as she huddled against him. He had a magnificent body, lithe and strong, and his temperature, like all werewolves, ran high. The dawn air coming through the window was cool, but with his arm wrapped around her she wasn't cold.

She was very hot.

She was nearly naked against him. It had seemed like a good idea to take her clothes off while she cleaned him up, so they wouldn't get bloody, but now she was wondering what on earth she'd been intending to do if he woke up while she was licking him. Her sanity was rapidly disappearing. What had she been *thinking*?

That he was really hot, and she hadn't been thinking with her brain at all.

He was still speaking with the policeman, who didn't seem angry or annoyed. In fact he seemed to be quite amused.

"Sweetheart?"

She looked up from the werewolf's shoulder -- reluctantly, because it was a very nice shoulder.

"He wants to know if we're staying around here."

"We?"

He raised his eyebrows, and she realized, blushing, that "we" was reasonably appropriate given the circumstances.

"I -- no, I was going to…" What had she been going to do? A vague plan to find a B&B or something where he could rest, and she could leave and go home, conscience clear, wafted to the front of her mind.

"We were going to look for a hotel," she said slowly, turning to look at the policeman, not sure how much English he understood. "As soon as the hour was decent."

The policeman frowned and looked confused.

"*Nous cherchaient un hôtel tout près*," said the incredibly hot naked man on whose lap she was sitting. Inevitably, his smooth command of the language only made her hotter. Why was French so sexy? She could feel his cock pressing between them, hot and gently pulsing, and it made her lose her breath.

The gendarme said something, pointing down the road, apparently giving directions. The werewolf thanked him, the policeman nodded and wished them a good day (that part she could remember) and drove off.

Magda found herself still sitting in the lap of a very attractive man with longish dark hair and broad shoulders and the most innocent, beautiful, puppyish eyes she'd ever seen. She was in her underwear and he was stark naked, and both of their bodies seemed to be aware of the fact.

His eyes dropped, not quite so innocent any more, and regarded Magda's not insubstantial cleavage. Her nipples obligingly sat up and begged for attention. Magda frowned at her treacherous body. It wasn't shy about asking for what it wanted, even if she was.

"He said there's a hotel up the road."

"Oh." Magda gulped. "That -- I guess that would be a --" he shifted beneath her, pressing his cock against the rapidly dampening material of her panties "-- a good idea," she finished weakly.

"I guess it would. I don't suppose you'd know where my clothes might be?"

She shook her head. "You weren't wearing any when I... found you."

He nodded resignedly. "Right. And did you see what did all this?" He gestured to the healing wounds all over his body.

Magda swallowed. "Er, yes," she said.

"God. It must be dead by now. Did it hurt you?" he asked, and his hands started investigating, making Magda's blood pressure shoot up.

"Not as such," she squeaked.

"What was it? Did you see what it looked like?"

"Um," Magda swallowed again, "yes. It looked like *me*."

Chapter Two

Elek looked at the petite woman sitting about six inches away, her hands gripping the wheel as she stared straight ahead at the road. Make that *glared* at the road. But she definitely wasn't looking at him.

Thank God she'd put some clothes on, because he really couldn't concentrate with her soft, full, round breasts jiggling at him, threatening to fall out of their lacy little bra.

"Let me get this straight," he said as the car bounced over a pothole, and he watched her jiggle under her sweater. "You were driving through rural France in the middle of the night because…"

She tucked her hair behind her ears, a nervous gesture. "I was visiting my mother."

"Who lives in France?"

"No, she lives in Germany."

"And you live…"

"London."

He thought about this a while. "And it wasn't easier to fly?"

She shot him a sideways look. "At the full moon?"

He already knew she was a werewolf. And clearly, she knew he was -- so she wasn't shy about advertising the fact. After all, any wolf with half a nose could smell it. "You couldn't do a daylight flight?"

"No," she said shortly. There was a pause, then she added, "I have a day job, you know."

"Right." He didn't believe her for a second. "So you're driving home, in the middle of the night -- didn't you need to change?"

"I did change," she said, and glanced very, very briefly at the gash on his collarbone.

"Before or after I crashed into your car?"

They both avoided looking at the broken passenger window and crumpled bodywork.

"After," she said. "Very shortly after."

Elek was silent for a while as she piloted the car along the dark road. He had no recollection of the night's events -- mercifully, he never did. He only remembered waking up in the back of this strange 4x4, naked and in the dark with a rather beautiful woman licking his balls.

He could think of worse ways to wake up.

However, it did mean one terrible thing. He'd escaped the circle. Never since he'd first changed had that ever happened. He remembered intoning the words of the ritual, as he had every night that he could remember, even just for practice, and he remembered the change coming upon him.

Then nothing, until this pretty woman with her dark hair and dark, guarded eyes had woken him in such a delightful way.

The policeman had been very understanding, as only the French could be, of the situation Elek had invented. How he and his girlfriend, having got a little more amorous than they should have in their carefully -- carefully, mind you -- parked car, had accidentally hit the handbrake and run into a tree. Since the car was a mess and no one was going to come out at this time of the night, Elek had bashfully told the gendarme he and his girlfriend -- he really must find out her name -- had just carried on as before while they waited for the sun to rise. The policeman directed them to a small nearby hotel and left.

Only in France.

"I'm sorry," Elek said. "About your car. I'll get it fixed."

"That's very kind of you, but I need to get home."

"Tell me how much it costs and I'll --"

"Thank you, but it's fine."

There was a silence. Elek drummed his fingers on the door handle and looked down at the tartan blanket covering his lap. She hadn't had any clothes that would fit him, apart from a huge Sunnydale High T-shirt she apparently slept in. Elek thought that was pretty funny, considering what they both were. He'd slipped the T-shirt on and wrapped the blanket around his waist, kilt-style, and now he looked like a crazed Scotsman.

"How far to the --"

"I think it's just down here."

Great, now she was barely talking to him. Elek tried to think of a polite way to ask why she'd been licking his balls with that hot little tongue of hers, and failed utterly. Just the recollection of it made him hard again.

She stopped the car outside a pretty stone house in a pretty little village and nervously fussed with her bangs. It was not much past dawn, and the place was empty, silent, a still fountain in the village square, café chairs upside-down on tables. Like something out of a postcard.

"Is this it?"

Elek nodded without looking at the building she indicated. The curve of her neck as she looked out of the window was utterly mesmerizing. Her hair fell away from her skin in a dark shining wave, coffee against cream, and the scent of her shampoo made him lightheaded. How could she still smell of shampoo when she'd been running around in wolf form all night?

"Stay with me," he heard himself say, and she looked back at him, startled. "I mean, I -- I don't mean you -- we -- oh, fuck. It's just, you must be tired, and you should get some rest before you drive on. You know how dangerous tiredness while driving can be…"

She was staring at him, and those dark eyes of hers looked just a little amused. He was rambling. Yeah. Real smooth there, Elek. "Two rooms," he said. "We don't have to… Look, I'll pay for the room, it's just I don't think you should be driving on. You've had a hard night."

He couldn't bear to let her go so quickly. Proof that a solitary lifestyle was not good for a man. Or a *loup-garou*.

She bit her lip, regarding him in the early morning light, and then she gave a very slight nod.

Elek's heart turned somersaults.

* * *

I must be mad, Magda thought as she followed Elek down the hall to the little bedroom they'd just been assigned. *Not only staying -- Johann's going to kill me if I take any more time off work -- but staying in his room. I should have said no the moment the landlady said she only had one available. In fact -- did she even say that? For all I know he could have only asked for one room in the first place. That's what you get for failing to learn the local language properly.*

"You okay?" he asked, glancing back at her as he unlocked the door.

"I'm fine." She gave him a very unconvincing smile. "I'm just tired."

"Me too. All that running around..." He looked like he was going to say something else, then thought better of it, and just opened the door instead.

The room was small, pretty, unremarkable. There was a double bed, and a door leading to a tiny bathroom, and that was about it. Magda figured that since all she planned to do here was catch a few hours' sleep then it didn't matter -- although it occurred to her that with that fine body and puppy dog eyes lying a few feet away from her, she wasn't going to get much sleep at all.

"I'm going to take a quick shower," he said, and she tried very hard not to think about him all naked and soapy. "Unless you want the bathroom first...?"

"No, I'm fine. Thank you."

Now resorting to over-politeness because she was nervous, Magda felt like a teenager. This was insane. She'd been married. She had children, for God's sake. She didn't need to feel nervous around a strange man, even if he did have eyes she could drown in and a body she wanted to lick all over. Again.

He went into the bathroom and closed the door, and instead of changing into something she could sleep in, Magda lay on the bed and fantasized about his glorious, naked body and what it would feel like wrapped around hers, his strong hands, hard muscle, the hair on his legs rough against her soft skin. His mouth. She wondered how he kissed, what he'd taste like.

Wondered if he'd be as rough as his insane *loup-garou* form, or as gentle as those beautiful eyes promised.

Thinking of his beast made Magda remember the wounds he'd inflicted on her earlier. She shouldn't have even gotten out of her car to tackle him, but then that was a bit like saying the kids in *Jurassic Park* should have stayed where they were. The dinosaur would definitely have eaten them then.

The *loup-garou* would have smashed through Magda's windshield and ripped her to shreds before she could defend herself. He wouldn't have killed her, because she was pretty sure he didn't have silver in his teeth or claws, but she sure as hell wouldn't have been winning any athletic tournaments when he was done with her.

She peeled off her sweater and looked over her shoulder into the mirror over the little dresser. There was a big gash on her side and another on her leg. It was a miracle the gendarme hadn't seen them. Wide, deep, raw and bloody, they hurt like hell, and Magda knew the only thing that would heal them at all was her own saliva -- or that of another werewolf.

When she'd mentioned to her husband that her saliva could heal, he'd said it was disgusting. Magda was surprised. She'd always thought it was pretty neat. Saved a fortune on first aid supplies. The only problem was that she couldn't lick herself on her side -- and she really wasn't up to asking ol' puppy-dog eyes to do it for her.

She took off the rest of her clothes, concentrated, and turned herself to wolf form.

That was how he found her, curled on the bed, licking the gash on her side.

"Oh God, are you all right?"

Magda looked up, and froze. She might be wolf-shaped but her brain was definitely human, and definitely female, and he was definitely very wet and nearly naked.

Hamana. Hamana, hamana, hamana. At least being in this shape gave her an excuse for drooling.

"You're hurt," he said, coming closer, and Magda started to pant. "Let me see."

She started to tell him it was nothing, heard herself barking, and realized their landlady might not take kindly to hearing doggy noises coming from their room. So she took a deep breath and changed back to human form -- after all, she'd seen him naked and he'd seen her in her underwear, so it wasn't a huge step.

He stared at her, his pupils wide.

Okay, maybe it was a huge step.

"I," he began. "Er, you, um, we, er, you, uh..."

Magda bit her lip. He was pretty adorable when he was flustered.

"Are you, uh." He ran his hand through his damp hair, sending a fine spray of water over her naked skin. Magda shivered at the feel of it. "What happened?"

"You did."

"I hurt you?"

She nodded wordlessly. His eyes were rooted to her naked body, and she felt her breath coming faster. Under the little towel he wore about his waist, things were stirring. A drop of water ran down his beautiful chest. Magda licked her lips, which suddenly felt very dry. And hot. All of her was hot.

"I was trying to heal myself," she said, and her voice came out all husky.

"Uh-huh."

"I can't lick myself there," she said, and felt herself blush deep crimson as she heard her own words. "I mean -- to heal. Because werewolf saliva heals. Which you know, because you are one," she babbled.

"Yes," he said, stepping closer, his eyes still on her. "I do. I am. I could."

"Could?"

"Heal you."

Magda swallowed. The cut on her side wasn't too bad -- it ran for a good six or seven inches but it didn't hit anywhere embarrassing -- but the one on her leg ran up the front of her thigh. The top of it was an inch or two from her groin. If he licked her there he'd be getting very close to ground zero, and Magda wasn't sure she could take that. It had been a long, long time since anyone went anywhere near there.

"You don't need to --"

"You healed me."

She blushed even deeper. "I -- well, yes, but I hurt you, so..."

"I hurt you. I owe you." He put one knee on the bed. "I won't bite."

Magda nearly swooned. "I should put something on," she said pathetically, and his eyes gleamed.

"Why? It'll just get bloody." He cocked his head. "That's why you were in your underwear earlier?"

"I don't have many spare clothes," Magda whispered. Whispering was all her voice seemed capable of right now.

"Then don't waste them," he said. Then he was on the bed with her, and turning her gently onto her side, and then his mouth was on her, and Magda shuddered.

He had soft, gentle lips that just brushed her throbbing flesh, and a hot tongue that trailed fire across her skin. Magda forgot her hurts, forgot why he was doing this, and just let him lick her, run his tongue all over her side, little flicks and long sweeps, drenching her, tasting her, making her moan.

He tensed and stopped. "Am I hurting you?"

She'd moaned out loud. Argh. "No," Magda gasped, "it's good. I mean, I'm fine." She wasn't sure, but she thought she saw a smile cross his lips as he bent his head again.

"So this is why you were licking... er, me?"

Magda's fingers clenched in the bedsheets. "I was trying to heal you before you came around."

"Where was I hurt?"

Oh God. "Everywhere."

"You fight dirty."

"You were hardly playing by Queensbury rules yourself."

His tongue played over her hip. "Fair enough."

"Look," Magda tried to extricate herself from her deep embarrassment, "I didn't kick you *there* on purpose. In my defense, you were trying to rip my throat out."

"Looks like you got there ahead of me." He touched his neck, where the skin was still pink and raw.

"I'm sorry."

"I'm not." He looked up at her again. "There aren't many people out there who could take down a *loup-garou* in full strength. I'm only sorry I hurt you in the first place. If you hadn't been such a dirty fighter, you might be dead."

Magda met eyes with him and saw all the sorrow there, the pain, the regret. "It's not your fault," she said quietly. "No one ever becomes a *loup-garou* by choice."

He looked up, as if he hadn't quite realized she knew exactly what he was. "If I'd had the choice, I never would." Something blazed behind his eyes as he spoke. "I hate it. I hate this loss of control, I hate not knowing what's happened or what's going to happen."

"All werewolves lose control a little when they change --"

"Yes, but they keep their minds. When you change form you still know who you are. You'd no more kill a man in wolf form than you would as a human."

Magda said nothing.

"I don't know what's going to happen to me after dark," he said.

"Not every night?"

"No, just at the full moon. Three nights. The sun goes down and I lose my mind until dawn. The worst thing is that I don't even remember what happens." He gave a snort. "Or maybe that's the best thing. I have a circle," he went on, "a magic circle, to keep me in. It can only be broken by speaking a pretty lengthy enchantment. I remember going into it last night, but I don't... Something must have gone wrong."

"Is it far from here?" Magda asked, wondering at the surreality of having this conversation lying naked on the bed.

"I don't think so. I asked the gendarme. About a hundred kilometers -- fifty or sixty miles, I think. I don't come out this way much."

Magda didn't know what to say, so she said nothing and stroked his shoulder for solidarity. After a moment he gave her a brief smile, then bent his head again and started on the cut on her leg.

In a second the air got heavier, and whatever sexual tension had been dissipated by their conversation shot back into the room. Magda was lying naked on the bed, her nipples standing up for attention, her pussy getting wetter and wetter, and the worst thing was that she knew he was just as aware of it as she was. He could smell her arousal, just as she could smell his.

The towel had come off at some point and he was kneeling over her naked, that fine ass of his bare for her viewing pleasure. She couldn't see the impressive length of his cock from where she lay, but she was pretty sure she felt it brush her leg, long and stiff.

He was getting hard. Over her. This incredibly beautiful man was aroused by her!

Of course, Magda reasoned with herself, *he's probably a pretty isolated sort of guy. Trying to do the decent thing and keep himself away from the public when he's dangerous. He probably doesn't date much. Probably been a while since he's seen a naked woman. And he did wake up to me licking his balls. He probably thinks I'm a sure thing.*

Am I a sure thing?

He was moving up the cut on her leg now, getting higher, closer. Magda realized her bosom was actually heaving as he cupped her thigh to bring it closer to his mouth. It wasn't necessary, but she sure appreciated the gesture.

He wanted her. And God knew she wanted him. Her body was a quivering mass of hot, wanton nerve endings, all screaming for his touch. Magda knew that it wouldn't be a smart thing to do, and she also knew she wasn't that kind of girl. She was the kind of girl who made nutritious breakfasts for her kids and always kept a spare pair of stockings in her bag -- although the fact that she wore stockings was probably a clue that she really needed to be the other kind of girl.

The kind who let a naked man lick her thigh, and inched her legs open in invitation for him to lick something else.

It wasn't as if they were ever going to see each other again, anyway, she reasoned. They didn't even know each other's names.

His tongue flickered over her groin, and Magda sucked in a breath. He hesitated, just for a second, and she knew he was looking for her reaction. Would he stop if she asked him to?

She thought about those gentle eyes, and knew he would.

But did she want him to?

Chapter Three

In the boldest move she'd ever made in her life, Magda moved her thighs further apart, her heart thumping, and opened herself to him. He let out a soft sigh, and licked closer, and then his tongue was on her, brushing her labia, darting between her folds, seeking out her clit and licking, gently sucking.

Magda heard noises that she could only assume were coming from her. Gasps and moans and sighs that she wasn't at all aware of making, but she wasn't surprised to hear. Dimly she tried to recall if any man had ever done this for her, and if it had ever felt like this, but she couldn't remember, because nothing had ever felt this good and her brain was melting with the pleasure of it. Dear God, this man was a genius!

His hands cupped her hips, her buttocks, lifting her to him as his mouth moved over her. Magda was glad he was supporting her because her body had taken on a mind of its own. She writhed and bucked and pushed closer to him, greedy, wanting more, wanting everything. His fingers slipped into play, two of them sliding inside her as he sucked and licked her clit, and she sobbed in delight.

"Oh God, don't stop!" That voice again, the same woman who was moaning and wailing. Magda had no clue if it was her or not. She had absolutely no control over her mouth at all. No control over any part of her body. It knew what it wanted, and it was getting it, too.

He curved his fingers inside her, hit that sweet, sweet spot, and with a cry Magda came, convulsing, gasping, mindless, her whole being consumed by the total pleasure he was licking into her, thrusting with his fingers, melting her with his heat.

He didn't stop straight away, just carried on gently licking her so that the orgasm didn't fade, but kept crashing over her, making her weak, making her full, replete, satisfied.

It seemed like hours before she came back down again, could open eyes she didn't remember shutting, could look at the man who'd given her the best sex of her life without even fucking her.

He kissed the inside of her thigh, and even after all he'd done for her, that still made Magda shiver.

"Wow," she croaked, and he smiled. Not a leering smile, not a smug smile, just a real, honest smile, like he was glad he'd pleased her. "Who are you and what planet did you come from?" she asked. "I think I'll take a trip there."

He laughed and stretched out beside her, muscles flexing, before gathering her into his arms and kissing her mouth.

"I was just returning the favor. You taste delicious," he said.

He felt just as good as she'd imagined. Better, maybe, harder and hotter, the contrast of his rougher skin against hers so delightful it made her tingle. His mouth was as delightful up here as it had been down below five minutes ago. Soft and hot, sharp teeth and clever tongue. She'd have kissed him for hours if there hadn't been something else she wanted even more.

His cock nudged against her thigh, thick and hard, and Magda shivered at the thought of it filling her. She was just starting to feel like moving was a good idea, instead of the impossible dream it had been when he'd first lifted his head from her pussy, and she gently nudged him with her hips until he was on his back, and she sat up, straddling him.

"Whoa." Maybe the movement was too soon, because she felt a little dizzy up here. Or maybe it was the extremely hot naked man reclining below her, his fat juicy cock just there for the taking, his fingers stroking her ribcage, coming up to play with her breasts.

"My sentiments exactly." He smiled at her, and Magda lost her breath, which he took advantage of when he grasped her by the shoulders and pulled her down for another kiss, long and deep, making her squirm for more. His hands slid down the length of her back, and her skin rippled with pleasure as he cupped her buttocks and shifted beneath her, and then he was inside her, stretching and filling her, and Magda just couldn't breathe with the glory of it.

"Oh," she said. "*Oh.*"

He nuzzled her neck, nipping at the skin, and pushed a little deeper inside her.

"Yes," Magda breathed. "Oh God, *yes.*"

Elek looked up at the goddess above him, her head thrown back, her shiny dark hair tousled and tangled, her eyes closed and her lips swollen and parted, and nearly came there and then. She was so beautiful, her skin like heavy cream stained pink with a blush, strawberries and cream, edible. She had round hips and a soft belly, and there were tiny marks under her skin, stretch marks he thought. A mother, like the primal figure ancient tribes worshipped. Life-giver. Beautiful. Her full breasts thrust out as she arched her back, nipples standing proud. He caressed one of them with his fingertips.

She opened her eyes, brought her head back, smiling at him, and he slid his hand to her back. Using it to pull her to him, he kissed her, taking that sweet hot mouth of hers and plunging into it, making love to her mouth like he was doing to her body, because she was intoxicating and he couldn't think of anything else.

He flipped her on her back and she bounced as she hit the mattress, various interesting parts of her bouncing too. Elek slid deeper, loving the tight heat that surrounded him. If it wasn't for the fact that he was going to come soon, hard, deep inside her, he'd stay like this forever, sheathed inside her, gloved, held tight and wonderful in her heat.

She stretched beneath him, lifting her arms, her body shifting against his in a way that made him shudder. Her nipples grazed his chest and he moved in her, long and deep, the relief of being inside her almost too much to bear.

"You feel so good," he told her, trying to get some control over himself. He buried his face in her neck but that was no good. She smelled delicious, hot and wild and sweet and salty, all at the same time. She was all things to him, everything, and he gave in to his body's loud demands and started moving inside her, deeper and faster and harder. She moved with him, wrapping her legs high around him, taking him so deep inside her that his balls slammed against her hot, slippery folds with each thrust and he thought he'd found heaven.

I can't last much longer, he thought, and he looked down at her, saw her eyes closed, her lips parted, felt the tight clench of her pussy around his throbbing cock, and felt her orgasm rip through her.

It was a beautiful thing, even better for knowing he was the cause. She cried out, her fingers gripping him so hard he knew he'd be bruised, but he didn't care. He barely felt it, because he was consumed by the sight and the feel of this beautiful woman coming undone beneath him, around him, writhing and crying and clutching him. Before he knew it he was coming too, surprised by it, glorying in it nonetheless, holding her tight as pleasure overtook him, the power of their bodies and the perfect fit they made together.

He shuddered against her, feeling like he'd never move again and not caring. He'd never felt this way with any woman, and he never wanted to lose the feeling.

When he woke up, the sun was high and she was gone.

Chapter Four

"Oh my gods! Stop everything!" Masika cried as soon as Magda walked into the offices of Sundown, Inc., on Monday morning.

"What?" Magda said, alarmed.

"You got *laid*!"

Magda scowled at her and dropped her handbag on her desk.

Masika moved closer, sniffing like a cat. "Wow. Mags! I'm so proud of you!"

"What happened to my desk while I was gone? Nothing's where I left it."

"Tell me everything. Human?" Masika sniffed. "I can't tell for all that werewolfy smell you have all over you."

"Stop that, it's disgusting," Magda said, swatting absently at the vampire like she would one of her children. She tucked her hair behind her ears and looked around. "Where's my pen-tidy?"

"Where you left it. Don't change the subject." Masika hitched herself up on the edge of the desk, leather-clad legs swinging. "Was he hot?"

"Someone has rearranged everything on here. Where are all the paper-clips?"

"Was he good? Fit bod?"

"I can't find my pencil sharpener."

"Mag-*derr*. Where did you meet him?"

"I know I had it right here. Where is it?"

"In Germany? I have this image of someone very geometric. Teutonic men never really did it for me, but each to their own."

"Masika, what happened to my pencil sharpener?"

Masika blinked long-lashed eyes at her. "You threw it away three years ago and switched to mechanical pencils," she said. "I'm sensing you don't want to talk about this."

"No shit, Sherlock."

"Oh my gods! Magda swore. *Johann!*"

Magda scowled some more as her boss stuck his head out of his office. "What?"

"Magda *swore.*"

"Miracles happen. Now that you're finally back you can get me some fucking coffee."

"Get it yourself," Magda and Masika said together, and Johann glared at them and retreated back inside, slamming the door.

"Will you grow up?" Magda said, pushing things around on her desk in annoyance.

"Says the woman who proclaimed to the entire office last time I got laid."

"Oh *please.* Last time you got laid was about thirty minutes ago."

Masika looked a little smug. "Okay, but you know what I meant."

"Yes, when you got together with Dare, your soulmate, the man of your dreams, the forever guy. Literally." Masika was a vampire who remembered the days of the pharaohs, and her lover, Darien, was just a little older. They'd only been together a short while and were clearly still besotted with each other. Magda tried not to show it, but she was envious as hell, and not just because Dare was criminally hot.

Masika frowned and hopped off the desk. "Is that it? You just had a one nighter?"

Magda shrugged and reached for a hair tie. "Yeah. That's all."

"And it wasn't any good?" Masika asked, a thread of sympathy in her voice.

Magda silently cursed her mother for instilling in her the virtue of honesty. "No, it was fabulous," she said miserably, tying up her hair.

"Then... Why not make more of it? You could have stayed longer. Johann's all talk. You're the best secretary this firm's ever had, and I'm not just saying that because you're my best friend."

Magda sank into her chair and rubbed her face with the heel of her hand. "I couldn't have stayed," she said, swatting at her ponytail. "Not really. I... It wouldn't work. It wouldn't ever work."

"Why not? Human?"

"No. Worse."

"What's worse than a human?"

"A *loup-garou*."

Masika blinked. "Uh, a French werewolf? Is this one of those You Frog, *Je Suis Rosbif* things? Honey, get over it. Besides, you're not even English. You're German."

"I was born in Germany. Difference."

"Still, Mags..."

"That's not it. He could be from Mars for all I care."

"Then what is it? What does '*loup-garou*' mean that I don't know about? Is this pack politics?"

Magda looked up at her friend and considered saying yes, just to end it, but suddenly she really wanted to talk about it. "No," she said, "it's not. It's just... Well, it's bad."

Masika sat down in the other chair, her face serious now. "How bad?"

"Werewolves are... Well, there's really only one way to become a werewolf, when you come down to it. A true werewolf. You have to be bitten."

"You weren't. You were born to it."

"Yes, but somewhere in my ancestry someone was bitten. And don't ask me how the first werewolf was created, I don't know. All I know is that even if you're born to it, somewhere back in your family tree, someone got bitten. All werewolf children will be born full-blood, even if they have one human parent."

"Like yours?"

"Like mine."

"How're they doing, by the way?"

"Good. Speaking German like natives. I talked with my mother last night when I got in."

Masika nodded. It had been her suggestion that Magda send her children to live with her mother during the summer, the first summer since they'd started school, and their grandmother had moved away. Finding daycare for three active young werewolves was virtually impossible, and Johann had quickly banned them from the office.

"So how's this *loup-garou* thing different from a regular werewolf?"

Magda blew out a breath. She already missed the kids like hell, but she'd far rather discuss that than her one-night stand. "For a start, he wasn't bitten. He was cursed."

"That's a charming way to put it."

"But true. Someone with a really bad grudge against him, or one of his ancestors, put a curse on him to turn into a snarling beast at the full moon."

Masika raised her eyebrows. "Snarling beast?"

"Literally. When I change shape, that's all I do. It's still my brain inside the wolf's body. When he changes, he loses his mind. It's as if someone took a wolf and put it in a cage and starved it and beat it and stabbed it with cattle prods and just tortured it into insanity until all it knew was rage and anger and a horrible urge to kill." She took a breath. "And for three nights of the moon, that's what happens to the *loup-garou*. When he wakes up he has no idea what's happened, no memory of it at all."

Masika whistled. "That's one hell of a curse."

"Yep. And it's hereditary."

"How charming."

"I didn't think there were any left anywhere. Guess he's been hiding."

"And this is your one-night stand?"

Magda nodded miserably.

"Well, there's something to be said for him being an animal in bed," Masika joked weakly. She stood up. "Look, I have to go. I've been up all night -- I just stayed up to say welcome home."

"Thanks." Magda hugged her friend. "Good to be home. Felt like I was driving on the wrong side of the road, you know?"

After Masika disappeared down the Sundown tunnels, back to her home and her lover, Magda cleared her desk of all the work that had come in while she'd been away, called her mother again and chatted with the kids, and started to go through the accounts. If she left Johann to his own devices for even a day, things got in a horrible mess.

But her mind wasn't on accounts. It wasn't on anything, except for the incredibly hot werewolf who'd made her come so hard she saw stars, held her close in his arms, looked at her with those soft, sweet eyes of his. It wasn't fair, it just wasn't bloody *fair*, that someone as gentle and noble as him should have such a thing happen. That he should have to closet himself away like that. It just wasn't fair.

She stared blankly at her computer screen, thinking. Then she picked up the phone.

* * *

Con Devlin lived by the sea in a fisherman's cottage that was filled to the rafters with magical crap. By his own admission, most of it was useless, but he kept it on the basis that one day he might figure out what to do with it. He wasn't a very good wizard, but he knew a lot about theory, and he had good contacts, which kept him on retainer with Sundown. Besides which, Magda kind of liked him. It didn't hurt that he had deep blue eyes and a bucketful of Irish charm, either.

"Sorry, darlin', but I have to get this potion done before sunset tonight, and it's very sensitive," he apologized as he opened the door to Magda, already darting back inside.

"Sure," she said, "I just need some --" she blinked at the cloud of smoke billowing from the work table in his living room, "-- advice."

"Is it about invisibility potions? 'Cos I tell you, I'm all --"

"No, it's not." Magda waved her hand in front of her face, trying to find some air to breathe.

"Good." Con picked something up with a pair of tongs, held it at arm's length and dropped it into the steaming beaker, then immediately leapt back. "You wouldn't believe what people expect I know."

Magda eyed his torn jeans and the debris scattered all over the table, and held her tongue on that. "Do you know anything about werewolves?"

He glanced at her nervously. "Is that a veiled threat?"

"No." She smiled. "I need some advice on a *loup-garou*."

"Silver bullets." He poured something silvery into a tiny crucible. "Anything else projectile -- and silver -- will work, but you'll need to practice. Once it knows you're shooting, it'll come after you. And once it comes after you..."

Magda shivered at the memory of the huge black wolf crashing down on her. She'd fought other wolves in the pack before, but never anything so big, so strong, so terrifying. He'd been all claws and fangs and fury, blood and fur, and he hadn't stopped until she'd clawed at his belly and his balls and ripped out his throat.

And then, too hurt to sustain the change, he'd shimmered back to human form, and just for a second, those big brown eyes had blinked at her, hurt and confused.

"I don't want to kill it, Con," she said quietly.

He looked up at her, surprised, then dropped the crucible he was carrying and leapt backwards with a yelp as it burst into flame.

"Mags," he said, blotting out the fire with a rag, "you're a werewolf. You of all people should know what these creatures are."

"Yes," she said, "they're ordinary people tortured beyond their control."

He frowned at her for a moment. "You know someone?"

She nodded.

"Ah, feck, Magda. This is not a good idea."

"I know," she said. "That's why I'm here."

"I am not handing out dating advice to werewolves. I have enough problems of my own."

"I don't want dating advice. I want advice on curses."

"Oh." He dropped the rag in a bucket and wiped his hands on his jeans. "What kind of curses?"

"The kind that might turn a person into a *loup-garou*."

Con sighed, peered at his beaker, and sighed again. "It's not the sort you can undo with a few abracadabras."

"I was guessing that."

He slouched out of the room, went back into the kitchen. "Coffee?"

"Curse," Magda said.

"Fuck, bollocks, shit --"

"Not funny."

"Ah, come on, where's your sense of humor?" He came back out with two mugs and handed one to her. Coffee so instant she doubted it had ever seen real coffee beans. "Do you really want to know how to lift a *loup-garou* curse?"

"Yes."

"It's a lot like most hereditary curses."

"Tell me."

"Kill the last scion."

She blinked at him. "What?"

"The last scion. The last remaining family member with the curse."

She closed her eyes for a second. "No. Tell me something else."

"I can't, darlin'. Sorry. Unless you know who made the curse --"

"I could find out," she said, not sure if she could but willing to try.

"Then you either kill him, or get him to unsay it."

She stared. It had probably first been said hundreds of years ago. "The person who made the curse?"

"Yep. They're not supposed to be easy to rescind, Mags. That's the point."

She looked at the floor. At her coffee. At the wall. There had to be another way. "The actual person who said the curse?"

"Yeah." He blew out a sigh. "Unless --"

"*Yes?*"

"Well --" Con scratched the back of his neck, "-- it is sometimes known for a curse to be bound to an object. This is particularly true for long-running curses."

"Like this one."

"Well, yes. Reason being, that once the curser is dead, the curse dies with him, unless he binds it to something. Find the something, destroy it, end the curse."

"So..." This was good. This was something she could work with. "So I just have to find out what he bound the curse to --"

"Or who."

"Or -- what?"

Con shrugged and slurped his coffee. "Objects are fragile, hard to keep track of. People, now -- that's something you can use. Bind the curse to a person, to their blood -- and so long as that bloodline is active, so's the curse. It's a fairly common thing to bind the curse to a descendant."

"So I should look for the curser's descendant?"

"You could try," Con said miserably. "Magda. Don't do this." He looked right at her. "He's not worth it."

"How do you know?"

"Because -- this is going to cause you a lot of grief, and you've had enough of that."

Magda felt herself bristle. "And what would you know about that?"

He shrugged. "Wizard, remember?"

She scowled at him.

"You're welcome. Look, just promise you'll be careful."

Magda thought where being careful had got her so far, and didn't reply.

Chapter Five

Elek looked up at the rather grand offices of Sundown, Inc., and took a deep breath. The chances of them being able to help him were rather slim, but there just really wasn't anyone else who was even remotely qualified. Sundown had a reputation, a good one, as the only investigative firm in the paranormal world. And not just investigations. Word had it that they carried out assassinations and cover-ups and other kinds of wetwork. It was all a little *Angel Investigations* for Elek, but he was willing to try anything.

He'd been in the shadows long enough.

Upstairs he found an empty room with a very tidy desk and a reception area holding sofas, chairs, and magazines with titles like *Hot Leather* and *Today's Werewolf*. One of them held a bookmark.

"Hello?" Elek called.

Nothing. It was the middle of the day, and there was no one here. But then it was a firm staffed largely by vampires, werewolves, wizards, Fae, and other creatures of the night, so he shouldn't really be surprised.

"Anyone? I have an appointment…"

A tiny sound to his left that wouldn't have been caught by human ears, and Elek's head snapped toward it. A woman stood in the center of the large room, her slender body wrapped around with tight metallic leather, six-inch heels on her feet, straps of leather on her arms holding stakes and daggers. Part of her face and the visible part of one arm were puckered with pink scars, as if her dark bronze skin had been splashed with acid. In her hand was a small automatic pistol.

He'd never heard footsteps, and all the doors were still closed.

"Nice hearing," she said, her voice cool.

"Werewolf," he said. "Nice entrance."

"Vampire," she said. "Your name, wolf?"

"Sólyom," he said. "Elek Sólyom. I have an appointment with Johann Eriksson."

Her head cocked to one side. She was a very beautiful woman, even with the horrible scarring, but there was something absolutely terrifying in her lithe, precise movements.

"Johann!" she yelled, a sudden burst of volume.

A door opened, and a human man poked his head out. "Christ, do you have to be so bloody silent? What are you even doing here, Mas?"

"Forgot my purse," the vampire said. "You have an appointment with a werewolf?"

Johann looked at Elek. "Oh fuck, yeah. Gimme a minute," he said. "Mas, come in here, I need you to translate this for me."

"From what into what?"

"I dunno, Aramaic or something. One of those dead languages. Into English, if you please."

The vampire rolled her dark eyes at Elek, who gave her a polite smile.

"He'll be with you in a minute," she said, sounding as if she was speaking someone else's words, and vanished into Johann's office, shutting the door.

Elek frowned, and looked around again. Now that he paid attention, there were things about the room -- apart from the magazines -- that were more than a little eccentric. The decor and lighting were modern, sleek, attractive, but there was something in the placement of the thirteen spotlights that gave him pause. As did the apparently abstract prints around the room that all seemed to have some variety of casually included religious symbol in them. The coffee counter also held a microwave and bottles of deep red liquid, and other substances he couldn't even begin to guess at.

Riiight.

He went over to the receptionist's desk and picked up a set of dolls lying there. Two girls and a boy doll, soft cloth things, tied loosely together with white ribbons decorated with little hearts. Across the foreheads of each doll were tied gem stones, and there were more pressed against the hearts of the dolls, held in place with the same white ribbon.

The door to the street stairs opened behind him and he turned to hear a voice begin, "Can I help --"

Then she stopped, frozen, staring at him. His werewolf! Her glossy dark hair swinging in a shining curtain about her shoulders, petite frame beautifully dressed in a pale pink suit, pearls at her pretty throat. Her dark eyes wide as she stared at him.

"You're here," he said, because he couldn't think of anything else to say. His brain wouldn't work at all.

She smelled so good, even from a distance. "You're here too," she said, her voice husky, uncertain. Incredibly distracting.

"Business," he said, unable at present to remember what it was. "You?"

"Business," she said, and clarified, "I work here."

"Oh."

She took a step toward him, then another, then seemed to gain confidence and walked around him to take the dolls from his hand. But then she bent to put them in a desk drawer, and her butt in that tight pink skirt was more than he could stand, and when she stood up he swept her toward him and kissed her, desperately.

And she kissed him back.

Elek wrapped his arms around her and held her close, tight, in case he lost her again. She tasted so good, her own sweet taste and coffee and mints, her mouth hot, her body so soft under those clothes.

He drew back after a second or two -- or maybe it was several hours, hard to tell -- and tried to get his breath back. Probably he should let her go. She wouldn't appreciate being manhandled. "I thought I'd never see you again," he tried to explain.

She wrapped her arms around his neck and clung to him. Maybe she did appreciate the manhandling. "I should have gotten your name --" she began.

"I woke up and you were gone --"

"Or left you mine --"

"You taste *so* good..."

He nipped at her throat, tasted the perfume on her skin and her own taste underneath it, sweet and salty, a strong taste, his beautiful lady wolf. She moaned and pulled his mouth back to hers, and he went dizzy from the heat of it, lost balance and swung her against the desk to keep from falling over.

She arched against him, full breasts straining against that proper suit, and worked her hands under his jacket, burning him through his shirt, touching his chest, his stomach, his back, pulling him closer.

Elek reached for the buttons of her jacket and fumbled them open -- when had it gotten so hard to unfasten a button? -- slipped his hands under her blouse and felt her hot, smooth skin. She let out a small moan, buried her head against his shoulder, and let him touch her.

Her breasts were heavy, nipples pushing hard against the lace of her bra, pushing even harder when he ran his thumbs over them. She was breathing hard now, holding him close, slipping her fingers below his waistband and caressing his bare skin.

"God, you're so beautiful," she murmured, her voice husky, and Elek nearly bit through his lip in an effort to keep some tiny shred of control.

An effort that was entirely unnecessary, because a second later someone gave a little cough from just behind Elek, and they both froze.

"Sorry to intrude," Masika said. She sounded like she was laughing. "There are some private rooms you could use upstairs."

Magda wondered if her face really was on fire or if she was just imagining it. She had her legs wrapped round the *loup-garou*'s waist, her hands in his pants, and her breasts in his palms. And she still didn't even know his name!

"I'll hold Johann off if you want," Masika added.

"Thank you," the *loup-garou* said, not looking at her.

"You're welcome," Masika said, and added slyly as she vanished, "Elek."

Elek? That was his name? Magda tried not to look like she was studying him as he took his hands out of under her blouse and stepped back, straightening his clothing. It sounded Slavic, not that she was surprised with those cheekbones. His incredibly beautiful cheekbones.

She licked her lips, and he groaned. Stood up and brushed against him, and he closed his eyes.

"About those private rooms..."

She nearly giggled, feeling heady. "How about the ones in my house?"

"Is it far?"

Was she really suggesting this?

Elek's long fingers stroked her neck.

Yes, she really was. "Not far at all."

"Then they sound good." He nibbled on her ear. "Really good."

Her car was parked outside on the street, too far away, and she nearly fell down the steps in her haste to get there. She'd left Elek -- Elek, what a fabulous name! -- to reschedule with Johann. She wouldn't have fancied his chances if Masika hadn't been there to bully their boss along.

Brainless with desire, it took three tries to get her car key in the lock, and then she remembered she had a remote key anyway. She couldn't start the ignition. Her hands were trembling. She wanted him so damn much!

Magda made herself calm down, taking deep breaths and thinking about filing cabinets and other boring things. If she didn't get her head in order she'd crash, and then she'd never get to have sex with Elek again.

She put the car in gear, and drove it around the corner to the front of the Sundown building. Elek was there, coming down the steps, elegant in a dark gray suit, his shirt very white against his olive skin, his hair tied back, his beautiful eyes searching the street. When he saw her car, he smiled and loped over, hung his arms on the window frame and looked inside.

He smelled so good Magda lost her breath.

"Ready to go?"

She nodded, wordless, and he swung inside the car.

Magda was usually investigated by the tax office every year, because they couldn't understand how someone who gave her occupation as "secretary" could afford a beautiful house in Primrose Hill worth over a million, and send her children to a good school, and afford childcare every day after school. The answer was simple. Sundown paid her a fortune. She had a damn nice house, and it was even looking clean and shiny now she didn't have to pick up after the kids every day, and she was on the verge of forgetting its location because Elek was sitting there beside her in the car, smelling fantastic and looking unbelievably edible.

They were halfway around Regent's Park, stopped in traffic, when his hand slipped to her knee and caressed her through her stockings. She gulped, and tried to keep her eyes on the road.

"Am I distracting you?" he whispered, and Magda only just managed to shake her head.

His fingers inched a little higher. Magda gripped the steering wheel hard and kept her eyes on the lights, although if they'd suddenly turned pink and blue she wouldn't have noticed.

"Tell me it's not far now," Elek breathed.

Magda was about to tell him it was about six inches away, but then she realized he meant the house, and gulped out, "Just around the corner."

His hand was under her skirt now, on the inside of her thigh, stroking higher with agonizing slowness. Caressing her stocking-top, just brushing the bare skin above. Magda started panting, for once grateful that traffic lights in London were so slow.

When his fingers reached the lace of her panties, she let out a gasp of breath she didn't realize she'd been holding. He stroked the soft strip of skin at the edge of her underwear, and she closed her eyes, whimpering.

Elek's fingers slipped under the lace edge, Magda held her breath, and a loud blast from behind her ripped her eyes open in shock.

The light was green.

She stared wildly at Elek, who looked down at his hand, up at the light, then across at her. He didn't move.

Magda put the car into gear and lurched forward, each movement of her foot on the clutch shifting her leg, and therefore his hand, just a little, easing against her, stroking and caressing.

She had no idea how she made it home without crashing.

"You," she said as she pulled up the handbrake and he swept her toward him for a kiss, "are a very bad man."

"If you'd asked me to stop, I would," he said.

"I know," she said, and he grinned at her, and kissed her so long and deep she just melted into him. And when she came up for air he pulled her back and kissed her again, deeper, longer, wave upon wave of gorgeous kisses until she couldn't breathe with wanting him any more.

"We need to get inside," she gasped, "before we get arrested."

Elek just nodded, releasing her to get out of the car, managing it a lot more smoothly than Magda, who had to fight with her seatbelt and nearly lost. She stumbled up the steps to her house, fumbling through her keys, Elek behind her, his arms around her waist, his breath hot in her ear, murmuring all the things he'd like to do to her.

"And then some," Magda murmured, kicking the door open, finally stumbling inside, and pinning him to the wall as the door swung shut with a heavy clunk.

She kissed him this time, long, desperate kisses, even as she was fumbling with his clothes and her own, urgently undressing right there in the hall. Elek's hands were driving her skirt up, cupping her ass, stroking her through her panties. He slipped one hand around inside the lace, found her pussy swollen and drenched with desire and stroked her, made her cry out in desperation and frustration as she wrenched at his clothes, eventually unfastening his fly with shaking fingers and reaching inside to his thick, upright cock.

Elek groaned, lifted her up, and pushed the lace of her underwear to one side, rubbing the head of his cock against her pussy lips, making her shudder.

"Oh God, now, please, now," she moaned, and he lifted her leg around his waist and pushed into her, finally filling her, the tightest fit, so hot inside her. Magda gripped his hips, burying her head in his shoulder, trying to contain herself, trying not to come there and then.

Then Elek thrust, and she lost her balance, and he swung her around against the wall and pushed harder into her. She gave in and moaned, clutched him to her, and let him fuck her, hard, the way she wanted it, right there in the hallway with the door barely closed.

His hands ripped at her blouse, pulling it open, reaching for her breasts and stroking, squeezing. He dipped his head and sucked at her nipple through the fabric of her bra, ran his teeth over it, and Magda felt her orgasm starting, hot crashing waves that made her body shake and her mind melt into pure, brainless pleasure.

She only vaguely realized she was screaming when she came down, felt Elek thrust into her once, twice more, then come deep inside her with a howl of satisfaction.

For a long moment they rested there, his body pinning hers to the wall, still mostly clothed but for the jacket he'd shucked and the shoes she'd kicked across the floor.

She started to giggle.

"What?" Elek raised his head.

"We still have our clothes on."

He looked down at her bared breasts, a smile tugging at his lips. "Well, in a manner of speaking."

She giggled a bit more.

"I don't even know your name," he said.

"It's Magda. Magda Braun," she said.

He lifted his hand from her breast and offered it to her. Magda took it, laughing, as he said solemnly, "I am Elek Sólyom."

"It's nice to meet you," Magda said, thinking that this was the first time she'd ever made introductions to someone who was inside her.

"It's *very* nice to meet you," he replied, his eyes laughing even as he tried to keep his tone earnest.

The phone rang, just down the hall in the kitchen, and Magda looped her arms around Elek's neck for a lazy kiss, murmuring, "Leave it, the machine'll get it."

He was more than happy to oblige, cupping her face with his hands and kissing her with total tenderness, sweet and lovely, and she sighed with the rightness of it. She could spend the rest of her life kissing this man.

The answering machine kicked in, and Magda kissed Elek through her whole recorded message, until it bleeped and a child's voice called, "*Hallo, Mama!*"

Magda froze.

"*Wie geht es Ihnen?*" The child -- it was Anya, Magda recognized -- laughed, and carried on in English, "Nanna's been teaching us German. I mean *Großmutter* has! How come you never speak German? It's fun. You get to make all these sounds --" Anya broke off into throat-clearing noises "-- and spit, and it's great." Someone spoke off-stage, and Anya came back, "Oh. She says you'll probably be at work. I thought the time was different in England? Okay. Then call me back -- *Großmutter*, does she have the number? She says you do. Okay, *Auf Wiedersehen, Mama!*"

The phone clicked off. Magda swallowed.

Elek pulled out of her, and started fastening his clothes.

Chapter Six

Mortified, angry with herself for not making the situation clear beforehand, her head still fuzzy with sex, Magda tried to straighten her own clothes.

"How old is she?" Elek asked, his voice calm.

"Five."

"Sounds older."

"Werewolf children grow quickly. Elek --"

"And the others?"

She blinked at him.

"The dolls on your desk," he said. "Two girls and a boy -- protection dolls, I thought?"

She nodded, surprised at his insight. "Yes. Anya, Lucinda, and Robert. They're all the same age -- we tend to have, uh, litters..."

He nodded. Still he looked calm. Magda was puzzled. "You don't seem surprised," she said.

"I guessed." He gave her a lopsided smile, and gestured to the blouse she still hadn't fastened. "Stretch marks."

"Oh." Magda colored, and wrapped the shirt around herself. "Look, I'm sorry --"

"For what?" He tugged at the tie she'd loosened, and pulled it off.

"I should have told you..." Because now he wouldn't be interested, he'd get pissed off and he'd leave, and then...

"It's all right, Magda, I don't mind. I told you, I'd guessed. I like kids."

She frowned. "You're not angry."

"Should I be?"

"Well, no, I just... expected..."

He smiled, cupped her face, and kissed her again. "Expected?"

"You started getting dressed and I..."

"I started getting dressed because I thought we might be civilized and have a cup of coffee, and I didn't want to wander around your house naked and scandalize your neighbors."

"Oh." She watched him go into the kitchen, taking his fine ass with him, and felt a smile spread across her face. "Oh."

She followed, and found him in front of the fridge, studying the kids' pictures she'd stuck there by letter magnets.

"There is one thing," Elek began, worrying his lip between his teeth.

Magda made a face. "Yes?"

"Their father? My plans for tonight do not include fighting some other man for you."

"Oh." She relaxed, and slipped her arms about his waist. "No. No fighting. He's well out of the picture."

"Good," Elek said. "I want you all to myself."

Next morning Magda went into the office with a big smile on her face, and even the huge pile of filing Johann gave her didn't make it go away.

Two weeks later, with Magda working late at Sundown, Elek let himself into the austere building and up the steps to meet her. Two weeks of fantastic sex, of closeness, of waking up and seeing her head nestled close on his chest. Two weeks of being in love.

There had been other women in Elek's life, mostly at university, before the curse took him, but right now they were hard to remember. He'd never felt such a desperate need to be close to anyone before. He'd never known with such finality that it would never work between them, either.

At the end of the week he had to leave, go home to his derelict castle in France and lock himself inside the magic circle. If it failed this time...

If it failed...

He was as good as dead.

There was another man in the outer office when Elek arrived. Big, blond, eyes like sapphires. Face like a Greek god. Cold, coppery scent. Vampire.

"You must be Dare," he said, and the Greek god nodded. He sniffed.

"Werewolf," he said. "Not the usual flavor. I'm guessing you're Elek."

Pleased that Magda had mentioned him to her friends, he nodded.

"Let's hope you last longer than the last one," Dare continued, and Elek froze.

"Be nice," Masika's voice came from behind him, and she stalked out in her leather and heels to slide an arm around Dare's waist. "Don't frighten him."

"The last one?" Elek asked. "You mean her husband?"

Masika nodded. "You're nothing like him. Don't worry."

"I'm glad to hear it," Elek said. "If he'd leave her and the children --"

Dare snorted. Masika winced.

"He didn't leave?" Elek said, a sinking feeling in his stomach.

"Not voluntarily," Dare said.

"Magda hasn't told him," Masika said.

"No shit. What happened?" Elek's voice came out hoarse.

"Maybe you should sit down," Masika said, and her sudden kindness unnerved him. He took a seat on one of the sofas, and they sat down opposite, eerily synchronized.

"Magda's husband was --" Masika paused.

"A total shit," Dare supplied.

"Pretty much. None of us knew, or we'd have done something about it." She frowned. "That is to say -- her mother never liked him. But you know Magda. She's very independent. And when it started to get bad, I think she was too ashamed to tell anyone she'd made such a bad call."

"How bad?" Elek asked.

"Not very bad, not anything she could have really got him for," Masika said, leaving Elek wondering what she meant by "got him." "Until she got pregnant, and he knew she was vulnerable. You don't provoke a she-wolf."

"Normally a she-wolf will retreat into the pack when she's pregnant," Dare explained. "They protect her while she's vulnerable, when she can't protect herself."

"But Magda had pretty much left the pack by then," Masika said. "She really went into herself. And when he started beating on her --"

"Wait. Whoa. He did *what*?" Elek said.

"Beat her so badly she lost two babies," Masika said. "She should have had five."

Elek just stared at her. How had Magda, his beautiful strong Magda, been cowed like that?

"She didn't want to risk them," Masika said, reading his face. "Didn't want to risk changing shape -- that's the only time when the moon doesn't affect a she-wolf -- and she wasn't strong enough in human form. She is now, though. I wouldn't pick a fight with her."

"You would," Dare said, fondly.

"Well, yes, but that's me. What I'm saying is, you shouldn't, Elek. I like you. I'd like to see you live a long and healthy life with your viscera still intact."

"With my -- what?"

"Viscera," Dare said helpfully. "All the slimy stuff inside."

"I know what it is," Elek said. "Are you threatening me?"

"No," Masika said, then considered. "Well, yes. I don't want Magda to have to kill you. I'll do it instead. I should have got there last time, but... well, this time I won't let it get so bad."

"It won't get bad," Elek said, depressed. It wouldn't get bad because he'd have to leave. And he wouldn't be able to risk coming back.

He stood up. "Just to frighten me even further, what did she do to him?"

"She ripped out his guts," Masika said, as if she was describing a recipe. "Clawed open his arms and legs and watched him bleed. And before he lost consciousness, she tore out his throat."

Elek put his hand to his neck, which still bore the scar of Magda's attack on him.

"We called the pack, her mother and I, killed an animal there to disguise the blood, disposed of the body. Best you don't ask how," Masika added, and beside her, Dare made eating motions.

"Just so you know," Elek said, "I would never hurt her."

"But your beast would."

He closed his eyes.

"I know you love her, Elek. I can see it in your face, in every move you make, the way you hold her. A human could figure it. But I also know you can't control your beast. If you ever hurt her or her children, then she, or I, or both, will end you."

She said it simply, a matter of pure fact, no malice in her voice. When Elek opened his eyes she was looking at him steadily.

Dare raised his hand. "I'll help," he added cheerfully. "No hard feelings, wolf, but sometimes I miss the killing."

Elek stared at the two vampires. "I'll bear that in mind," he said, as the door to Johann's office opened and Magda came out, looking tired.

"Been having a chat?" she asked warily, her gaze darting between her lover and her friends.

"Swapping horror stories," Elek told her, and steered her out without looking back.

When they got home the phone was ringing, and Magda picked up to her mother's voice. Elek stood watching her for a moment or two, then disappeared into the kitchen.

Something smelled delicious.

Really delicious.

And it wasn't just the food that was cooking.

Magda kicked off her shoes, sat down and peeled off her stockings, and rubbed her aching feet as she talked with the children. Every now and then, Elek passed her with a dish or some cutlery, and she watched him, so mesmerized by the way he moved and how good he looked in his jeans that she lost the thread of conversation.

"You're probably hungry," her mother eventually said. "Have you eaten yet?"

"Elek's cooking," Magda murmured, admiring his feet -- his feet, for God's sake! -- as he passed.

"Elek?"

Oh, crap.

"Uh, he's just a -- just, uh -- crap," Magda said, and her mother laughed.

"Magda, *Liebling*, I won't say a single thing. Except that you must bring him to me. I want to meet this man who cooks you dinner."

Magda winced. She could just imagine it. '*Hallo Mama*, this is Elek, who fucks me silly three times a night and turns into a violent killer at the full moon. Elek, this is my mother. She's going to kill you now.'

"Uh, I'm not sure --"

"Magda," her mother barked, and Magda remembered she'd been the Alpha bitch of the pack when her father was alive. "I want to meet him. If there's any reason why I shouldn't, then break it off right now. I will not have you ashamed of your mate again."

Dammit, she had a point. As always. "*Ja, Mama*," she said. "I have to go now, okay?"

"Magda --"

"Bad line, breaking up, can't hear you, love you, bye."

She put the phone down and looked up to see Elek holding out a hand to pull her to her feet. She smiled at just that simple courtesy and slipped her arms around his waist, kissing his neck and breathing in his delicious scent.

"Keep doing that and we'll have to skip dinner," he said.

She laughed against him. "Wouldn't want to waste your effort."

He handed her a glass of wine and led her into the dining room, which she hardly used, and now barely recognized. The table was set with her special tableware, the stuff she only brought out at Christmas or if the pack Alpha was visiting. It had been damn difficult to find quality silverware that wasn't, in fact, silver.

There were candles everywhere. On the table, the dresser, the bookshelves, the window ledge. On the floor around the edges of the room. In the soft, flickering light, Elek's eyes gleamed. Her messy, junk-room dining room had been transformed into the most romantic place she'd ever seen.

"Oh," she said.

"Do you like it?"

She nodded, speechless.

He smiled, curled her into his arms, and kissed her softly. "You've been working so late, I wanted to do something nice for you."

Her heart melted. "Have I told you lately that I love you?" she said without thinking, and she saw the surprise flicker across his face before he smiled and kissed her again, deeper this time, more thorough, holding her close against his hard body.

Which was getting harder.

"I love you too," he murmured, and she glanced at the sofa under the window. Usually covered with schoolbooks and laundry, it looked like a new piece of furniture, standing there all plump and uncluttered.

"Seriously," she said, "will the food spoil if we leave it?"

He smiled, and then he laughed, and said, "Two seconds."

Her face fell. "That's all the time we have?"

"No," he laughed harder, "that's how long it will take me to turn the oven off."

He undressed her slowly by candlelight, kissing each bit of skin he revealed until Magda was breathless with wanting him. Pushing him onto the sofa, she straddled his lap and kissed him, long and slow, unbuttoning his shirt and smoothing her hands across his hot skin.

Maybe she'd slipped up telling him she loved him. Maybe it was true. Right now, it certainly was. Two weeks of companionship, like spending time with her best friend -- who was incidentally a red-hot lover. She'd never felt this way about anyone before. No one had ever done for her the things that Elek did.

She kissed her way down his chest, his adorable flat stomach, following the line of hair that disappeared into his jeans.

Her eyes flickered up and met his, and she unfastened the top button. Elek licked his lips. She licked the skin she'd just revealed.

It was a shame his jeans were zipped, not buttoned, because a girl could have more fun unfastening them slowly. Although with the mood she was in, the quicker the better. Magda stripped off the rest of his clothes, leaving him sitting there naked on the sofa, his eyes dark, his breath coming fast, his cock standing tall and rigid and beckoning to her.

She knelt before him, and took it into her mouth.

Elek let out a fast breath, his hand sliding over her hair, cupping her head. She licked down the length of his cock and then back up, enjoying his groan. She ran her tongue around the head of his cock, and he made a small noise that sounded very much like he was trying not to cry out.

She sucked his cock in as far as she could and worked her mouth over it, in and out, fondling his balls, and he moaned, "Christ, Magda."

She smiled and wriggled her body so her breasts were pressing against the insides of his thighs.

"Stop," he said, "please stop."

She looked up at him enquiringly.

"I want to be inside you."

She released his cock and smiled. "I think that's something I can work with."

She slid onto his lap, kissing his mouth, wrapping her arms around him and rubbing her wet pussy against his cock, gliding her aching clit against his hot flesh, faster and faster because it felt so good. Elek slipped his hands between them and massaged her breasts, full and heavy with wanting, and bit on her lower lip, a new ache to distract her from the one deep inside.

She moved, reached down and guided his cock into her, slid down onto him and closed her eyes as he filled her, little by little, slowly, until she rested on his lap, as close as she could be, feeling the swell of his balls against her cunt.

For a moment they were still, savoring it, and then Elek brushed his lips over hers, a tiny thrill that she relished, and she smiled and started moving, and he moved too, capturing her mouth and kissing her deeply, his tongue thrusting just as his cock drove into her.

Her head rolled back. How could anything feel this good? Body to body, her breasts rubbing his chest with every movement, the friction against her nipples an almost unbearable excitement, the slide of his cock deep inside her, his hands on her hips, guiding her.

He ran his fingers up her back and pulled her head back to him, kissing her, and she opened her eyes and looked into his and knew right then that she'd never loved anyone like she loved him, and she never would again.

When she came she cried his name and buried her face in his neck, and he held her as she shook with the pleasure he'd given her.

"I love you," she whispered against his skin. "I love you."

Chapter Seven

"So what would you have done if the phone hadn't rung?" Magda asked as Elek fed her from the dish of plum dumplings that had been keeping warm in the oven.

"I'd have sent your mother another text."

She blinked. He grinned.

"You set this up!"

He laughed. "I called her earlier and she agreed to phone on my signal and keep you talking until I had everything set up. I sent a text just as we were leaving the car."

"You sneaky little adorable sweetheart," Magda said, which made him laugh even more. "You spoke to my mother? She never said."

"It was supposed to be a surprise."

"Well, it is." She thought back over her conversation with her mother. "So when she told me I had to bring you for a visit..."

"She asked me earlier if we were coming over the weekend."

Magda thought of a few choice words for her mother, none of which would get her into heaven. "She asked me too. I thought I'd have to talk you round."

He smiled. "I haven't been to Germany in a while. Your mother's quite a woman. She said your father used to be pack Alpha."

Magda nodded, accepting another spoonful of dessert. "He was. He was magnificent," she said, remembering the huge, proud wolf. "He died when I was thirteen, of cancer."

"I didn't know --"

"That werewolves could get cancer? Sure. We can get a lot of things. It's just physical damage that can't harm us, unless it's silver. But because he was a werewolf, and his physiology was different to a human, he couldn't go to the hospital for treatment."

Elek covered her hand, then wrapped his arms around her and hugged her tight. He didn't say anything, didn't say he was sorry, just held her, and Magda appreciated that more than anything.

"Tell me about your curse," she said, and Elek, who was more open than anyone she'd ever met, did so.

"It's been in my family for generations. A thousand years or more."

Her heart sank. "Does it hit every generation?"

"No, or we'd never procreate. Who'd mate with a *loup-garou*?"

I would, she thought, but said, "So how often?"

"I don't know. It seems to be random. And always males -- or so we thought, until my grandmother became the beast."

"What happened to her?"

He was silent a while. "She took her own life when my father was young," he said. "Most of them do."

Magda didn't know what to say to that.

"But she married and had children, obviously," she tried.

"Before the curse took her. My grandfather died in France, in the war, and she was alone in the chateau, where I live now. It's usually the home of the *loup-garou*, but there hadn't been one for a while. My father was only small so he doesn't remember it well, but he says the first time she turned was when the Germans came. They wanted to take over the chateau, so she hid my father and my uncle in the cellar and tried to fight them herself. But they took the house anyway."

"And?"

"And that night -- my father says it sounded as if someone was massacring the troops. When morning came my grandmother took them from the cellar and made them cover their eyes as she took them through the house. She took them to the village and left them there in the care of the schoolteacher, and she never came back. There were reports of a dreadful killing at the chateau, as if a wild animal had got in there and just slaughtered all the German troops. But it was her. When the family heard, they knew it was her."

Magda was silent a while, watching the flicker of candlelight reflected in her wineglass.

"What about you?" she asked, forgetting that she was supposed to be learning about the origin of the curse. "How old were you?"

"Twenty-two. I came to London to study journalism at university, and got a placement at one of the big papers. They sent me to Africa to report on the famine and corruption there."

"It happened in Africa?"

Elek nodded, his eyes on a distant view. "People were starving, there were children with guns, and these fat cats in their glossy compounds with Mercedes and designer clothes were just taking everything. The first time it happened, when I realized I'd killed one of the rich men who was stealing Western aid, I told myself it was for the good anyway."

"It was," Magda assured him.

"But the next night... I killed innocent people. I didn't even know until I woke up and heard the stories, about an animal, a lion or something, that had destroyed a village. A whole village. I didn't know what to do. I couldn't fly home, there was still one more night of the moon. No cage, no jail, has ever held a *loup-garou*. Then I remembered the incantation my father had taught me, in case the curse ever did come on me. For a magic circle. It held me then -- just. After that I came home and used the one set into the floor in a turret of the chateau. It's a double circle of iron and silver, and I repeat the incantation three times when I'm inside, and seal it with blood. Every night of the moon."

"Except for the last one," Magda said.

"No, even then," Elek said, looking at her, his eyes blazing. Magda was taken aback. She'd never seen those beautiful eyes of his looking anything but gentle.

It made her hot.

"The circle can't hold me forever, Magda," he said, and there was pain causing the fire in his eyes. She put her arms around him and kissed him. His hands slid over her bare skin, and then he was laying her down on the sofa and sliding inside her, not gentle this time at all, but fierce. She knew he was trying to tell her something, that his words had meant something more, but she couldn't think when he was touching her and as her orgasm swept over her, she didn't care any more anyway.

* * *

Magda sat on the terrace with her mother, watching Elek roll around on the grass with her children, and found herself wondering what he'd have looked like as a puppy. Then she remembered that unlike herself, unlike her children -- one of whom presently *was* a puppy -- Elek had never changed shape as a child. Until the curse had taken him, he'd been human.

It was only the curse that made him like her, and only the curse that made them so different.

"Full moon night tomorrow," her mother remarked.

"Yeah." Magda swirled the ice in her glass.

"We can introduce you to the local pack. And Elek, of course. They've accepted me very warmly. I promised the children an introduction."

Magda closed her eyes. There was something in the way her mother was watching her that made her think she knew something. Elek couldn't be introduced to the pack, of course. Not now, not ever.

Not even to her own pack at home.

"Magda?" her mother said.

"Sorry, I was thinking."

"Elek's a fine man."

"Yes, he is." She watched him tussling with Robert, Lucy running around in cub form, nipping at his heels, while Anya jumped up and down laughing at them. "Maybe more of a fine boy," she said, watching the man she loved play tug with his teeth.

Her mother laughed. "He loves you."

Magda's heart swelled. "Yes. I think he does."

"And you love him?"

"Yes."

"But?"

Magda sighed. "Why do you have to be so clever?"

"You wait until those three grow up and you'll see."

She made a face. "Now I see why parents used to arrange their children's marriages. I thought you liked Elek?"

"I do. I like him very much. He even gets on with the children."

"So?"

Her mother regarded her patiently. Magda tucked her hair behind her ears and concentrated on watching Elek and the children.

"Will you tell me?" her mother said.

"Tell you what?"

"Why it will never be right between you?"

Magda's vision blurred, her eyes stinging. "I'm working on that," she said. "I am."

But later in bed when she tried to ask Elek about the curse, he distracted her by burying his head between her legs. As distractions went, it was a pretty good one, and Magda forgot all about it. Elek fucked her so hard she forgot her own name, forgot everything but the power and pleasure of being in his arms.

Chapter Eight

She lay sleeping, incredibly beautiful in the moonlight. Strange how the moon could make her so lovely and him so foul. Every instinct of Elek's body screamed for him to touch her, to stroke her soft pale cheek, brush the fall of dark hair from her neck, kiss her sweet skin -- but he forced himself to move away. If he touched her now he'd spend the night, and the next night, and the longer they spent together the harder it would be to leave her. It had already been too long.

He slung his bag onto his shoulder and walked out, eyes stinging, heart breaking.

* * *

In the morning, Elek's side of the bed was empty, and when Magda wandered sleepily into the kitchen for coffee, he wasn't there either. Nor was he in the bathroom, or in the garden, and when she asked her mother if he'd gone for a paper or a walk, she just shook her head.

Panic prickled inside Magda.

"Then where is he?"

"He's gone."

Magda gripped the edge of the table. "Gone?"

"It's the full moon tomorrow," her mother said, looking sad. "Tonight's a change night."

Magda closed her eyes. Couldn't he do his circle thing anywhere? Maybe he was trying to protect the children. In three days he'd be back. He wasn't gone for good. It would all be okay.

When she went to get dressed she saw that his passport was gone, and something inside her snapped. Without thinking, she started throwing her own things into a suitcase.

"*Liebling*, what are you doing?" asked her mother from the doorway.

"I have to go find Elek."

"I don't think --"

"His passport is gone."

"Well, he's going to France."

"Doesn't need a passport. He's a French citizen. All he needs is ID." Magda threw her underwear into the suitcase. "If he's taken his passport, he's gone for good. He hasn't left anything."

Her mother was silent for a moment.

"*Liebling*, don't do this."

"I thought you liked Elek?"

"I do. I like him very much. But you can't stay with him. You know that. Your relationship will suffer from this curse, and you can't put the children at risk."

Magda slammed her suitcase shut. "Then I'll have to find a way around the curse, won't I?"

"How will you do that? Elek's been trying for years. He told me yesterday that his ancestor made the curse over a thousand years ago."

Magda straightened, and blinked at her mother. "Say that again?"

"The curse is over a thousand years old."

"No, the part about his ancestor."

Her mother shrugged. "Some grandsire back in the dark ages. When Europe was constantly at war, somewhere or other. I think it was a defense. The strength of a berserker in a time of war. Magda?"

Magda was standing very still.

Corruption in Africa. Nazis taking over the house. War and poverty and pain and anger. A defense.

"Equally blessed and cursed," she murmured.

"What did you say?"

"I have to go and find him," Magda said, yanking on her shoes. "He can lift his own curse."

* * *

Elek had never hated the sight of his family's chateau before now. Huge, crumbling, in desperate need of heavy repairs, it was largely unlivable. He'd been occupying a few remaining rooms in the east wing. The family didn't have the money to pour into the place and they couldn't sell it. Where else would the cursed ones go?

Now he loathed it. A crumbling prison, especially the tower room on the fourth floor with the silver and iron circle laid into the floor. He'd happily lay it all to waste, burn it to the ground, this decaying masterpiece of architecture, trash the remaining works of art and antique furniture, destroy it all if he could just go back to Magda.

Damn it, he should never have gone to Germany with her. Should never have met her mother, who was wise and kind and possessed of a very dry sense of humor -- or the children, who made him laugh and ache to be a part of their lives. What would it be like to have more children with Magda?

He closed his eyes and leaned against the cool stone of the house. If he thought about that he'd go crazy. He couldn't stay with her, couldn't leave this place. Couldn't risk hurting her or her family, not when they'd been hurt before so badly.

He couldn't risk hurting anyone. If the circle didn't hold tonight, if he woke and found himself anywhere but safe inside the iron and silver rings, it was time to end the curse, the only way he knew how.

As the sun sank in the sky, he dragged himself on heavy feet up to the tower room, already rehearsing the incantation inside his head.

Chapter Nine

"Okay, run this by me again," Con said through the speakerphone. "You're dashing across Europe to get to a chateau in France before the sun sets because…"

"I have to save Elek from the curse."

"Why tonight? Why the hurry?"

Because if I don't do it tonight, Magda thought, *he might not be there tomorrow. That's what he was trying to tell me.* "It just has to be tonight," she said. "Con, if I know who made the curse and I know who it's bound to, what do they have to do to rescind it?"

"It varies," he said. "Usually some sort of undoing spell."

"Such as?"

"You got a pen?"

"I'm driving."

"You can't write while you're driving?" Con asked, sounding genuinely confused.

"Not if I want to stay alive. I've got British plates and I'm going about ninety miles an hour. I don't need to get pulled over for bloody writing."

"Okay, all right. I'll text it to you, yeah?"

"Yes," Magda said. "Thank you, Con. I mean it."

"No problem," he said. "Take care, Mags. I mean that."

The sun was getting lower as she approached the French border. Dammit, they were stopping people, and there was a queue. Didn't they know she was in a hurry?

She fidgeted in her seat for twenty minutes under a blood-red sky while someone up ahead had an argument with the crossing guards. The guards were in a foul mood by the time Magda got there, and proceeded to argue with her about everything from the purpose of her visit -- family, she told them -- to the damage she still hadn't got fixed on her car. They seemed insistent that she was leaving the country after an unreported car accident.

By the time she got through it was nearly dark, and she was almost in tears. What if she was too late and he'd already changed? The pull of the moon was driving her crazy and she couldn't concentrate on finding the small village where they'd spent that first amazing night.

When she finally did, she stripped off her clothes and bounded out into the night on all fours, phone between her teeth, nose to the ground, trying to find Elek's scent. It was a month old, but she traced his path from the last time he'd been in the woods, right back to a huge crumbling chateau in the middle of a weed-choked lawn.

There were candles burning in a high tower room. Magda leapt through a broken window and raced up to the top floor, following Elek's scent, hurling herself against a locked door until the wood splintered and gave and she rolled and skidded to a halt on the stone floor of a large circular room.

In the center was a double circle of iron and silver, and in it stood Elek, naked and startled, silver chains on his wrists and ankles.

Magda shook herself and turned human with an effort of will. "That door will never hold you," she said.

"Magda, what are you doing here? You have to leave," Elek said urgently.

"No."

"What do you mean, no? The moon's almost fully up. A few more minutes and the curse --"

"You can rescind it," Magda told him breathlessly, trying not to get distracted by his nakedness. "I've been talking to the resident wizard at Sundown and he told me if I can find the descendant of the person who made the curse then they can unmake it. That's *you*, Elek. You can break the curse."

He stared at her for a long second.

"It was your ancestor, wasn't it?" Magda said, suddenly wondering if her mother had misunderstood.

He nodded slowly. "But I never understood why he'd do such a thing."

"Misguided, probably," Magda said. "Never make a spell unless you know exactly what the consequences will be. With that in mind," she grabbed the phone that had tumbled from her jaws when she changed shape, and quickly scrolled to the text Con had sent, "repeat this."

He looked at her as if she was mad.

"It's a counter-curse. One of the best. Come on, Elek, please."

"Where'd you get it?"

"Con, the wizard." Magda was hopping from foot to foot now, her nerves in pieces, desperate for it to be over.

His eyes widened. "Bastard wouldn't see me, he said his schedule was --"

"Elek, please!"

He glanced at her face, then at the phone, and started repeating the weird, twisting words.

Nothing happened.

"Is there supposed to be like a clap of thunder or something?" Elek asked, a feeble smile on his face.

"I don't know." Magda felt a tugging on her skin and glanced out the window to see the moon gliding out from behind a cloud. In direct moonlight, she couldn't resist the change.

Neither, apparently, could Elek. She watched in horror as his fingers lengthened to claws, his spine bowed, and he groaned through elongated canines, "Get out, Magda! If this doesn't hold you won't be safe. Get away, as far as you can."

"I don't want to leave you," she said, tears in her eyes.

Fur prickled through Elek's skin. "I love you," he said. "I always will. Now get the fuck out of here!"

His eyes clouded over to a stormy amber and his face changed, bones remolding themselves under his skin. Magda felt the pull of the moon on her own flesh and slid easily into her wolf shape. Her eyes met his, but he didn't seem to see her.

I love you, she thought, and turned and ran.

She ran across the lawn, into the woods, knowing he could trace her scent if he wanted to, if he got loose. Knowing the counter-curse hadn't worked and he was doomed. After tonight she knew he wouldn't live with the curse any longer, one way or another.

She stumbled on her front leg, went down with a howl, and buried her nose under her paws. Elek, oh God, her sweet Elek.

She didn't know how long she'd been there when she heard the noise behind her, smelled another wolf approaching. A wolf scent of a different flavor. A flavor she knew.

Elek had gotten loose.

Magda gritted her teeth, got to all fours, turned ready for him, and growled. If he was going to track her, by God she was going to fight him.

A second later the huge black wolf crashed out of the undergrowth a few feet from her, tumbled over once, twice, and righted himself. He shook out his fur, sniffed, and turned to face her.

He looked like he was smiling.

Magda faltered, and then the wolf howled and bounded over to her, his jaws wide open, teeth flashing.

She braced herself.

He licked her.

Magda was so astonished that she lost her balance and fell to her side, and the black wolf followed her, whining anxiously.

And she understood him.

"Magda!" Elek's voice sounded in her head, the way she heard other wolves speaking to her. "Are you all right? Did I hurt you?"

She stared at him. His eyes weren't amber, they were brown. Rich, deep brown. Elek's eyes.

"Magda, what did I do?"

"You know me," she said weakly.

"Yes." A wide doggy grin split his wolfish face. "I know you. Intimately."

"But -- you said -- the beast --"

"Is gone." He nuzzled her neck. "The counter-curse worked."

"But you're a freaking *wolf*!"

Elek let out a bark that sounded a lot like laughter. "I *am* a wolf!" he echoed. "Don't you remember? You bit me. A month ago, you bit me. I'm a werewolf."

She stared some more.

"Are you badly hurt?" Elek asked anxiously.

She shook her head.

"Can you stand?"

She got shakily to her paws. "I'm not hurt at all. I'm just shocked out of my mind."

Elek barked laughter again. "And I'm in my mind," he said delightedly, nuzzling her again. "Do you know what this means?"

"The curse is ended."

"I'm safe at the full moon."

"I can introduce you to the pack," Magda said.

"Really?"

"As my mate," she added, and Elek howled at the moon. Magda howled too, a sound of pure joy, and wrestled him to the ground.

"Have you ever had sex as a wolf?" Elek asked as she licked his fur.

"Nope."

"Me neither. You want to try it?"

"Yes. Oh, *yes*."

Sundown, Inc.: What Wizards Want

Cat Marsters

Chapter One

It rained the day the pirate queen came into my life. Since I live in England, however, I missed the significance.

It's possible there are wizards out there who actually don't begrudge every single spell they have to do. Sadly, I ain't one of them. Ever since my first love turned out to be an insane faery with purple teeth and blood red eyes, I've been beholden to the Unseelie Court and bound to perform any magical service they just can't be bothered to do themselves. This involves a lot of tramping around soggy marshes in Scotland, looking for the bones of Fionnbar the Slightly Hysterical because the faery queen thinks they'd make a nice decoration for her bedroom.

In order to make money, I do séances and junk like that. The parlor of my little house is set up with dark curtains and dribbly candles and all the shit people expect. I found a couple of reproduction human skulls that looked okay once they'd been swiped with tea bags and dribbled with wax. They look nice next to the genuine sheep skull I found on Bodmin Moor when I was searching for the Holy Chalice of Julia Caesar -- according to the faeries, the only female Caesar of Rome. Funny how I didn't fully believe them on that.

Tonight's séance had a double purpose -- saves time and gets me more money. I was contacting the spirit of Mrs. Croggle's late husband, Bert, and freeing Dr. Wishbourne's son from the clutches of his biker girlfriend. I had an inkling Dr. Wishbourne's son was quite happy in the clutches of said girlfriend, who I understood to be six feet tall with a torrent of red hair and breasts the size of the Himalayas, but money was money, and I had rent to pay.

A lot of magic is making things up. At least, the way I do it, it is. Thanks to Eibhlis of the Unseelie, I never really completed my formal training. Well. That is to say, I never started it either. I may have made a bargain with her to the effect of a lot of magical prowess for me, and my eternal slave-like devotion for her. Yes, I know, but can you honestly say you were sensible when you were eighteen? I go on instinct a lot of the time, and when I don't get results I pretend I have. Just don't tell anyone, 'kay?

Bert Croggle didn't want to talk to me today. Oh, he was out there, but he didn't have anything to say. At least not anything his wife would want to hear.

"Tell the silly old biddy to shut up and leave me in peace," he said. "Go back to her knitting. There's a swimsuit parade on telly."

"What channel?" I asked.

"One you don't get down there." And off he wafted.

Look. I'm not a charlatan. Well, maybe I am, but… I don't do this to hurt people. I don't pretend I can see things I can't. Far from it. It's just that what I see isn't always what they want to know about. Face it, would you rather hear that your dear old grandma was standing beside you on your wedding day, or that she thought your fiancé was a dolt and you looked fat in your wedding dress?

Thought so.

So I made up something vaguely comforting about Bert watching over her and added that she looked very nice in her new violet hat. Mrs. Croggle, who clearly wasn't the brightest crayon in the box, cried, "Oh, he really can see me!"

She seemed to have forgotten that I could too.

Still, she went off happy, and I got paid. I turned to Dr. Wishbourne and said, "So. A freeing spell."

"Yes," he said, looking doubtfully after the retreating Mrs. Croggle. "Do you know my son, Mr. Devlin?"

I never tell clients my real name, and it's not to do with that thrice-calling business. It's because no one would ever trust a wizard named Con Marks.

Yeah. Apparently my parents had a worse sense of humor than anyone realized. I use my mother's maiden name of Devlin for trading purposes. Besides, it sounds so much more dashing and wizardly than Marks, don't you think?

"I don't think I've met him," I told the doctor.

He nodded to the fishing float I'd set up as a crystal ball. "Tell me if you can see him."

He was testing me. I knew that. He didn't trust me after the stunt I'd pulled with Mrs. Croggle. Can you blame him?

So I pulled the float toward me, started to make some mystical type motions with my hands, and caught the good doctor's eye. All righty then. No mystical motions. I concentrated on the improvised ball, which I was using because I'd broken my proper one earlier, and felt the familiar crackle of power building behind my eyes. I might make a lot of stuff up, but I really do actually have some ability at this. Just not as much as I pretend to.

I concentrated on what the doctor had told me about his son, his name and age and what he was studying at college, and eventually brought up a picture of him. He was making out with a busty redhead in the dark corner of a bar somewhere.

The image was a little foggy, green around the edges, but that's fishing floats for you. I didn't feel easy using this, to be honest -- it had the mark of someone else's use on it. I couldn't figure out if that was real fisherman type use, or mystic magical type use. Either way, I didn't want to dwell on it.

I cleared my throat, and gave the doctor a brief physical description of the boy. Lucky for me, the kid had a dagger-shaped earring in his left ear, and that seemed to convince the doctor that I was being genuine.

His pager suddenly bleeped.

"Blast, I've got to go," he said. "Devlin, can you do this spell without me?"

"Yes," I said, and didn't add that it'd probably be easier without him breathing down my neck the whole time.

After the doctor had gone I sat at the round table in my front room, candles flickering on the dark drapes, and drummed my fingers on the tablecloth. Something about that float didn't feel right, but I couldn't put my finger on what. I'd been given it by a faery of my acquaintance a while ago as a sort of joke, I think. That's how the Fae seemed to regard me: as a sort of joke. I got used to it a long time ago, but that doesn't mean I have to like it.

I reached for the incense burning on the dresser, and prepared to do the freeing spell. It wasn't hard -- a few words to focus the spell, a symbol of freedom -- in this case my car keys -- and an effort of will. Had I company, I would've made it fancier. It seems to reassure people to see a lot of props being used -- maybe because it stops them thinking I can do magic on the spot, without any preparation.

I brought up the image of Dr. Wishbourne's son again in the fishing float, and concentrated on freeing him from the clutches of this evil red-haired harpy. The image I brought up was, unfortunately, of the boy with the harpy, getting hot and heavy in that bar -- did they not have bouncers in this place? -- so I have to say my thoughts were less and less pure as I ran through the spell. I said the words in Latin, which I suck at, but that doesn't matter, because the words are just there to give the magic focus. I could be reciting a shopping list for all the relevance the actual words have, but it makes it easier if they vaguely correspond to the spell I'm doing.

"*Extrico de ligatio,*" I said, and concentrated my will on the float, which sort of lit up, and pulsed, and grew hotter and brighter as I concentrated on it, until it hurt to look and the light was blinding me. Sweat ran down my face from the heat of it. What the hell was happening? I'd never felt this before.

"*Extrico,*" I cried, and there was a huge flash, like lightning, and then everything went dull.

When I opened my eyes, there was a naked woman lying on the hearth rug.

* * *

I sat there, eyes watering, blinking in the sudden darkness, staring at her. Because you know, the most surprising thing about this woman was not that she'd suddenly appeared, or even that she was totally naked.

It was that I knew her, although I'd never in my life met her. I mean, I *knew* her. Biblically. And before you go thinking icky things about webcams and the like, let me explain that that's not it at all. I knew her from my dreams.

She had dusky skin that might have been the product of a lot of sun, or might have come from mixed ancestry. Probably the latter. She'd never spoken much so I couldn't discern her accent -- our encounters together had never really been of the conversational kind. Her eyes were closed, and her face looked younger than I remembered. Her teeth were a flash of white between shapely, soft lips. Her hair splayed around her head, Medusa-like, a tangle of long braids threaded with beads.

She had soft, round breasts just the right size to cup in my hand, and plump juicy dark nipples that tasted quite delicious. Between her long, lean thighs was a patch of dark hair that I knew was concealing the tightest, hottest little pussy I'd ever had the pleasure to meet.

My cock hardened even as my brain told me I was seeing things. She wasn't real, this woman. She came to me in dreams, tangling with me in silken sheets or on pure shores, the scent of the ocean on her skin. She tasted salty, like the sea; she smelled hot; she felt like fire. She was a dream, a fantasy, one I'd been entertaining for maybe a year now, the hottest dreams I'd ever had in my whole life.

She stirred, and I closed my eyes. No! That was it! Clearly when I'd done the spell I'd done something wrong and knocked myself out. I was dreaming now!

I looked at the lithe body curled on my hearth rug, and licked my lips.

"Hi," I said, and her eyes came open.

Then, in a movement so fast I barely caught it, she was on her feet, half-crouched like she was going to pounce, braids flying around her, eyes flashing. Those eyes were so beautiful, deep dark pools, tip-tilted, sultry eyes.

They scanned me, took in my clothes, my hair, also black but a lot less tidy, the three or four days of stubble shadowing my face, evidence that the Fae had me working overtime.

She relaxed a little. "It's you."

"It's me," I agreed.

"What are you wearing?"

I looked down at my "professional" outfit of black dress slacks and silk shirt -- smarter than my usual jeans and T-shirt but just not as silly as a robe and pointy hat -- and back up at her.

"I never saw you in clothes before," she clarified.

"I can amend that."

She grinned, a slow smile that took over her whole face. "I can help you amend it."

This was probably the longest conversation we'd ever had, and it allowed me to assess her accent with the tiny little fraction of my brain that still had blood flowing to it. She sounded West Indian, Caribbean, all hard t's and musical lilt. It was pretty sexy.

Then again, she was standing there naked, offering to help me take my clothes off. There wasn't much about her I didn't currently find sexy.

She licked her lips and moved closer. The candlelight glinted off her dark caramel skin and her beaded hair clicked softly.

"This is clearer than I ever remember," she said, and I reached for her, touched her hot skin.

"Hotter than I remember," I said.

"I'm always hot for you," she said with a wicked smile, and I slid my arms around her and kissed her. Her mouth was cool and she tasted like -- I don't know, like rum or something. I'm more of a beer guy personally.

Her skin was hot and smooth under my hands, the long lines of her back uninterrupted by pesky things like bra straps. My fingers glided down to her high, round little bottom and pulled her against me, felt her body flush against mine, her soft round breasts and her stomach and her thigh, curling around mine like a tango dancer.

She had a clever little tongue and hot hands, hands that made short work of my shirt buttons by ripping them off. In another situation I might have been annoyed, because silk shirts don't grow on trees and the Fae don't exactly pay me much, but I figured I was dreaming right now, so we could rip up as many shirts as we wanted.

With that in mind, I shucked the ruined silk and helped her unfasten my fly. I believe in being chivalrous: why let the woman do all the work? Her hands smoothed down my body, past my stomach to the dark hair between my legs, slower, slower, making me lose my breath and my concentration, and then her fingers brushed the aching length of my cock, and I think I moaned.

She smiled another slow smile that said she knew she had all the power here, and stroked one finger right from root to tip. Then back.

I closed my eyes and she laughed, a deep throaty sound, and pushed the rest of my clothes away. I stood there naked, hot and wanting, and she ran one hand over my shoulder, my arm, as if testing me for strength. Like you might check out a horse.

"You're so white," she said, and I frowned, because I'd thought my tan was pretty decent this year. I come from solid Irish stock, and we don't tan well, as a rule. "You don't see the sun enough," she added.

Too much gathering wildflowers by the light of the moon, I thought, but I didn't say anything, because how manly is it to gather flowers?

"One day we will make love under the sun," she said, and traced her finger in a circle around my nipple. Her eyes sparkled mischievously. "Then your back at least will be more brown."

"We'll have to find a way to tan my chest as well," I said thoughtfully. "You know, if you just get on your knees I'll get brown all over."

She gave me a look of mock outrage. "I don't get on my knees for anyone."

I ran my hands under the delicious curve of her bottom, stroked the tops of her thighs, slipped my fingers between her buttocks. "Not even if I ask nicely?" I said, and she shivered delightfully against me.

"Very nicely," she murmured, her face against my shoulder, and I took the opportunity to move her back against the table, perch her on the edge of it, so I could lean forward and take one of those gorgeous plump nipples into my mouth.

Her breath came out in a hard gasp. "Nicer than that," she said, her hand betraying her words by clutching at my shoulder, sliding up my neck and clenching in my hair. I ran my tongue around her nipple and her fingers dug in my scalp. When I nibbled gently her leg curled around my waist and squeezed my bare stomach against her hot, wet pussy.

Hmm. I sucked thoughtfully on her nipple a while longer. It was ripe and sweet and delicious but, I recalled, so was the aforementioned pussy. Even sweeter, I think.

Of course, I couldn't be sure, so in the interests of research I abandoned the nipple and slid a little further down her body, laying her back on the table. Then I felt bad about the nipple and sent one hand to keep it company while the other helped me part her long dark thighs and nuzzle between them.

She let out a gasp of indeterminate wordage as I licked the inside of her thigh, tasted arousal on her skin, hot and salty and sweet, and moved up for some more.

Her pussy was slippery wet, her folds hot and swollen. I decided to lick them clean, and she moaned her appreciation. Her taste was delicious, and the more I licked the more there was of it. I moved up a little, found her clit practically standing up and waving for attention, and ran my tongue around it.

She squeaked, and I tried not to laugh.

"Is this asking nice enough?" I inquired, licking my lips.

She made a moan that could possibly have been construed as *no*. I chose to take it that way, and tried harder, by investigating just how tight her pussy really was.

I slid one finger inside. Hmm, pretty tight. Room for another finger though.

She clenched around my fingers. It felt pretty good to me.

"Nice enough, darlin'?"

"A -- little -- more --"

A third finger, and I went back to licking her clit, curling my tongue around it and sucking on it. She was writhing in earnest now, making little noises that were nowhere near words, wrapping her thighs around my shoulders, pressing her feet into my back. Her hand covered mine at her breast, molded my fingers to pinch her nipple, stroke and squeeze it.

I curved my fingers inside her, seeking out the sensitive flesh at the front of her pussy. Evidently I found it, because she suddenly bucked and cried out, and her pussy clenched hard around my fingers, and with a sob and a flood of sweetness on my tongue, she came.

Nearly took my fingers off, too. I extracted them and carried on licking, cleaning her up. Well, that's my excuse anyway. Truth is she tasted delicious, and I was desperately trying to distract myself from the painful arousal she'd brought me to. I wanted to fuck her, badly, but I was trying to be a gentleman and let her recover.

Apparently she didn't want to, though, because she sat up and pushed me away, and leapt off the table to push me on my back on the floor and kneel over me.

"You asked nicely," she purred, dipping her head to my cock.

Christ, no! If she so much as licked me I'd come instantly, and I wanted to be inside her before I did that. "No," I stopped her with half an inch to go. She looked up, confusion on her beautiful features. "Not like that."

She sat back on her haunches and regarded me expectantly, and I smiled. On her knees? That suggested a few things to me.

One of them involved a mirror.

But right now I was far too desperate to get inside her to think about props. I got her on her knees, knelt behind her, and tried to think of boring things. Fae rituals. Gathering seventeen hundred daisies for a prosperity spell. Dr. Wishbourne. Cricket.

She dropped forward so she was on her hands and knees and wiggled that gorgeous round ass at me.

The hell with it.

I plunged into her, her cunt hot and smooth and tight around my aching cock, and nearly died of pleasure. She gave a little moan as I pushed deeper into her, pushed back against me, and I grasped her hips with both hands and pulled out, then thrust back in again. It was good, it was so fucking good, better than all the other times, she just felt more… *real*, hotter and wetter and tighter and my God, the sounds she made. I slid my hands up her body, felt her breasts heavy in my hands as I slammed into her, harder and faster. Ran one hand back down her stomach, slick with sweat, and found her clit all slippery and hot.

She started rocking harder against me, urging me on faster, and I pretty much lost my mind. Her pussy tightened around my cock and I felt her whole body buck and spasm, and then I completely lost my mind, coming hard, so hard I nearly blacked out.

I hardly remember falling to the floor, holding her to me, her body hot and soft against mine. But I do remember falling asleep with her cradled in my arms. She felt really good there. Not as good as she had coming around my cock, but still. Pretty good.

Chapter Two

When I woke up I yelped, because I was lying naked on the floor and there was someone standing over me, holding my laptop, screaming at me.

Actually, I didn't yelp, I bellowed in a manly fashion. *She* screamed. Okay? She was the one being girlie, not me. But come on, I thought she was a robber or something. Laptops are expensive things.

She screamed, and then she stopped, and looked at me, and giggled. Which made me shut up.

"You scream like a pickney," she said.

"A what?"

"A child. A little girl," she clarified, and I scowled.

"I didn't scream, I... bellowed," I said, and she giggled again. It did interesting things to her chest which, I couldn't help noticing, was as naked as the rest of her. She was naked and beautiful, caramel skin and beaded braids, standing there laughing at me. What the hell was going on? Was I still dreaming?

I shifted on the hearth rug and felt the patch of wax I'd spilt last week dig into my hip. No, I don't think I was dreaming. Her accent was softer this morning, not as intense as it had been when I'd had my face buried between her legs.

I sat up, tried to focus. "What are you doing with my laptop?"

"Your what?" Her eyes went straight to my groin. "I'm not doing anything."

"The computer," I said patiently, and she frowned.

"Never heard it called that before."

I rolled my eyes, and stood up. "No," I said, taking the offending piece of machinery from her, "this."

She watched me put it on the table -- the same table where I'd stretched her out and licked her pussy until she screamed -- and said, "I was just looking around. Is this your house?"

I nodded.

"It's strange."

"What, the candles and stuff? Yeah, a little bit."

"No," she said. "Well, the skulls are a little strange, but I meant the other rooms."

She thought this room was normal and the others were weird? Hookay. I'd shagged a nutcase.

"What's weird about the others?" I asked, trying to act as if we weren't both standing there naked having such a surreal conversation about my house.

She shrugged. "It's just different. I don't recognize a lot of things. Where are we?"

"Uh, my house."

"No, where is your house? You sound Irish to me."

"I am Irish. But this is England. Village of Blackchapel, on the east coast."

She nodded as if this was all very interesting, looking around at the books on the walls. "I've never been to the east coast of England. That's why it's strange."

"Uh-*huh*." I scratched my head. "Look -- I don't mean to sound rude, but what's your name?"

"Lily."

"Lily. I'm Con."

She smiled, a sudden, dazzling smile. "It's nice to meet you, Mr. Con."

"Er, yes." I didn't want to go into how nice it was to meet her, not with us both standing here all naked. I should probably have a conversation with her before I started thinking about just how *nice* it was to meet her. "Look, Lily. D'you have any clothes?"

She shrugged, no.

"Right. Okay. You're just kind of distracting right now. Er." I needed to know one thing before we went any further. "How did you get here?"

She looked at the bits of broken glass on the far side of the table. "I don't know," she said, a little distantly. "I was hoping you could tell me."

* * *

My black silk shirt was lying there on the floor, so I got her to put it on. Unfortunately she looked even sexier with the silk sliding against her skin, skimming the tops of her thighs, her nipples pushing against the fabric. I swallowed and steered her up the stairs to put some of my regular clothes on before I started ravishing her. I needed answers from her, and sex probably wasn't the best way to get them.

She still looked pretty cute in my sweatpants and T-shirt, but at least she was covered up. The clothes seemed to fascinate her completely, so much so that she didn't seem to notice me washing and dressing.

"Breakfast," I said, and she looked up from examining the hem of the T-shirt. "Are you hungry?"

She admitted she was, which made my heart sink because I had no decent food in the house at all. There was plenty of coffee though, which seemed to make her happy.

I thought about going on to the bakery to get some croissants or bread rolls, but some instinct told me that right now, keeping her in the house was the best thing to do. So I made some toast while she stared around the kitchen in some sort of awe. She was weird. Hot, very hot, but also undeniably weird.

"Okay." I sat down at the kitchen table with her and pushed the butter in her direction. She stared at it a while, and then when I took the lid off she stared some more. "Lily?"

"Hmm?"

"It's butter. Spreadable butter. Comes standard in a tub."

She poked at it. "It's cold!"

"Yep. That'll be the fridge."

"Fridge?"

I sighed.

"Con?" she said, scraping up some butter with an experimental look on her face.

"Yes, darlin'?"

"What year is this?"

"2005."

She blinked and looked startled. Had she been watching a lot of *Quantum Leap*? *Back to the Future*?

"Two thousand and five?" She seemed to be working this out. "Two *thousand*? After one thousand, nine hundred and ninety-nine?"

"Or nineteen-ninety-nine, yes," I said.

"Why don't you say twenty-oh-five?"

"We just don't. What year do you think it is?"

She frowned and spread some butter on her toast. "I think you are probably right and it is 2005."

Okay, change of mental gears. "What year do you, er, are you familiar with?"

She smiled at that. "Last time I saw the sun it was 1723."

Right.

Riiight.

She saw my face, and put her hand on my arm. "You think I'm crazy, don't you?"

I don't know. I was the one seeing her. "No, darlin'. I think I am."

She glanced toward the front of the house, where she'd first appeared. "The broken glass in there. It was a fishing float, yeah?"

I nodded.

"What did you do to it?"

"I... uh..." Usually I'm cautious about talking about magic to regular people, but then she wasn't a regular person. "I was using it as a crystal ball. You know... to do magic."

"What sort of magic?"

"A freeing spell."

She drew back.

"I was supposed to be freeing someone from a relationship. I didn't think..."

But wait a minute. The float had borne the mark of someone else's use. And I'd used it for a freeing spell.

"You were in the float?" I said slowly. Lily nodded. "How long?"

Her fingers moved as if she was counting. "Two hundred and eighty-two years."

"It was really 1723?"

She nodded again.

"How? Why?" I thought about the float, about as big around as a teapot. "How?"

"Magic. Faery magic."

Ah.

She was watching me. "You know the Fae."

"Yes," I said flatly.

"But you aren't Fae. Are you?"

"Sweet fuck, no. I just work for them."

Her lovely eyes narrowed. "Willingly?"

"Ha!"

Lily relaxed a little. "I was banished there by a Fae princess."

"Why?"

She shrugged. "She wanted a man. He wanted me."

Irrational jealousy rose in me. "Did you want him?"

Another shrug. "A little."

I scowled. She laughed. "You're not getting possessive, are you? You don't even know me."

"Hey, I know you, woman," I sulked. I knew she liked me to kiss her neck and that she tasted like the sea. I knew she had the softest, ripest, sweetest mouth I'd ever kissed. I knew she could trigger an orgasm in me just by coming herself.

"You don't even know my last name," she said.

"What is it?"

She looked proud. "I don't have one."

Fine. Great. Wonderful.

I stood up, pushing back my chair, and gathered up the breakfast things. Lily had been imprisoned in that fishing float. Implausible, yes, but believe me when I say that where the Fae are concerned, nothing is impossible. Well. It's supposed to be impossible for them to tamper with free will, but they have so many ways and means that it doesn't really matter what the rules are.

But the fishing float. It had been given to me by a faery, and a faery had imprisoned Lily in it. Coincidence? Yes, and I'm David Copperfield.

I picked up the phone and dialed Aura's number. The Fae can use any method they like to get a hold of me, but being a mere mortal, if I want them, I have to use the phone.

It rang out. Bloody Fae.

Lily was sitting there looking mildly puzzled as to why I was holding a piece of plastic to my ear. I glanced past her to the detritus of my everyday life, the candles, the pizza boxes, the massive piles of books, and the half-finished Eye of Splendida that I was constructing for the Unseelie Queen.

I drummed my fingers on the counter.

"Con?" Lily said.

I turned and gave her a smile. "Let's take a trip," I said. "You ever been to London?"

* * *

Turns out Lily had been to London, but you know, cities change in three hundred years. Methods of transport certainly do, although I have a sneaking suspicion that my car, ancient hunk of junk that it is, was around when Lily was born. It didn't feel like working today, just sat there coughing and whirring while Lily asked if it was supposed to be making such a noise.

"Yes," I growled, "that's the noise it makes when it thinks we need to take the train."

Trains were, needless to say, a revelation to Lily. I didn't think they'd been invented in her lifetime; she certainly hadn't been on one before. She was amazed by the little Victorian station with its wrought iron fixtures and hanging baskets, and she asked me endless questions about the ticket machine that I was forced to answer with "I don't know." Well, I don't. I do magic, not mechanics.

The train stunned her to silence. As she stared in awe, I wondered if this was the closest Lily ever came to fear. She hadn't seemed remotely frightened when I told her what year it was. She hadn't been fazed by my magic, or by any of my modern household items. But the huge, noisy, dirty train had her staring like a child.

I took her hand and towed her aboard. When it started to move, she let out a squeak and clutched my arm.

"It's okay," I said, "it's supposed to do that."

"It moves like a ship," she said, relaxing just a tiny bit.

"It does?"

"The motion. The way it rocks."

"I suppose so." I led her to a pair of seats and pulled her down beside me. "You sail a lot?"

She blinked those big eyes at me. "You do magic a lot?"

What was that supposed to mean?

"I'm a pirate," she said, looking past me, through the window at the rapidly moving scenery.

"Really?"

"Had my own ship since I was fifteen." A misty smile came over her face. "The captain wagered it in a game of cards. When he lost he didn't want to hand it over, so I shot him in the knee and took it anyway."

Rightiho.

"What was it called?"

"*The Valley.*"

"Lily of the Valley? Cute."

She smiled, bringing her gaze back to me. "You think I'm cute?"

Uh-oh. "Do you want to be cute?"

She laid her head on my shoulder, surprising the hell out of me. "I don't know. I don't think I mind."

Right.

The train made a gazillion stops on the way into town, during which time I tried to remember anything at all from school that might help me explain to Lily the internal combustion engine.

I got halfway through massacring the principles of the steam engine when I remembered that modern trains were electric. It's the wizard thing, we don't get out much. Electricity was a complete mystery to me, so I left that part out.

Negotiating the London Underground is, at the best of times, a little tricky for me. It seems unnatural, dwarfish even, to be so far from clean air. Plus I have no sense of direction. Okay, but how many pirate queens have you freed lately? I don't need no stinkin' sense of direction.

The endless tunnels and sickly lighting subdued Lily, too. She looked around a lot, at the endless variety of life flowing past. Businessmen in suits, women in heels and makeup, students in holey cardigans, tourists with their shiny clothes, a party of Japanese kids with matching backpacks, the homeless guy playing guitar. I never look at people on the Tube. Well, you just don't. But Lily looked at everyone, took everything in, silently.

It was a relief to emerge into the relatively clean air of Marylebone and make our way to the Sundown, Inc. offices. I could have phoned, could even have e-mailed, but to be honest I sort of wanted reassurance that I wasn't going crazy. Johann, the Sundown boss, didn't take any mystical shit from anyone, which was interesting, since he ran a paranormal business. If he could see and hear Lily, I'd know I wasn't imagining things.

The offices were above a row of shops. I let us in, escorted Lily up the stairs, and walked into some kind of hell.

Magda, the secretary, was standing there with half a dozen fabric swatches thrown over her shoulder. She was draping some red silk around one of Sundown's best operatives, Masika, who was dressed in leather with half a dozen knives attached to her person, looking mildly murderous. Leaning against the desk, laden down with yards and yards of silk and taffeta, was Masika's boyfriend, Dare. The pair of them were both wearing shades, looking surprisingly un-ridiculous in the middle of the day.

"All I'm saying, Mags, is that you have to think about the other guests."

Magda, pristine as ever, was in a suit and pearls and had a mouthful of pins. She took them out and held them like a bunch of cigarettes as she spoke. "The other guests who will mostly be werewolves, vampires, demons and faeries?"

"And the perfectly ordinary people who live on your street. People you went to school with. Your kids' friends. Clients. Human ones."

Magda laid some pink silk over the red, made a face, and removed it. "Well, so long as you promise not to eat anyone we should be all right."

"Mags, look at me. I'll scare the living daylights out of everyone there."

"Try leaving your throwing knives at home," Dare advised, and she shot him a filthy look. He grinned.

"You'll be dressed in perfectly ordinary clothes," Magda said. "Well, ordinary bridesmaid clothes, anyway."

"And I'll still have holy water scars all over my face and arms."

"Long sleeves?" Magda said desperately.

"Mask?" Dare said idly.

"Hello, children," I said, and they all looked up, surprised. I gave them a bit of a smug smile. Not one of them is used to being ambushed.

"Con," Masika said gratefully, "tell Magda why I can't be her bridesmaid."

"You'll combust when you enter the church?"

"Haha. I mean, yes," Masika said, snatching this eagerly and turning to Magda.

"I have seen you enter many churches and exit completely unscathed," Magda said, twitching the silk off Masika's shoulder. "Stop making excuses."

"I don't want to wear pink," Masika whined.

"Con, you're coming, aren't you?" Magda said anxiously.

"Uh," I said. Weddings are so not my thing. "I'll have to check my schedule."

"Hey, if I have to go, you have to go," Dare said.

"What about me? I have to wear a *dress*," Masika grumbled, as if Magda had asked her to attire herself in burlap and blood larvae.

"Is it the dress?" Magda asked. "We could have you in something else..."

Masika held up her hands. "Spare me," she said. "Con, did you want something?"

I glanced at Lily, who seemed utterly bemused by the whole thing.

"I need to get hold of Aura," I said, and diverted my gaze to Magda. "If the wedding planning is over?"

"It's never over," Magda said, going behind her desk and doing something at her computer.

"Remind me when the big date is?" Dare asked.

"Six months tomorrow," Magda fretted, and Masika threw up her hands.

"I've seen her eat people's entrails," she said, "and *this* scares her." She glanced back in my direction, saw Lily, and her demeanor changed subtly. She stalked over. I mean really *stalked*. Masika embodies the word "predator."

Lily stood up a little straighter, and gave Masika a once-over.

Masika made a sidestep and moved around Lily, watching her warily. Lily moved the other way, so they were circling each other. The air suddenly became tight with tension and I half expected both women to unsheathe claws.

"Oh boy," Dare said softly, and Magda looked up from her computer.

"Who is this?" Masika never took her eyes from Lily's.

"This is my, er, friend Lily."

"Friend?" Dare said doubtfully.

Masika sniffed. "Fuck-buddy," she said.

Magda sniffed too. "Con," she said, "didn't you even shower?"

I felt myself color. Vampires and werewolves and sex, oh my.

Lily never took her eyes from Masika. "Enough with the sniffing," I said. "We all know you're Alpha females. There's no need for --"

I was interrupted by a metallic sound as Lily suddenly produced a knife that seemed to have been hidden under her shirt.

"-- theatrics," I finished, a little lamely. "Uh, Lily -- is that my carving knife?"

Masika gave a little smile. It displayed her fangs. "That won't hurt me, little girl," she said.

"No, but it slow yuh down while I cut a stake," Lily said, and as her accent got thicker my panic increased.

Soundlessly, Dare appeared behind Lily, fangs out.

Chapter Three

"Whoa," I said, suddenly seeing Lily's time in the twenty-first century cut far too short. "Stop!"

"Yes," Magda brandished hands that seemed to have very, very long nails, "stop."

"If yuh choble 'im me a-go hit yuh," Lily spat at her, and while I had no idea what her actual words meant, I got the meaning loud and clear. I tried to remember a spell -- any spell! -- that might get us out of this.

"If she doesn't put that knife away in five seconds I'm going to rip her throat out," Dare growled.

"There will be no throat-ripping," I said, somewhat desperately. "Lily, put the knife away."

"When de duppy put 'er fangs away."

"Masika. Please."

"She got her knife out first."

"*Children*," Magda said, and then Johann's door banged open and he scowled at us all.

"Oi," he said, "you two, stop terrorizing clients. You lose me far too much fucking business that way."

I reached out and closed my hand around Lily's wrist, and in a lightning move she had me pinned against the floor, the knife to my throat.

For a second everything was still. Lily was straddling my chest, which in other circumstances might have been a pleasurable experience. The blade of the knife pressed into my skin, and my eyes met Lily's.

Johann made a disgusted sound and slammed back into his office. Masika sniggered.

Lily let up. "Don't interrupt me when I have a knife in my hand," she said, and got off me, holding out a hand to pull me to my feet. Since she was talking in understandable syllables again, I figured she was controlling herself better. Useful barometer.

"Don't pull a knife on a vampire," I replied. "Especially when her boyfriend is in the room."

Magda rolled her eyes and extended her hand to Lily. "Welcome to the madhouse," she said. "How did you know Masika is a vamp?"

"The teeth sort of give it away," Lily said.

"You didn't know until you pulled the knife?" I said, and she shrugged. "So why did you?"

"I didn't like the way she was looking at me," Lily said, her chin out, and Masika snarled and made a lunge toward her. Magda put out a hand to hold her back.

"Lily, let me introduce you to my friends," I said, a little desperately. "This is Magda. She's a werewolf with three little werewolves of her own, and six months tomorrow she's marrying another werewolf, after disposing of her first husband by eating him."

Magda adjusted her pearls and gave Lily a smile. To her credit, Lily smiled back.

"This is Masika," I gestured to the leather-wrapped goddess now leaning (or possibly restrained) in Dare's arms. "She was born about two and a half thousand years ago in Egypt and recently decapitated the oldest vampire in all the world. Behind her is Dare, her... mate, a former Greek soldier, and possibly the only person who could beat Masika in a fight."

"Only if I had a stake in my chest," muttered Masika.

"Guys," I took a breath, "this is Lily. Lily has been imprisoned in a fishing float for nearly three hundred years, before which she captained a pirate ship that she kneecapped a man for."

"And she's boffing you," Masika put in.

"That's our own personal business," I said.

"He has a very talented tongue," Lily said at the same time, and I know I blushed. Masika laughed out loud.

"Seriously?" she said. "A fishing float?"

"Got on the bad side of a faery," I explained, and that was all they needed to hear from me. Most people who know me -- well, most people in the paranormal world, anyway -- know I'm the Unseelie butt-monkey. Some of them think it's funny. A lot of them, usually the ones who've had run-ins with the Fae themselves, sympathize.

"Wasn't Aura, was it?" Magda asked.

"I don't know her name," Lily said. She stood beside me and her hand rested on my waist. It felt good, nice, companionable.

"Aura gave me the float," I said. "Her idea of a joke," I explained, "to use it as a crystal ball."

Lily's hand caressed my butt.

"We don't want to know about your balls," Magda said crisply, and wrote something down on a piece of paper. "Here. Her address and phone number."

"I have the number," I said, thinking I needed to get out of there before Lily gave me a hard-on. Seeing her all tense and ready to fight had been sexier than it ought to. "She wasn't answering."

"She should be at home," Magda said, consulting her computer.

"Right. Okay then. Lily, we're off to see a faery."

"Oh, joy." She turned to Masika and said with false sweetness, "It was nice meeting you."

"Charming," Masika said in the same tone.

"Con," Magda called as we turned to go. "Seriously, take a shower. You turn up at Aura's place smelling of sex like that, she'll have you for dinner."

What was with all the smelling? I did not smell! Bloody werewolves with their hypersensitive noses.

"Sure," I said, "I'll just pop all the way back home and bathe. Think I should shave too?"

"First time for everything," Masika murmured.

Magda rolled her eyes. "Go to my place. Elek should be in." She picked up the phone. "I'll tell him you're coming."

I hesitated, then nodded. Magda might have some clothes Lily could borrow.

Her house was in Primrose Hill, not far from the office, a big house on a leafy street. Sundown paid well. I did work for them occasionally, mostly on a consultancy basis. Even a wizard like me who's not too stellar at the actual spells knows a lot about the history and theory of magic. It was me who lifted the curse on Elek, Magda's intended.

He doesn't like me much, though, mostly because I ignored his initial request for help. I was up to my ears in faery magic and I just didn't have the time to go around helping strangers. Usually I would though. When faeries aren't involved, I can be quite a kind soul. Really.

Lily stood on the pavement outside Sundown, Inc. and put her hands on her hips.

"What?" I said, squinting at the sun.

"You're friends with vampires and werewolves?"

"Well, not friends, per se --"

"I thought they were made-up creatures!"

I frowned at her. "Like faeries and wizards, you mean?"

She glowered. She did a nice line in glowering.

" 'There are more things in heaven and earth, Horatio, than are dreamt of in your philosophy'."

"Who's Horatio?"

"Some dude Hamlet knew."

"Who's Hamlet?"

"Not a Shakespeare fan?"

"Who's --"

"Never mind," I said, and set off down the street.

She ran after me, catching up and striding along with a gait that was sexy as hell. "I don't understand your world," she said. "People talk strangely and dress very strangely."

"What, Masika? She's not what you might call normal."

"Other women on the journey here. They wear breeches and -- skirts like petticoats. No one is surprised by what I'm wearing.

In my... time, respectable women covered themselves. Have things changed so much?"

"Well," I said, trying to think of a way to put it that she might understand, "okay, three hundred years before your time, the fifteenth century. Things would have been pretty different then. Clothes certainly were. No printing press -- or, er, not much of one," I said, trying to remember when it was invented. When was Geoffrey Chaucer around? "And the Americas," I said. "Is that where you're from?" She nodded. "Not even discovered by most of the world. They'd never have seen someone who looked like you."

She was quiet a moment. "I expected things would be different," she said. "I'm not surprised by it. I just don't understand a lot of things. The way we came here. These things," she gestured to the cars rolling by, and I marveled that she hadn't been freaked out by them. Probably the train took care of that. "Are vampires and werewolves normal now?"

I laughed, mostly at the prospect of anyone calling Masika et al. "normal." "Christ, no. The complete opposite. Most people have no idea they exist."

"And they work for that... place?"

"Yeah. Actually I think the staff is about fifty-fifty. Half human, half... other."

She was silent a while longer. "I think I have a lot to learn," she said, and the way she said "tink," not to mention her sentiments, made me go "Awww" inside my head. Then she slipped her hand into my back pocket, and all cute thoughts fled my mind. There were a couple of layers of clothing between her hand and my skin, but that didn't matter. I remembered what it was like without the clothes. Last night's sex wasn't the only hot stuff in my memory. In my dreams I'd spent hours exploring her body, falling in love with every inch of it. We'd have sex for hours. We'd even occasionally make love. Lily could be surprisingly tender sometimes.

I slipped my arm about her shoulders, wondering if she was going to throw me off, but she leaned into me and we walked along together like that.

"Con?" she said as we made our way through Regent's Park, leafy and pleasant in the afternoon sun.

"Hmm?"

"Last night. It… was real, wasn't it?"

"Felt real enough to me, darlin'," I said, getting warm just thinking about it.

"I thought… to begin with, I thought it was a dream again. Then I realized there had never been anything else in the dreams, furniture or anything. Just you and me."

I frowned. "No, you're right. I hadn't thought about that."

"You remember the dreams?"

Oh, sweetheart. Do I remember! Hours of soft, sensory pleasure, drowning in her, her taste and her smell, surrounded by satiny skin and warm flesh. Her mouth on mine. Her hands caressing my skin, her hot, tight pussy welcoming me in. Her high, round butt tempting me, her beautiful breasts, those big dark eyes of hers. They turned liquid when she came. Darker and softer the more pleasure she was getting.

"I think I can bring them to mind," I said, and my voice sounded almost normal.

I got us mildly lost on the way to Magda's house, preoccupied with thoughts of Lily's hot little body, wondering if I'd make it as far as a cold shower or if I'd give in to temptation and ravish her on the bathroom floor, and when we got there Elek was flying out the door, looking impatient.

"Here," he thrust a key at me. "I have to go pick the kids up and run some errands. If you're done before I'm back, post the key back through, okay?"

"Sure," I said, and he jumped in his car and roared off. House to ourselves. Have mercy!

"Is everyone now in such a hurry?" Lily asked.

"Seems like," I said.

"You're not."

Ha-bloody-ha. Right now I was desperately impatient to either get into a cold shower or get inside Lily.

"Well," I tried to look as laid-back as possible, "when you have to wait three weeks for the exact phase of the moon you want, or three years for a certain flower to bloom, you can't be impatient."

We went into Magda's pleasant house and found our way upstairs. I tried to figure out if Lily and Magda might be the same clothes size and gave up. I knew Lily's body intimately, but I'd never spent that much time ogling Magda.

Thinking about Lily's body didn't help with the wanting of her. It brought a rush of blood to places that missed her very much. I swallowed down my lust and showed Lily the bathroom, which amazed her.

"I don't recognize any of these things," she said, looking around in awe.

"You don't recognize a toilet?"

She shrugged and stared at it.

"I guess you, er... it's what you might call a chamber pot," I said, trying not to be embarrassed and failing.

Lily kicked it. "It doesn't move."

"No, they usually don't."

"How do you empty it?"

I pressed the flush. Her eyes went wide.

"This is the sink," I said, and demonstrated the taps. Whenever piped water had been invented, it clearly hadn't made it to early eighteenth century pirate ships. "And this is the shower."

She looked at the tub. "We called that a bath."

"Well, yes, it is a bath, but this part is called a shower."

I switched the water on and she marveled at the power and cleanliness of it. I showed her soaps and shampoos, warned her not to get them in her eyes, and retreated, trying not to think about her all naked and wet, and failing completely. Hopefully a house of this size would have more than one bathroom. I needed some cold water, and I needed it now.

"Con?"

I spun around so fast it made me dizzy. Or maybe that was all the blood rushing south from my brain. "Yeah?"

"Which one did you say was for my hair?"

I pointed. She bit her lip and nodded, then she peeled her T-shirt off, and my cock got so hard so quickly it hurt. She was so perfect, those high round breasts of hers, dark nipples, flat stomach, soft smooth skin.

"You maybe want a hand with that?" I heard my own voice asking. Oh please oh please say yes.

She smiled. "Yes."

I was on her in seconds, grabbing her half-naked body and running my hands all over her beautiful bare back as I kissed her. She kissed me back, tugging at my T-shirt.

"Showering can be tricky," I managed between kisses. "I wouldn't want you to get soap in your eyes."

"Mmm," she agreed, biting my lip.

"Or…" She pulled my T-shirt off me and applied her lips to my chest. Sweet Jesus. "Or, you know, fall…"

"You better hold onto me," she agreed solemnly.

Oh, I'd hold on all right. I tugged the rest of her clothes off and she did the same for me until we were naked in each other's arms, kissing hotly, her nipples hard against my chest, her stomach soft against my cock.

I picked her up and stood her in the bath, and she moved under the water and smiled. Then she laughed.

"It's so hot and clean!"

"Hot and clean sounds good to me," I said, and joined her. She was all wet, and when I smoothed shower gel all over her she was pretty slippery too. We slid against each other, hot skin and busy hands, and she pressed me back against the wall and kissed me, rubbing her soapy body against mine.

I slid my hands down her back, admiring the curve of her back into her buttocks, and cupped her deliciously curvy butt in my hands, pressing her closer. She went up on her toes, her arms around me, and lifted one leg to prop her thigh on my hip. Her hot, slippery pussy caressed my cock and a groan escaped me.

"Christ, Lily!"

She looked up at me, her eyes heavy-lidded and soft, and she moved against me, rubbing her swollen folds against my aching cock. Her breath quickened and her little white teeth bit down on her lip.

Any more of this and I'd come in seconds.

I lifted her and spun us around so her back was against the wall, and slipped my hand down between us, finding her clit and stroking it. She let out a gasp, her eyes closing, and I slid one finger inside her. She was so wet, so tight, so hot.

I took my finger out and replaced it with my cock, and it's hard to say which of us moaned the louder. For purposes of machismo, I'm going to say her.

I pushed deep, and she lifted her other leg to lock around my waist so she was just resting on my cock, propped up by the wall and her arms around my neck. Dear, sweet heaven, it felt incredible.

I should probably have taken it slower, but I don't think I could have even if my life had depended on it. I found her mouth and her tongue thrust into mine and I took that as a sign to thrust into her cunt, faster and deeper, dizzy with pleasure as her tight little pussy clenched around me, hot and sweet and perfect.

One day, I thought as I came, one day I'll get around to taking it slow. When I'm not so frantic for her. Say, in maybe ten or twenty years?

Her body cushioned mine, the water beat down on my back, and her fingers played with the hair at the nape of my neck.

"Hey, lover," she murmured, and I looked up and her eyes were bright. Not soft. She hadn't come yet. Crap! See, this is why slow is good. Right now I felt as if I could hardly move, and there she was, squished up against the bathroom wall with me panting into her neck.

"Sorry," I murmured, straightening up and sliding out of her. "I should've --"

Her finger slid over my lips, and she took my hand and placed it over her pussy.

"I'm almost there," she whispered, and I stroked her wet, swollen folds, found her clit and ran my thumb around it, slipped two fingers inside her and thrust with them.

She kept her eyes on mine the whole time, looking right at me, and it was the most intense thing I'd ever experienced. I saw the softness take over her gaze, saw the pleasure cloud over those rich dark eyes of hers, and then her pussy was gripping my hand hard and she was coming, gasping and panting. Holding onto me with her arm around my neck, gripping me tight as her orgasm shook her.

Then it was over, and I held her in my arms. Her soft, lush body warm and wet and perfect. Her head tucked under my chin, feeling pretty fucking good.

Chapter Four

I introduced Lily to the joys of shampoo, fluffy towels and toothpaste, and left her drawing in the steam on the mirror while I went in search of some clothes for her. I would, of course, be more than happy to have her wander around completely naked all the time, but there were laws about that sort of thing, and the weather was turning a bit chilly.

I figured Magda probably wouldn't mind us taking some clothes for Lily. I'd wash them and bring them back. It was just for a short while anyway, until I got around to buying her some. Besides, who knew what might happen when we found Aura? Maybe Lily would get zapped back to her own time. I didn't know if that was possible, but faery magic is weird stuff.

Thinking about sending Lily home sent a twinge of pain through me. It was stupid, since I hardly knew the girl, and all we had was fabulous sex, and I could get that anywhere, right?

Right. I'm a wizard geek who spends half his life tramping round moonlit fields gathering fucking daisies. Great sex does not wash up on my hearth rug every day.

I sighed, staring at Magda's clothes. It was silly to get involved with someone who might disappear any moment. It was just sex. Really, really hot sex, but just sex all the same.

Scowling, I found her some underwear and went back to the bathroom. She was sniffing at her hair and grinning.

"That stuff smells great! It's been so long since my hair smelled of anything but sea water."

I smiled and handed over the underwear. "I haven't got a clue what you should wear, darlin'," I said. "Come and have a look."

"Why should I know?" Lily asked. "I never wore women's clothes even in my own century."

"Never?"

"No." She frowned at the bra I held out. "Too hot and restricting. Besides, everyone thinks it's bad luck to have a woman on board. Until I got my own ship no one knew I was a woman."

I took pity and put the bra on her. This turned out to be a bad move, since it involved much touching of her breasts. At least, it did the way I did it. "What about when you were a kid?"

"I wore boys' clothes," she said. "Easier to run away in."

"Run away?"

"Sure. A kid on the streets always needs to know how to run."

Right. Excellent.

I towed her to Magda's wardrobe where she stared in awe at all the clothes, and eventually picked out a summer dress and cowboy boots. Yeah, and I'd been worried I'd choose a ridiculous outfit. The weird thing is, she looked pretty good in it. Go figure.

It was turning cold outside, so I persuaded her to borrow a coat too. She chose a long, bright red one. Ah, that's my girl.

So attired, and having borrowed -- okay, stolen -- some food from Magda's kitchen, we left the house. And I honestly started out with the full intention of going to Aura's place, but then some little demon inside my head said, "Go to Aura's place now and you might never see Lily again."

So we went shopping.

* * *

I know. I hate shopping. Well, not hate it, so much as don't understand it. How can girls shop for recreation? You shop for stuff you need. Handing over money is painful, not fun.

Thankfully, shopping wasn't considered a recreational activity where Lily was from. She studied women in the street, stood and stared at shop window displays, and by the time we'd arrived somewhere I figured I could actually afford something for her, she knew exactly what she wanted. Jeans, boots, T-shirts, sweaters. A coat. Running shoes. A scarf, a hat, a dress, and she was done. Wonderful girl. She was mildly astonished that all the clothes were ready-to-wear, but took it all in stride and had a full wardrobe in less than the time it takes most women I know to get dressed. It cost me a small fortune, but I figured I could lean on Magda to get me some Sundown work.

I even treated Lily to dinner. Sure, I was delaying the inevitable. And yes, I'm aware that buying a girl lots of clothes when she might disappear is not the smartest thing to do. But where Lily was concerned, I'm afraid smartness just went out of the window. I knew I was quite in love with her body: was I falling in love with the rest of her, too?

Lily regaled me with tales of the high seas as we ate. She seemed pleased with my description of her as a pirate queen; her crew, she said, were all men and all under her thumb. I wasn't surprised. Not only was Lily beautiful, she was smart and sharp and she didn't take shit from anyone. It would be an extremely stupid sailor who would question Lily's authority.

She had chocolate cake for dessert, served with ice cream, and the look on her face when she tasted it was just like the look on her face when she came. I couldn't eat a bite, too transfixed by her heavy-lidded eyes, full lips parted in a sigh, the long sleek lines of her throat as her head dropped back.

"You want some?" she offered.

"Yes," I moaned, and she laughed.

I called Aura's house again as we left the restaurant. This time she answered.

"Darling," she said languidly, "I was busy. You know how hard I work."

"You're a sex faery," I said, causing Lily's eyebrows to shoot up. "It sounds like all play and no work to me."

"Is there something you need help with?" she asked, her voice like rich velvet.

"Yes," I said. "But you can keep your clothes on for this."

"I'm intrigued," she said. "Do stop by."

"I intend to."

"Sex faery?" Lily asked as I ended the call, having explained the basics of telecommunication to her in the restaurant.

"Yeah. She helps people with sexual problems. Couples and stuff. People who don't enjoy sex."

"You mean she's a whore?"

I shrugged. In all fairness to Aura, what she did was more of a calling than a job, part of who she was as a faery. As far as I knew, she didn't get paid for it. Her income, like a large portion of mine, came from consultancy services for Sundown.

We got back on the Tube and rode to Kensington. Okay, maybe Aura's income was supplemented by something else. You don't live in Kensington on a peanut salary like mine. Her house was part of a high, grand crescent, the sort of place Oscar Wilde films are set. I felt kinda scruffy in my beat-up leather jacket and jeans, but Lily walked along as if she owned the place.

Hell, twenty-four hours ago she'd never seen the twenty-first century. Now here she was, moving like royalty, looking like a goddess, totally at home in the richest part of one of the world's biggest 21st century cities. What a woman.

I caught her arm at the bottom of the steps to Aura's grand front door. "Lily…"

"Yes?" Her eyes were flashing. She was gearing up for a fight.

"Look. I don't know… I don't know what's going to happen when we talk to Aura. She's not bad, for a faery. I mean, she's reasonable. But she might… she might send you back. To your own time."

Her face was unreadable. "Oh."

"I just wanted you to be prepared for that."

"I'm always prepared." She flashed me a smile.

"Yes, I suppose you are." I hesitated, then said, "I -- look, if you do go back, I want you to know… I want to say… I'm glad you were here. That I met you."

She touched my face. "I'm glad I met you too. It was nice to have real sex after that dream stuff when I was in the float."

With that, she turned and went up the steps, leaving me feeling like I'd been slapped in the face. Sex. Yes, of course.

Lily hammered on the door with more strength than you'd expect in someone so small, and a minute later it was opened by a willowy goddess in a silk robe. Aura, her red-gold hair falling in

Marilyn waves to her shoulders, her green eyes shining with sex and magic.

Lily looked as if she was about to hit her. "You trapped me for three hundred years!"

"I did no such thing." Aura took a drag on her cigarette, carried in a long ivory holder, and her eyes flickered to me. "Darling," she waved the cigarette holder at me, "who is this gorgeous creature you've brought to see me?"

"Hi, Aura," I said. "This is Lily. Did you trap her in a fishing float in 1723?"

Aura stared at me. Then she laughed. "Darling, I'm not that old. Come in, and do tell me what this is about."

Her home was beautiful, full of beautiful things. Such as the couple fucking on the floor by the fireplace in her lovely sitting room. At first I thought it was a woman riding a skinny man, and then I saw that the man had tiny breasts and straps around his hips, and realized he was a woman wearing a dildo. Nice.

Lily's eyes bugged out. I guess homosexuality on the high seas didn't extend to girl-on-girl action, huh?

"Yes, darling, that's it," Aura encouraged, stroking the woman on top. "Doesn't that feel good?"

I tried to find my voice. "Isn't that defeating the object?"

"What, the dildo? Takes all sorts. Just because Marie here prefers women doesn't mean she doesn't want a little bit of cock every now and then."

Marie threw back her head and thrust out her breasts. If she knew we were here, she didn't seem to mind. Below her, her skinny lover thrust up with her hips.

"What sort of place is this?" Lily murmured, looking around. On the walls, most of the pictures were Kama Sutra type prints of couples, and even groups, fucking happily.

"I told you, Aura's a sex faery," I said, as Aura bent down and slid her hand beneath Marie's shapely bottom to fondle the pussy of the woman wearing the dildo. From the way the woman started shaking and moaning, I'd say the action was appreciated.

"Is there somewhere else we can talk about this?" I asked as the dildo woman thrashed about orgasmically.

"If you're going to be a prude, darling," Aura said, "pop into the kitchen. I'll be in in a minute."

She picked up Marie, turned her round on the dildo and bent to lick both pussies at once. I hustled Lily out of there, more turned on than I wanted to admit. I'm a guy, okay, lesbians do it for me. Three hot women getting down and dirty? Oh, hell yes.

I gripped the kitchen counter and stared out the window, needing to get some focus before I talked to Aura. But all I could think about was hot naked women. And when Lily pressed her body against my back, all I could think about was hot naked Lily.

"I'm seeing so many new things today," she murmured against my back, her hands sneaking round my hips. "Trains, cars, women fucking with a fake cock."

"That one's new to me too," I said. Her hands were straying dangerously close to my cock.

"You liked it," she said, feeling the hardness under my clothes.

"Is it that obvious?" I asked desperately.

Her hands caressed my cock through my clothes. I closed my eyes. "I don't understand why she isn't fucking a man with a real cock," Lily mused, her fingers finding my fly and unzipping it a little.

"Lily, please stop."

"Don't you like it?"

"Oh hell, yes, but you're making me so hard I can't think."

She grabbed my shoulders and spun me around. "Then I'll have to make you soft again," she said, and her eyes sparkled.

I had a moment to wonder what she meant before she dropped to her knees and unfastened my fly, taking my cock out and running her little hands all over it.

"What are you -- oh," I said, as she licked the tip. "*Oh.*"

She smiled, then ran her tongue along the underside. I held onto the counter, feeling like my knees were going to buckle.

"When I said..." she kissed my balls, "...that I don't get on my knees for anyone..." she slid her tongue around the head of my penis, "...I forgot to add that I will if they earn it."

With that, she took my cock into her mouth, as much of it as she could, and wrapped her hand around the rest. Dear, sweet Lord, what had I done to deserve this? It was heaven! If I never saw Lily after this, she was making sure we went out with a bang.

"Oh, God." I tangled my hand in her braids. "Christ, Lily, that's good."

Her head bobbed up and down, her beads clicking as she sucked and licked. Her mouth was glorious, so hot and deep and soft. Better than her cunt? Hell, I didn't know. All I knew was I never wanted her to stop. As she sucked my cock she fondled my balls, and I thought I might die then, a happy man.

More noises were coming from the sitting room. Apparently Aura was imparting the joys of sex very eloquently to those two women. One of them was screaming, "Yes! Yes!" over and over. I started to sweat. Between the thought of the three women fucking in the next room and the wonderful heat of Lily's mouth on my cock, I was about ready to burst.

"You're incredible," I gasped as she deep-throated me. "Lily, oh God, Lily. I think I love you."

Was I babbling? Did I mean it? In my defense, this was the best damn blow job I'd ever, ever had. She really was incredible, her lips and tongue doing the most amazing things to me.

I held her head in both hands and started to thrust into her mouth, lost in glorious pleasure. I think I was mumbling her name. I might have been crying. The only thing I know is that the kitchen door opened just as I came, and Aura stood there, her robe falling open to reveal perfect pearly breasts that weren't half as appealing as Lily's soft, dark ones. It was Lily I cried out for when I came, and Lily who sucked down every drop of come, holding my hips as I jerked into her.

Aura left, displaying unusual tact, and as the world returned I heard her ushering the lesbian couple out. When she came back in, I was dressed again and Lily was drinking water from a glass.

"Didn't mean to intrude," Aura said. "Nice to see you two have no need of my services."

Lily licked her lips. "None whatsoever," she said, and put her glass down. She eyed Aura distrustfully. "You gave that fishing float to Con."

Aura nodded. "Yes, and aren't you glad I did?"

"You knew she was in there?" I asked.

"Of course, darling."

"And you didn't feel any inclination to let her out yourself?"

Aura shrugged beautifully. "Mmm, no. Eibhlis would have known if I'd done it. Any trace of faery magic would have shown up. Besides, I'm not sure I could. I make sexual magic, darling, not --"

"What did you say?" I said, feeling suddenly queasy.

She blinked. "Don't tell everyone, will you, darling? I don't want it common knowledge that my magic is limited."

I shook my head. "No. About Eibhlis."

"Oh. Well, that's who I got the float from. That's who put her in there." She gave me an innocent look that made my stomach churn. "Didn't you know?"

Before I knew what I was doing, the curse "*Inlaqueare!*" had flung itself from my lips and pinned Aura against the wall by her throat.

"No," I hissed, stalking over, "you didn't say. You somehow managed to miss out the fact that the faery who made me her bitch, my old *girlfriend*, in case you'd forgotten, is the one who imprisoned Lily in that float for three hundred fucking years."

Behind me, I heard Lily gasp. Yeah, see, I can be tough sometimes. And I'm not totally useless at magic.

"But you have to admit there's a nice irony to it," I said. "If I hadn't made that bargain with her, I'd never be able to do this to you."

"And you'd never have had those dreams, either," Aura said, her hand going to her neck. But my spell was holding her there, and there wasn't anything she could physically do about it.

"How do you know about the dreams?" Lily demanded.

"They were my gift to you, darling. I couldn't get you out, but I could make you connect. I'm a sex faery," she repeated. "It's the only way I could do it."

"You couldn't have told me?" I said.

She shrugged. "Sorry. Now, could you release me? I think you've made your point."

I glowered at her, but let her go, and she sagged to the ground in a silky, graceful heap, massaging her throat.

"I can't interfere with another faery's magic," she said, getting to her feet. "And I'm far lesser than her. I have no place at the Unseelie court."

"And your little sex-dream spell wasn't interfering?" I said.

Aura frowned, and crossed to the freezer. She took out a bottle of Polish vodka, frozen to a thick syrup, and slugged straight from it. "I was sort of hoping it would come to the attention of a higher power," she said. "You know what the courts are like, Con. It's all back-stabbing and subterfuge. The rules are there, but they might as well not be for the way everyone bends around them."

Lily and I glared at her.

"I couldn't challenge Eibhlis over what she did to Lily," Aura said, sighing. "I don't have the authority. I needed to bring it to someone else's notice, and I was sort of hoping that if -- when -- you freed her, the Unseelie Queen might notice and reprimand Eibhlis."

"What do you have against her?" I asked, and Aura snorted.

"She's a vicious little bitch," she said, which true enough. "And she shouldn't have imprisoned a mortal like that. Lily, did she ever bargain with you? Offer you anything?"

"No, she just turned up with her mad red eyes and cursed me into the float."

"That's against the rules," Aura said with a nod. "She should at least have tried to trick you into something."

"But if it's against the rules --" I began, and Aura waved her hand.

"Eibhlis is royalty," she said. "I can't challenge her. Only other royals can do..." she suddenly looked thoughtful, "...that."

"What?" I said.

"Elline," she said, and Lily and I exchanged a look.

"Who or what is Elline?" I said.

"Seelie prince," Aura said, her lovely eyes distant. "It's the wrong court, but he might be willing to speak out if I ask him nicely."

"Yeah?" I said. "And what's he going to ask in return for that?"

"Oh, he's not like that, darling." Aura fussed with the lapel of her gown, not looking at me.

"Uh-huh," I said. "No. I don't believe you. The Fae always want something." I drummed my fingers on the counter. This information was highly interesting, but I wasn't sure how to act on it. If Aura didn't have the authority to challenge Eibhlis, then I sure as hell wouldn't. And there was no other faery who would even talk to me.

The only way I had of clearing this was to go straight to the queen herself. And she would never, ever respond to a summons from me.

I glanced at Lily, standing there looking so beautiful and defiant, and considered asking her just how much she wanted to avenge this. But I knew the answer. Lily wouldn't let her tormentor just go on living in peace. She wanted retribution. And damn it, so did I, even if I hadn't a clue how to get it.

"I need to get to the queen," I said.

"Yes," Aura agreed, "but she'll never talk to you. She doesn't even think of humans unless she wants something from them."

I blinked. Wants something? My mind flashed back to the Eye of Splendida in my front room. I might be able to do this. At a price, of course, because this is the Fae we're talking about, but still…

I glanced at Lily again. Price, hell. What was a little more servitude?

"Can you get a message to the queen for me?" I asked Aura heavily.

She blinked. "What sort of message?"

"The Eye of Splendida. Tell her… tell her that I need her presence to finish it. And Eibhlis's, too. Females of the blood royal or something."

Aura cocked her head. "You want me to do this thing for you? For free?"

"I'll bargain," I said.

"No, Con." Lily grabbed my wrist. "No, it's not worth it."

I looked at her big brown eyes, stroked her palm with my thumb, and smiled. "Yes," I told her, "it is." I turned to Aura. "Name your price."

She put her hand to her heart. "I am so touched," she said. "I really am."

"Yeah, yeah. And don't say a firstborn child. That one is such a cliché."

Aura regarded me a while. Regarded us. My heart beat faster and faster. What the fuck was I doing? God only knows what she'd ask for. I could be signing away my soul. Again.

Eventually she spoke. "If this works," she said, "if you talk to the queen and tell her what Eibhlis did, she'll be punished. And that will mean taking all Eibhlis's property and obligations."

I made a circular motion with my hand, telling her to move on with it.

"Promise me the obligation you have to Eibhlis," Aura said, her eyes on mine, "and we'll be even."

I froze. Lily's hand tightened around mine.

"If it's promised to me, then the queen can't take it," Aura said.

"You swear that?"

"I do. Promises are things we can't break."

"No, Con. Don't do it," Lily whispered.

But if I didn't, then Aura was right, and I'd be directly beholden to the queen. And the Unseelie Queen was a pretty terrifying prospect. Aura... Well, Aura could be a bitch sometimes, but she'd said herself she had no influence in the Unseelie court. She hardly had any Fae friends, or else why would she associate with humans so much?

"Done," I said, and Aura smiled a wicked smile, and took my hand, and just like that, I signed my future away, all for the woman I loved. Again.

Chapter Five

Lily was quiet as we walked to the Tube and made our way back home. Well, my home. Probably not hers for much longer. She hardly said anything until we were on the mainline train, chugging slowly back to Blackchapel in the twilight. It was busy, the train full of commuters in suits, talking on their phones and tapping on their laptops. I found us a pair of seats together, and Lily contrived to sit as far away from me as she possibly could, which is quite a feat in the narrow seats.

"You okay?" I asked.

She shrugged, playing idly with the ends of her hair and staring out the window. "I'm fine."

Uh-oh. "Fine" from a woman is never really fine. Even I know that. "Lily?"

"Low me," she mumbled, turning further away.

"What does that mean?"

"Leave me alone."

The hell I would. "What did I do?" I asked.

She turned her angry, stubborn face to me. "What did you do? You promised yourself to a faery, that's what you did!"

"Well, could you think of another way to get hold of the Unseelie Queen?"

The man sitting opposite us gave us a strange look.

"Not *her*," Lily spat. "The other one. The one who trapped me in a fishing float for three hundred years!"

A woman on the other side of the aisle looked at us over her newspaper.

"Okay, but I can explain that one," I said, a touch desperately. "I was really young --"

"How young?"

"Eighteen --"

Her eyebrows shot up. "By the time I was eighteen I had raided four British and three French ships," she said scornfully.

"Well, that's just peachy," I said. "Unfortunately, I was getting tricked into love by an insane faery with purple teeth and mad red eyes."

The woman with the newspaper leaned over. "Excuse me, are you rehearsing for a play?"

"No," we both said, and glared at each other.

"So what, you promised to love, honor and obey her in return for unlimited powers?" Lily said.

"No." I glowered at the floor, and mumbled, "not unlimited."

She let out a low laugh.

"But I didn't promise to love, honor and obey, either," I said.

"Just to do whatever she wanted for the rest of your life?"

"Um. Yes."

The train rattled to a halt and there was a rush of people trying to get away from us. When it started moving again, Lily switched to the vacated seat opposite me, all the better to glare. "I can't believe you would be so stupid," she said.

"Well, believe it," I said, lamely. The truth is, I know I was stupid. But right now there's not a lot I can do about it.

"And now you're promised to another faery," Lily said in disgust. "Eibhlis won't leave you alone, you know. She'll try and get you to promise something else."

"Yes, thank you. I am acquainted with faery practices."

"And this Aura might be even worse," Lily went on.

"No, she's not."

"How do you know? Just because she looks human and lives in a human city, that doesn't mean she is human. She's *Fae*, Con. She will lie and cheat and manipulate you. That's what they do. And if you try to fight them they do something underhanded like stick you in a fishing float for three hundred years. Maybe more, because if you hadn't let me out I'd be trapped there still."

"And if I hadn't made that bargain with Eibhlis then you'd still be in the float," I said. "You ever think of that?"

She glared at me. I glared at her. The train rattled to a halt again, and Lily got up.

"Where are you going?"

She flicked her gaze at the sign outside. "This is where we got on, yeah?"

Damn it, she was right. I'd got so caught up in arguing with her I hadn't realized we were already at Blackchapel. I got up and stomped off the train. She stomped after me. We stomped down the platform.

"Who's to say this Aura isn't twice as bad as Eibhlis?" Lily burst out. "All she does is have sex all day."

"That's all we do," I pointed out.

"Because of her. She said she'd put a spell on us."

"You were sleeping with me because of a spell?"

"Yes." Defiant, she glared up at me.

"Well, so was I," I said, glaring back down.

We left the station and walked along the dark, quiet road to my house.

"Well, good. Now we know we don't have to do it any more."

"No," I said.

"Good."

"Good."

Wait. *What?*

"Wait," I said, stopping.

"What?"

My brain was broken. "You didn't want to have sex with me?"

She glanced sideways at me, then her eyes skittered away. "It was a way of passing time," she muttered.

"Oh, thank you. Thank you very much. I'm glad to know I was an adequate pastime," I huffed, and strode on ahead, more insulted than I think I've ever been.

"No, you weren't." Lily ran after me.

"I wasn't adequate? You really know how to insult a man, Lily."

"No, I mean, you weren't a pastime."

"Really? That's how it sounded to me. I'm so glad we've been relieved of this spell now, so you won't be forced to endure sex with me any more."

"I wasn't enduring it before," Lily cried. "Con, will you listen to me?"

I stopped again and glared sullenly at her. First she'd insulted my taste in women, then my magical prowess, and now this. I was gearing up for a terrific sulk now. Whatever she had to say couldn't possibly make it any better.

"What I meant was, maybe the spell had been making us have sex in our dreams. But now we're not dreaming, we don't have to have sex. We're doing it because we want to."

Oh bollocks, a great sulk ruined.

"At least, I did want to," she said, glaring at me, her hands on her hips. "Now you're being a lobcock and I'm not sure I do any more."

With that she turned and strode off, that pretty little ass of hers wiggling as she walked.

I blinked. "What the hell is a lobcock?"

"A limp dick," Lily said, not looking back at me as I followed her.

"Oh, cheers. Thanks very much."

I caught up. She was smiling.

"I'll have you know my dick is very rarely limp around you," I said.

"I'd noticed."

I glanced at her, and she was grinning, and just like that I forgot what we'd been arguing about. God, I love this woman. I slung my arm around her shoulders, and she leaned into me, and I thought how warm and wonderful she felt there, and prayed to any god I could think of that she wasn't going to be taken away from me.

I'd barely closed the front door behind us when she wrapped her arms around me and kissed me, long and slow. Her mouth was so soft, so hot. Her body pressed slowly into me, relaxing little by little, warm and right in my arms.

She pulled back and smiled. "I could take you right here," she said, and my blood pressure skyrocketed.

"Bed," I said, grabbing her hand and tugging her toward the stairs. "Now."

She laughed as I towed her after me. "We could do it anywhere," she said. "In the kitchen on the table."

"We did the parlor table," I said, remembering fondly.

"Outside in that car thing of yours."

I swallowed. "Too far."

"Right here on the stairs."

I stumbled. Lily caught me and pinned me down, straddling me, her hands holding mine above my head. Her hot core right above my cock, which was straining to meet her through our clothes.

"Here is good," I managed, and she laughed, her voice husky and low, the sound vibrating through me. She leaned down and kissed me, her hands already unfastening my jacket. I returned the favor, sliding my hands under the red wool of Magda's coat and feeling the heat of Lily's skin through her thin dress. Her skirt rode up on her thighs as she stripped off my T-shirt and I took a moment to appreciate the glide of the fabric over her smooth skin, before helping it on its way and pushing it up past her tiny little panties.

It probably should have been uncomfortable on the stairs, but to be honest I was focusing a lot more on the extremely hot woman above me. She was kissing my chest now, flicking her tongue across my nipples, making me gasp. I slid my hands up her legs, lingered a while on the sweet curve where thigh turned to buttock, then cupped her butt in my hands and just savored the feel of it.

Then Lily sat up and pulled off the dress, leaving her sitting there on my crotch in just her underwear. White lace against dark skin. She was so beautiful with those long beads spilling over her shoulders, her white teeth flashing as she laughed, her eyes soft and dark, looking down at me.

I ran my hands up her back, pulled her down and kissed her some more. She squirmed in my arms, doing extremely interesting things to my general state of arousal. Flicking open her bra, I freed her breasts and ran my hands over them, felt their weight, their softness. I rolled her nipples between my fingers, making her gasp. She kissed me with increasing urgency, taking charge of my mouth. Did I mind? Hell, no. Lily could boss me around any day of the week.

I moved one hand down the soft, smooth skin of her stomach, down beneath the lace that was the only thing separating her pussy from my skin, and slipped inside. Her folds were swollen and wet, so tempting. After the amazing tongue job she'd given me at Aura's, I wanted to return the favor. Besides, the taste of Lily's pussy on my lips, the feeling of her soft thighs cradling my face, the tightness of her cunt around my tongue, those were things I was eager to get reacquainted with.

But not right here, not right now. We had no room to maneuver for one thing. Instead I sat up, taking her with me, my hand still buried in her panties, and dipped my head to taste one of her beautiful plump nipples.

"Con," she moaned softly, the sound vibrating through her skin. I slipped one finger up into her pussy, my thumb circling her clit, felt her start to breathe faster. I switched to the other breast, sucking and licking her nipple, kissing her hot skin. She tasted like the ocean. She tasted hot.

Another finger in her pussy, and she arched against me, her head back, moving against my hand. Thrusting. Fucking my fingers. Her cunt was tight and hot, so slippery, so inviting. A third finger.

Lily let out a sound that was part gasp, part moan, and moved harder against my fingers. She was almost there. I could feel it. Her breath came in quick pants, her hands clutched my shoulders, short nails digging in. It was the second time today I'd brought her to orgasm with my hand, and I was feeling pretty pleased with myself when she ripped my head from her breast, stuck her tongue down my throat, and came with a terrific shudder, her cunt clenching so tight around my fingers that I thought she'd squeeze them off.

Then she sighed, her body going loose in my arms, soft and pliant, her head falling to my shoulder. Her head fit neatly under my chin and I held her there, sliding my hand out from her pussy to wrap both arms around her and hold her as she shuddered and shook against me.

For a while we stayed like that, quiet and still, warm skin and soft breathing. Her rapid heartbeat slowed, and eventually she looked up at me, smiling so beautifully I forgot how to breathe.

"Bed now," she said, and shifted in my arms, rubbing against my cock which was still hard, still straining against my jeans. It jumped around, going "Yes please!" and who was I to argue?

"Bossy woman," I said, and she lifted her chin and gave me a haughty look that was damn sexy.

"I am the captain," she said loftily.

"Of what ship?"

"Of this relationship," she said, and dissolved into giggles.

I groaned. "How long have you been waiting to say that?"

"Forever," she said, and got to her feet, breasts bouncing happily. "Come on," she ran her hand over my cock, "I want this inside me."

"And it wants to be inside you too, darlin'," I said, jumping up so fast I nearly fell over, and tugging her up the rest of the steps to my bedroom. She stopped me in the doorway, tugged me to her by my belt loops and kissed me. Goddamn, the woman could kiss. Her hands worked the fly on my jeans and pushed them down. I kicked them away and then I was naked, and there she was, almost as naked and right there in my arms.

One second and a slight tearing of lace later, she was naked too.

"You are so beautiful," I said, drawing her down to the bed, and she looked a little bashful. "No, really, you are."

"I never felt beautiful before," she said.

"Do you now?"

She stroked my cheek. "When you look at me like that, yes. I do."

She rolled soft and hot in my arms, kissing me, sliding her gorgeous body against mine and wrapping her legs around me. Slow, I reminded myself, take it slow. This might be the last time you ever get to do this with her. Make it last.

I slid inside her welcoming cunt, so hot, so tight around my aching cock, and she smiled at me, easing her legs higher around my waist to pull me in deeper. Christ, I thought as my balls brushed her hot slick pussy lips, slow is not going to happen unless I start thinking of really boring things. And I don't want to think about boring things, I want to think about how deep and silky Lily's cunt is.

"You're not moving," she whispered.

"I can't," I said.

"What do you mean, you can't?"

"If I move, I'll come."

She laughed, her belly shaking, the movement rather too delightful. "Then come, lover," she said.

"I want to make this last. It's been -- we've just been rushing and I wanted... you deserve..."

Her eyes filled with such softness it looked like she was going to cry. She pressed a quick kiss to my lips, then pulled me to her and rolled so I was on my back.

She sat up slowly, stretching out her back, her breasts pouting for attention.

"Oh God, I'm a dead man," I groaned.

Lily moved on me slowly, gently, her hands tracing unseen patterns on my chest, her body rocking, actually hardly moving. Just the tiniest friction where it mattered. I was surrounded by her glorious heat, looking up at her beautiful body. Moonlight gleamed through the window, shining on her sweat-dampened skin.

"My God, you're beautiful," I said again.

She smiled, closing her eyes. "You're just saying that because you're inside me."

"No, I'm saying it because it's true. If I was using it as a line, it'd be redundant, because as you pointed out, I'm already inside you."

"Hmm." She played with my left nipple. "I think if you're still managing to use words like 'redundant' then I need to move a little more."

Which she did, changing her rocking movement to a truly impressive up-and-down motion. Immediately, all words over one syllable fled my mind. In fact, all words other than "Oh God, *yes*" became complete strangers to me.

I closed my eyes, hoping that by blocking out the visual I might be able to concentrate better. It didn't work. Lily bent down and ran her tongue over my lips until I opened my mouth, whereupon she bit my lip, and I moaned, and opened my eyes.

She was grinning at me.

"Witch," I said.

"Wizard," she replied, straightening up and lifting off so far I thought I'd slip out of her. But then she slid down on me, taking me right to the balls, and my breath left in a whoosh of air. The sight of her, the amazing sight of her rising and falling, her breasts rolling with the motion, was so incredible. I watched her beautiful pussy swallow up my cock, over and over, faster and faster. Before I knew it she was rocking as she moved on me, and I was thrusting into her, my hands on her hips, lost in the rhythm.

Her pussy tightened around me, convulsed, and her body shuddered. I felt her come, watched her face change as pleasure overtook her and her fingers dug into my chest. She cried my name. My name.

I pulled her to my chest, rolled her to her back, and finished with a few thrusts inside her. She wrapped her legs around my waist and cradled me with her body, holding me to her as we came back down to earth again together.

Chapter Six

We lay together, arms and legs tangled, and then I figured I was squashing her and summoned a last reserve of energy to roll away. She came with me, clinging close, snuggling her head into the curve of my neck.

I will never get tired of making love to this woman.

It wasn't a startling revelation. Less than twenty-four hours after she'd materialized on my hearth rug, I was in love with her. I just didn't want to let her go. The Unseelie Queen could appear at any moment and spirit Lily away. If she had a mind to undo Eibhlis's meddlings, she'd just send Lily back to her pirate ship in 17-fucking-23.

I'd be free, but you know, I'd rather be beholden to every Fae in the world, Seelie and Unseelie, even the Wildfae, and keep Lily.

I wanted to call it all off. Ring Aura and tell her I didn't want to see the queen after all. Didn't want to square with Eibhlis. But then I looked at Lily, so warm and soft in my arms, so small and strong, and knew that even if I was content to let the Fae fuck me over for the rest of my life, I wasn't going to let them do it to Lily. She wanted revenge, she deserved revenge. And maybe it's the sex talking here, but I was of a mind to give her whatever the hell she wanted.

"Con?" Lily murmured.

"Yes, darlin'?"

"Do people still sail boats?"

I blinked at this unexpected question. "Well, yes, they do. Usually for pleasure, but yes."

She made a soft noise against my shoulder. "Why else would you sail but for pleasure?"

"To get somewhere."

"You have your cars and trains for that."

"But you didn't. If you wanted to get from..." I tried to think of places she might have actually traveled to and from, and drew a blank. I don't do geography. "Okay, from the Americas to England, you'd have to sail, right?"

"Is there another way now?"

"Yes." Oh crap, how do I explain flying? "It's, er. We have these things called planes. They, uh, fly."

"Like the ones on the pictures at the stations?"

"The what?"

"On the walls. Underground. There were pictures of things, books and clothes and other things I don't know. And one with a big machine, like a train with wings, in the sky. It said something about flying."

Her tone was calm, and again I marveled that she was taking all this in stride. "Yes," I said. "That's a plane."

"How does a machine fly?"

"God knows," I said honestly.

"Is it magic?"

"Of a sort," I said. "But that's how we travel long distances now."

She was quiet a while, curled there at my side, her hand on my chest, her thigh resting on my hip. It felt good, so good, so damn right, to be holding her like that.

"You miss sailing?" I said, knowing she did and she wanted to be back on her ship.

"Whenever I am on land I miss it," she said. "Sometimes it's hard to walk when the ground is so still."

I closed my eyes.

"Maybe I could get a boat," she said. "A little one. I'm sure I must have some buried treasure somewhere. Do you think it might still be worth something?"

"What kind of treasure?" I asked dully.

"Gold, jewelry, diamonds."

"They're always worth something," I said, and then her words caught up with me. "You mean, now? Would they be worth something now?"

Lily nodded, looking up at me with slight confusion. "Now is where I am. When I am," she corrected.

"But I thought… you want a boat now?"

She nodded again. My heart swelled.

And yes, *just* my heart swelled. Give a guy a break, will you?

"You want to stay here? Now?"

Again the look of confusion. "Why wouldn't I? I like your new world. I like this place." Her hand smoothed up my neck to cup my face. "I like you."

I kissed her at that, full of relief and happiness. Okay, it wasn't over yet, we still had to face the queen, but Lily wanted to stay. She wanted to be with me, and that was bloody fantastic.

After that it wasn't just my heart swelling. Lily shifted in my arms, all that hot soft flesh pressing against me, my arms full of her. We kissed more, endless kisses, long hot kisses that went on and on. Lily moved to my neck, my chest, sucked my nipple into her mouth and flicked her tongue over it. She started to go lower, but I pulled her back.

"I want to lick you," I said.

"I want to suck you," she said, and I couldn't really argue with that. I let her run her lips and tongue all over my cock, and before I lost my mind too much I pulled her over me, straddling my face, and licked her lovely pussy while she sucked my balls. It was heaven, absolutely glorious, and I'd have gone on forever -- or at least until we'd both come our brains out a few more times -- if we hadn't been interrupted.

For a moment I thought the flash of light meant I was coming, which was a bit of a surprise to me, but then a cold female voice said, "There's a fucking welcome for you," and I went cold all over.

Lily froze above me, and then she slowly sat up, leaving my cock all cold and friendless. Not that I really cared at that point. The presence of my ex-girlfriend had put a hell of a damper on my libido.

Lily moved off my face, and there she was, Eibhlis, standing at the foot of my bed, looking as chilly and beautiful as she ever had. She was draped in something ice blue and diaphanous, showing her slender body off to the best advantage. Her hair was ash blonde, her eyes calm and blue. A glamour, a false appearance -- but also the way I'd first seen her. The way I'd fallen in love with her.

The purple teeth and red eyes came later.

"I'm hurt," she said, looking down at me with mocking in her eyes. "You seem to have gotten over me."

"It wasn't hard," I said, wiping my mouth which was still full of Lily's taste. "You've done your best to ruin my life."

Beside me, Lily reached for the duvet and pulled it over us.

"At least she has some sense of propriety," Eibhlis said.

"Unlike you," I replied. "Don't you knock?"

Eibhlis gave a chilly smile. "I'm a princess of the Unseelie court," she said. "Of course I fucking don't."

"Why are you here?" I asked, completely not caring that I sounded rude. I wanted to sound rude.

"My mother never appears without fanfare," Eibhlis said, and clapped her hands.

I grabbed hold of Lily, and Eibhlis's low laughter filled the room as the temperature plummeted. Ice crawled across the windowpanes. The curtains shook and flapped in the sudden breeze. Lily shivered beside me, pulling the duvet tighter around us. We huddled together, skin like ice, while the air swirled around the foot of the bed, outlining the figure of a woman, coalescing into solid form, an ice statue standing there in my bedroom.

Dear God, I've never been so cold in my life, or so afraid. Not of the Unseelie Queen, but of what she might do. Of who she might take away from me.

I wrapped my arms around Lily and held her tight.

When the breeze died down, the air was still freezing, but the room was still. Very still. It felt as if everything had died, everything -- even the air itself -- had been frozen to death. The

Unseelie Queen stood there like the eye of the storm, a tall figure radiating a cold so severe I thought my feet were going to get frostbitten.

She was more than pale, her skin so white it hurt, almost blue, like ice. Her hair lay like frost against her shoulders. Her eyes were the color of a hole in the ice, the deepest cold, the bottom of a frozen sea. She was so beautiful it hurt to look at her, a chilling, violent beauty.

"Wizard," she said, and her *voice* was cold. Her actual voice. If ice sang, it would sound like this. Her words echoed, deep and terrible, just the sound of them so cold my skin crawled in fear. "You have summoned me."

Crap, the story about the Eye clearly didn't wash.

"I humbly desire your presence," I said, toadying as well as I could.

"To tell me words of treachery?"

Fuck. Five seconds in and already we were doomed.

"Your majesty," I said. "My lady. It doesn't please me to say them."

"It pleases me less to hear them."

"Mother?" Eibhlis said, and as I tore my eyes from the terrifying splendor of the queen, I wondered how I could have ever found her daughter beautiful. How anything could be beautiful when you'd seen such icy perfection.

"He charges against you," the queen said, never taking her eyes from mine. "That you have imprisoned a mortal against her will."

In that second Eibhlis's eyes widened, and Lily tightened her grip on me, and I remembered why I was here. The queen's beauty could be a glamour, or it could be real, but it would quite definitely kill me. She'd wrap me in her cold embrace and I'd slowly freeze to death, figuratively if not literally.

The woman shivering in my arms right now was real. She wasn't beautiful because of some glamour. She was beautiful because she was real, and she wasn't trying to trick me, or get anything from me but what I wanted to give.

Lily pressed her cold cheek against mine, and I turned to kiss it.

"He is a mortal, Mother, trying to break free of the promise he made me," Eibhlis said. "An honest bargain. His servitude for the power I supplied."

"Your bargain with him is not in dispute," the queen said. "What of the mortal woman?" Her terrible gaze fell on Lily. "This is she?"

"Yes, but --"

"What is your bargain with her?"

Eibhlis was silent. Her eyes burned with fury.

"She made no bargain," Lily said. Her voice shook with cold. Her teeth chattered. "She wanted something she couldn't have."

"And what was that?" The queen's voice was icily quiet.

"A man," Lily said. "A mortal man. But he didn't want her. She couldn't make him love her."

"We cannot interfere with the free will of mortals," the queen agreed. "But I fail to see why this involves you."

She made it sound as if Lily was so inconsequential as to be completely below Eibhlis's notice. In my arms, my pirate queen tensed.

"The man didn't want her," Lily said. "He wanted me. So she removed me."

There was silence. I felt the air thin out and start to crystallize. Any more of this and Lily and I would freeze to death. I wish I'd thought to buy arctic gear before I requested an audience with the Unseelie Queen.

"What bargain did she offer?" the queen asked, her voice a whisper like snowflakes falling.

"None," Lily said. "She didn't try to bargain. She just imprisoned me."

"Lies," Eibhlis cried. "Mother, she lies!"

"Ask Aura," I said quickly. "Eibhlis gave Aura the fishing float that Lily was trapped in."

"I traded that," Eibhlis jumped in before her mother could speak. "For some jewelry Aura had."

The queen clapped her hands and Aura suddenly appeared at our feet, sprawled on the bed, naked, legs open wide, cunt gleaming. She gave a shriek and scrambled backwards, away from the queen, onto me and Lily, who shoved her away and onto the floor.

Aura leapt to her feet with remarkable grace, and pulled a cloak around her shoulders that hadn't been there before. Faeries.

"Interrupt something?" I murmured, and she shot me a glare.

"You're on thin ice here, Devlin, don't make it worse."

Haha, great pun.

"Your majesty." Aura made a deep bow. "I am honored --"

The queen cut her off with a wave of her hand. "The 'fishing float'." She said the words as if she had no concept at all of what they meant. As she probably wouldn't.

"Eibhlis gave it to me in return for some jewelry," Aura said, and Eibhlis looked smug.

"And what is it?"

"A sphere of glass, yea big." Aura made a circle with her hands a few inches across. "Tied up with rope. Mortal fishermen use them to, er, weight --"

"Float," Lily muttered.

"-- their nets," Aura said.

The queen looked at Lily for a long moment. "This mortal human was trapped in a glass sphere of such a size?"

"Yes. For nearly three hundred mortal years."

"The blink of an eye to me," the queen dismissed.

"Four mortal lifetimes," I said, and her icy gaze swung back to me.

"And you, wizard, freed her?"

"Yes."

"Why?"

Might as well be honest. "It was an accident. I was using the float for another spell. I didn't know Lily was in it."

More silence. Even Eibhlis had the sense to say nothing.

"Daughter," the queen said. "What bargain did you offer the mortal before imprisoning her?"

Faeries can't lie. They just can't. They can twist the truth something chronic, and they are masters of evasion, but they just can't outright lie.

"None," Eibhlis said through clenched teeth.

"You trapped her against her will without recompense?"

Suddenly Eibhlis changed. Her beautiful white-blonde hair bled color, dark blue color. Her skin whitened out to translucence. Her eyes flashed red, blood red, and she gnashed her teeth, vivid purple fangs in a drooling mouth. "She was fucking the wizard when I found her," she snarled, "that's recompense."

"For three hundred years in a glass ball?" I said. "I'm flattered."

Lily nuzzled my shoulder. "For one or two hundred, maybe," she said. "Not three."

"Daughter, you must be punished," the queen said, and even before the sound had died Eibhlis let out a scream.

"*No!*"

"Yes." The queen's eyes glittered. Her skin sparkled like fresh snow. "Your powers stripped, your influence lost." Eibhlis howled and sank to the floor. "Your promises and obligations mine."

I cleared my throat and glanced at Aura.

"Wizard, your promise to Eibhlis is now to me. You are bound for the rest of your mortal life to do as my will dictates."

Lily clutched at me. Eibhlis sobbed on the floor.

"Your majesty," Aura said, bowing again. "He is promised to me."

Horrible silence. The queen's eyes bored real holes in my icy body.

"Promised?"

"He is mine if Eibhlis should lose him," Aura said carefully.

The queen was still as only ice can be.

"So mote it be," she said eventually, and turned her gaze to Lily. My heart thudded in my chest and my frozen arms clutched Lily to me. *I love you*, I thought fiercely.

"Mortal," the queen said, her voice a blizzard, harsh and cold, beyond cold. "You are owed a debt by my daughter, and now by me. It is within my power to return you to your own place and time."

"No," Lily whispered.

"You wish to remain here?"

"I do," Lily said, and looked up at me. "I do."

"Then your debt..." For the first time, the queen looked slightly lost.

"A future claim?" Aura suggested, and the queen frowned. Then she nodded irritably.

"Very well. Wizard, your debt is to the Wildfae Aura. Mortal, our debt is to you."

A crack like a glacier snapping in two, and then they were gone, the queen and poor sobbing Eibhlis, and the room immediately reheated.

"Jesus fucking Christ, that woman is scary," Aura said. She glanced at me and Lily. "You okay?"

"I may never be warm again," I said, "but yes. Lily?" Her head was tucked under my chin. Her body shook. "Lily?"

She was crying. Oh, fuck. Oh fuck, oh fuck.

"Maybe I should go," Aura said, and vanished.

"Lily, what's wrong?"

She raised her head, looking wretched. "I hate crying. I'm a pirate queen. We don't cry."

"But..." Oh Christ, something had to be really bad then.

"Especially when I'm not sad."

I blinked. "You're not sad?"

"No, you stupid clodpole." She wiped her eyes with the back of her hand. "I'm happy."

I stared stupidly.

"It's all over," Lily said, and her face split into a huge smile, and she took my face in her hands and kissed me. "It's all over," she said, pressing herself against me, kissing my face, her tears on my skin. She pulled me down under the covers, her skin icy against mine but warming up the more I touched it. My beautiful pirate queen, round and soft in my arms, all mine for the rest of forever.

I rolled her onto her back and kissed her fiercely with all the relief and love I felt for her. She was mine, and no one was taking her away from me. And she matched my passion. Kissed me back just as hard as I was kissing her, wrapped me tight in her arms, her legs, holding me to her with everything she had.

"Don't ever leave me," she gasped against my mouth.

"I won't," I said, pressing a kiss to her lips.

"And never stop fucking me."

I grinned. "I won't," I promised.

I kissed her mouth, the sweet curve of her neck, her pretty breasts. I held her in my arms and kissed her all over, because she was so perfect, so precious, and I'd been so scared of losing her.

When I licked the inside of her thigh she gasped and wriggled away, but before I could complain she'd thrown the covers back, wormed her way down my body, and taken my cock in her mouth. Back to where we were when the queen interrupted us.

I settled her thighs either side of my head and ran my tongue over her pussy from ass to clit. She was so wet, plump pussy lips just ripe for tasting. I ran my tongue around her clit and slipped a finger into her pussy.

Lily sighed around my cock and took it deeper into her mouth. That mouth was a fucking miracle, so hot, so wet. Her tongue swirled around me and I saw stars.

Concentrating hard on her pussy, I pumped two fingers in and out as I licked her clit. Her breathing quickened, her breasts heaving against my stomach. She'd warmed up considerably now and both of us were slick with sweat. I trailed my fingers from her pussy up to her ass and stroked the tight little bundle of nerves there.

Lily moaned, and I can tell you the vibrations felt pretty fucking good.

My fingers were slippery with her juices, and when I pressed one just a little bit into her asshole it went in easily.

Lily took her mouth from my cock and whimpered.

I smiled, curved my tongue around her clit, and felt my way into her ass. It was tight and as I stroked her from the inside, she whimpered and shook. I had a fleeting thought to ask if that meant she was enjoying herself, but then I figured she'd damn well let me know if she wasn't. Lily wasn't the sort to lie there and take an ass fucking if she didn't want to.

Still. It's only polite to ask.

"Is that good, darlin'? Do you want me to stop?"

"No," she moaned, her breath hot against my balls, "don't stop. It's good."

I pumped my finger in and out, then slid another in with it. Lily, who had my balls in her mouth, shook and writhed.

"You have the sweetest little ass," I told her, kissing her pussy lips.

"Will you --" she broke off to shudder as I stuck my tongue in her pussy "-- put your cock in it?"

"Now?"

"Yes. *Now.*"

I just can't deny this girl anything. I flipped her over onto her back, where she lay with legs open wide, breasts heaving, face flushed, looking like sex personified. She rolled slowly onto her front and presented her ass to me.

"I don't have any lubricant," I told her, trying to remember if I had anything we could substitute.

"Fuck my pussy," Lily said. "That's lube enough."

The lady had a point. I joyfully slid my throbbing cock inside her pussy, her tight, hot, slick little pussy, and we both moaned. A few thrusts were all I needed to get slicked up, but I did a few more because it felt so bloody good. Her little round ass was hot against my stomach, beautiful firm flesh to thrust against. I wanted to get inside that ass, but not yet. I slipped my two fingers back inside, and she moaned my name. A third finger to open her a little wider, and she whimpered.

I debated a fourth finger. Then I stuck it in as well.

"Oh, yes," she moaned. "Con, please!"

I pulled out of her pussy and was just about to plunge into her tight little asshole when it occurred to me that I rather liked seeing her face while I was fucking her. So I turned her over, slipped a cushion under her, and gently, slowly, pushed my cock into her ass, watching her face the whole time.

Her eyes were closed, her teeth digging into her lip.

"Lily? Are you all right? Is that okay?"

She gave a tiny nod and her eyes came open. "I don't know what okay is," she smiled, "but this is good."

I smiled, laughed and pushed further in. Her muscles relaxed their tight grip, and I moved inside her a little, stroking my cock inside that ass made for fucking.

"Yes," she whispered, and I bent to kiss her mouth.

I fucked her slowly. No, I didn't; I made love to her slowly. Stroking her breasts and her pussy as I pumped my cock in and out of her ass. She came first, crying out my name, her ass so tight around my cock, her pussy clenching on my fingers.

"Con," she cried, actual tears in her eyes. "Yes, oh! Never stop fucking me, Con!"

"I won't," I promised.

"I --" her whole body shuddered, "-- love you, Con."

And with that I came, shooting my load into her beautiful tight ass. "I love you too," I said as the world exploded, holding onto her so tight, my cock in her ass and my heart in her hands.

Chapter Seven

Three weeks later I stood at the bar of the Hotel Royale outside the village of Port Antonio in Jamaica, looking out at the private beach. It was a hell of a difference from cute, rainy Blackchapel, I can tell you. The beach was white sand, fringed with palms and decorated with incredibly beautiful women in tiny bikinis.

The most beautiful of whom had woken me that morning with her lips around my cock, before donning a few inches of white crochet and skipping off to go sailing.

Sometimes I was amazed how well Lily adapted to twenty-first century living. She'd taken the flight to Jamaica to find her treasure completely in stride, and was even learning to drive a car. The box of gold she'd dug up was worth a fortune, even to my eye. Enough for a boat of her own -- a fleet of her very own. She understood the Internet -- well, as much as anyone understands it -- and adored television.

She even found time for plenty of sex with me.

"Lily's enjoying herself," came a voice from beside me, and I turned to see Aura's red-gold hair shining in the bright sunshine.

"I didn't recognize you with your clothes on."

"Ha. Ha."

I looked back out at Lily, who had a motorboat out in the bay, whizzing around at the speed of light. "Never happier than when she's on a boat."

"Apart from when she's on you."

I couldn't help a smug smile.

"Why aren't you out there with her?"

The smile faded, replaced by embarrassment. "I get seasick."

Aura laughed. "Classic."

We stood and watched a little longer. There was a mild breeze to cool us off, a cold beer in my hand, and Lily seemed to be bringing her little boat back to shore. Sailing always made her highly exuberant, and more than once she'd hauled me into the cabin for some cramped ship sex. And more than once I'd had to drag her back to the hotel, because sex is a lot less fun when you're nauseous.

"Con," Aura said, "I have a bargain for you."

"Oh God. No. The answer is always no, to whatever you want."

"Even if it's a way to lift your horrible obligation to me?"

I glanced sideways at her. She hadn't once asked me to do anything in three weeks.

"No," I said. "No."

"I'm going to New York," Aura said, as if I hadn't spoken. Actually, as if we were having a different conversation. "I'm bored with London."

"Okay," I said cautiously.

"Of course there'll be a lot of Sundown stuff I can't do. So my bargain is this --"

"No," I said, "no bargains."

"You take on my Sundown clients while I'm out of the country, and I'll absolve you of any other debt to me."

"How long will you be gone?" I asked, thinking it'd be a decade or two at the least.

"Six months. A year, maybe. No more."

I stopped with my beer halfway to my lips, looked at her, and put it down.

"Your Sundown work for no more than a year, and you'll cancel my obligation to you?"

She nodded, a picture of innocence.

"There's a catch," I said, "there's always a catch. What horrors do you have lined up for the next year?"

"None, I swear. Darling, I'm not being underhanded here. I swear. Didn't I get you out of your obligation to the Unseelies? Have I asked anything of you since?"

"No, but that's what's making me suspicious."

"Fine," she said. "Call Magda and ask her."

I did. I got out my phone, called the Sundown offices, and asked Magda what Aura had lined up.

"Not much," Magda said. "She only does consultancy anyway."

"Nothing scary? No high courts? Taming Wildfae?"

"Nope. Some background info for a goblin assassination Mas is doing, and a centaur investigation."

I frowned. Goblins weren't that hard to deal with if you knew the right spells, which thankfully I did, and centaurs were famously dignified creatures. Nothing that was likely to get me in any hot water with either Fae court.

I thanked Magda and ended the call. At the little quay, Lily was tying up the boat. She saw me and waved, and I waved back.

"Nothing more than a year," I said to Aura. "Only the work Magda would have assigned you."

"Absolutely."

"And then we'd be clear? I'd owe you nothing?"

"That's right."

"Promise."

"I promise, Con."

I eyed her over my drink. "Why are you offering me this?"

"Because I'm a nice person. Don't spit that out, you'll make a mess. Con, I wasn't raised in the high courts. I don't enjoy all that bargaining crap. And hey, I'm the one who introduced you to your future wife --"

"Shh!" This time I nearly did spit my beer out. "She doesn't know yet."

Aura made a lip-zipping motion. "So, do we have a deal?"

"Say it out loud."

She made an elaborate sighing noise, but I wasn't going to be moved. No more Fae trickery.

"If you take on my non-threatening Sundown work for the duration of my stay in New York which will be less than one human year, I promise to absolve you of any other obligations to me. Okay?"

"When? When am I absolved?"

"As soon as you shake my hand."

"When are you going to New York?"

"Next week."

I could be home by then. Lily had said she was looking forward to taming the North Sea.

I held out my hand, Aura took it, and her green eyes sparkled at me. "Done," she said.

"Done."

She gave me a sunny smile and walked away. "Oh, and Con?"

"Yes?" I said, dread stealing back in. What had I forgotten to ask?

"Try a spell. For the seasickness."

With that she was gone, and I was left watching the movement of Lily's hips as she swayed up the beach. In her wake was a devastated trail of men, watching with their mouths hanging open. I smiled. My pirate was a damn fine looking woman.

A whistle sounded behind me, and I looked around to see the bartender shaking his head as he watched Lily move. She was wearing only a very, very small bikini that consisted of a few triangles of white crochet, contrasting so incredibly with her dark skin that it literally took my breath away.

"That is one hot lookin' mama," the bartender said, and I leaned back against the bar and watched her, deep satisfaction spreading through me.

"Tell me about it."

"Man, that woman is fine. I'd do anything for a taste of that."

Would you take on the Unseelie Queen? I wondered. Risk death, risk losing her, to get her what she wanted, what she needed? What she deserved?

"Look at that fine ass," the barman whistled as Lily worked the steps up into the bar. "Hey beautiful, you want something to drink?"

She looked up and smiled at him. Then she saw me, and her face lit up, just beaming, glorious, shining. She bounded over, her breasts bouncing, her freshly braided cornrows swinging, and planted a hot, wet kiss on my lips.

"Hello, lover," she said.

"It's nice to see you too."

She smelled like the sea, salty and fresh, and suddenly I wanted to test Aura's idea. A spell to combat seasickness? Why hadn't I thought of it before?

Because I'd been too busy having sex with Lily, that's why.

"This your woman?" the bartender said, seeming astonished.

"Yes," Lily said, draping her arms around me, and rattled off something in Jamaican patois that was way too fast for a white boy like me to understand. The barman laughed and backed off to get her a drink.

"What did you say?" I asked her, and she grinned and pressed her hot, nearly naked body against mine.

"I told him I only have eyes for you, lover." Aww, sweet. "And also you got the most skilled tongue I ever met."

I burst out laughing. That's my girl.

My phone rang, and it was Aura. "What now?" I asked cautiously.

"I'm spitting," she said. "Absolutely furious, darling."

Jolly good. "Why's that?"

"Magda will tell you." And she rang off.

"What did she want?" Lily asked, knocking back her thick, dark rum.

"I have no idea." I dialed the Sundown offices. "Magda? Why is Aura mad at me?"

Magda giggled. "Because apparently she's given you all her clients for the next year, right?"

"Right…"

"And Johann's just contracted us to track down a faery changeling."

I glanced at Lily, who was listening carefully, her cheek pressed against mine. She shrugged at me.

"Why is that bad?"

"Because I'm giving the assignment to you, and it's in Barbados."

My eyes met Lily's. She grinned.

Life is tough sometimes, eh?

Sundown, Inc: Baby Sham Faery Love

Cat Marsters

Chapter One

"I feel stupid," I said, prostrate on the couch with my head on a pillow.

"Well, you look divine. Now, open up."

I giggled. I couldn't help it. If it wasn't for the fact that I was fully clothed and I knew Tadgh was as bent as a nine bob note, I'd have thought he meant something else.

But for once in my life, the man asking me to open up was interested in my soul. Tadgh was a psychiatrist, a good one, whose clients were mostly women who were desperate for him to fall madly in love with them. Since Tadgh had been sleeping with the same guy since I met him, this seemed unlikely; but the girls could still stare at his massive shoulders and big dark eyes as they poured their souls out.

He was leaning against his desk, big and handsome in jeans and button-down shirt, watching me patiently. I crossed my ankles and admired my pretty mocha-and-cream polka-dot Choos while I thought about what to say.

"Come on, Tadgh, you know what it is," I sighed. "I've been bitching about it to you and Ell for years."

"Put it in words for me. What's the biggest reason you're unhappy?"

"I'm… invisible," I said.

"Define that for me."

"I… no one remembers me. I do all this stuff for them and make them all happy, then poof! I'm gone, and they have no idea I ever existed."

"So you want credit for what you're doing?"

"Well, no," I said, frowning. "Okay, yes. Maybe. I don't know."

"You don't know what you want?"

"Er. No."

"That's okay. Defining the problem is a big step."

I giggled again. "Is this you in shrink mode?"

"I have never shrunk in my life," Tadgh said mildly, and I thought about that image for a while and suppressed a shiver.

It occurred to me some time ago that I have a huge crush on Tadgh; but that's okay, it's a safe crush. Like I said, he's gay, so it's not like it could go anywhere. I can love Tadgh and he can love me, and neither of us are going to get our hearts broken.

As if reading my mind, Tadgh said, "Have you ever thought that maybe the reason you're unhappy is that you're too safe?"

"What?"

"Safe," he said. "You work with all these couples --"

"Not just couples," I said, "I've done my share of ménages."

There was an infinitesimal pause. "Right," Tadgh said calmly, "but you never get emotionally involved."

"Well, no," I said, "it'd be pointless. See above, regarding them forgetting me the instant it's over."

"So you get sex without emotional involvement," he said.

"Works for most men," I grumbled.

"And then, with Ell and me, you get the safety and security of not one but two men adoring you, but none of the risk of a love affair." He cocked his head. "I don't think you've been on a date since I've known you."

"I spend all my time having sex with strangers," I said. "How'd that look, if my boyfriend came around and found me at it on the floor with two girls wearing dildos?"

"I'd imagine he'd be overjoyed," Tadgh said.

I scowled. It's not what you think -- well, it's mostly not. I'm a sex fairy. Have been all my life, and please don't ask the hows and whys, because I'm not entirely sure myself. I bring sexual fulfillment to couples and singles of all varieties, just zoom in and make them happy, then vanish without a trace. I'm the catalyst for some mighty flammable relationships, I tell you.

My phone rang in my bag, and Tadgh frowned.

"I usually ask clients to turn those off," he said.

"I'm not a usual client," I replied, taking the phone out. I frowned at the number, then answered. "Magda?"

"Yes," she replied, her voice smooth and Moneypenny cultured. The line should have been dreadful since she was in London and I New York, but I guess the Sundown offices have ways and means of getting around that, too. "Aura, we had a client today I think you should know about."

"I'm not doing Sundown work any more," I told her. "Remember? Not while I'm over here. Give it to Con."

"Well, all right, but I really think you'll want to hear about this."

"Why? Someone taken out a hit on me?" It was a joke; I'm not important enough in the Fae Courts for them to employ an assassin. Especially not one of Sundown's caliber.

"No. It's about your friend Ell."

I went cold. Someone had taken a hit out on Ell? "What?"

She sighed. "His mother wants to find him a wife. Wants us to, at least. I told her we're not a matchmaking agency, but you know the Fae."

"Yes," I said grimly, "I do. But a wife? His --" I glanced up at Tadgh, who was pretending not to listen, and got to my feet. "Wait a sec, Magda. I'll just take this outside," I added to Tadgh, who nodded resignedly.

"Not interrupting, am I?" Magda asked.

"No, it's just I was with Tadgh," I told her once I was out in the corridor, where his secretary couldn't hear me either. "You know, Ell's boyfriend?"

Magda sighed. "Aura," she said, "I know he's gay. His mother knows he's gay. Small deaf animals in the middle of the Sahara desert know he's gay. That's the problem."

"Why is it a problem? He's a faery, Magda. We really don't care about orientation."

"I know --"

"And I'm pretty sure his mother doesn't care either."

"No," Magda said carefully, "but she does care about the succession of the Seelie throne."

I leaned against the wall, looked out at the treetops of Central Park. Succession I knew all about. "Ah," I said.

"You know, of course, that since the king and Ell's two brothers were killed, it's just been Ell and his sister?"

"Yeah," I said, trying to remember the sister's name. She was a sly creature, even for a faery, and I'd never really liked her too much.

"Well, it appears that recently she, uh, defected," Magda said.

"Defected?"

"Yes. She's eloped with an Unseelie prince."

I clutched the phone. "She *what*?"

"Yes, exactly. Apparently she's been embraced by the Unseelie Court."

Unlike my parents, who were only minor courtiers. My mother was Seelie, my father Unseelie. They'd been kicked out by both Courts and I'd never been accepted by either.

But if Ell's sister was now married to an Unseelie prince, then even if her mother disinherited her she'd still be the only one of the Seelie children likely to bear a child. And that child would stand to inherit the Seelie throne.

An Unseelie on the Seelie throne.

It really didn't bear thinking about.

"Aura?" Magda said. "You still there?"

"Yes," I said. "I was... thinking. So basically, if the future of the Seelie throne is to be secure, Ell needs a wife. Well, he needs an heir."

"The wife part is optional," Magda said. "Apparently the queen can tell parentage..."

Of course she could. "I suppose artificial insemination is out of the question?"

"You suppose correctly."

I slumped against the wall, in a mild state of shock.

"Aura?"

"I'll... I'll think about it," I said.

"The queen was adamant that this is very important," Magda said. "Most definitely... adamant."

"Yes," I said flatly. "It is important. Bye, Magda."

Tadgh was behind his desk when I went back in, reading some notes. I looked at him hard. Did he know about this? Had Ell shared the news? Did he even know about his sister? I hadn't asked how long ago she'd eloped.

He looked up. "A minute of your time, Aura. So kind."

"Sorry," I said, "it was important."

"And your sanity isn't?"

"Well, there's not much of it," I said dispiritedly, sitting back down on the couch.

"And that's why I'm here," Tadgh said. "Listen. You're a sex faery, right?"

"Top marks." I stared dully at my phone.

"You make other people's fantasies come true."

"Yep." How the fuck was I going to get Ell a girlfriend? He got all prissy if he saw a girl with too much cleavage. Said the girlie parts were a little nauseating.

"So, maybe you need to work on your own fantasies. Please yourself."

"That's what vibrators are for," I said absently.

"A vibrator doesn't kiss you," Tadgh said, coming round to the front of his desk and looking at me. "A vibrator doesn't cuddle you."

I said nothing, still frowning at my phone.

"Aura," Tadgh said quietly, reaching out and taking it from me. It looked really tiny in his big hand. Tadgh's father is a centaur, a massive creature, and Tadgh takes after him. Most of the time he takes human shape, but it's a damn big shape.

"Tell me what you want. The first thing that comes to you. What do you want in a lover?"

I spoke without thinking. "Well, first off, I want him to be two lovers."

There was a pause, and my mouth just kept on moving, filling the emptiness.

"I never get to be with two men -- well, why would they want a woman around? And even if I did, I'd be the one doing all the work. I want to be seduced, not to do the seducing. I want it to be all about me. I don't want to have to worry about anyone else's pleasure. Just two men, no waiting. Bang bang."

My words echoed in the silence. Tadgh was sitting very still on the edge of his desk, his gaze locked somewhere above my right shoulder. His big hand gripped my tiny, fragile phone. His knuckles were white.

Aw, crap. Mouth is open, Aura, should be shut.

"So, Ell needs a wife," I said desperately to change the subject, and almost immediately wished I hadn't.

Tadgh's eyes focused back on my face. "What?"

"Er, nothing. How is Ell?"

"He needs a wife," Tadgh said.

Bollocks.

"Sorry," I winced. "I shouldn't have..."

"How did you know?"

"Uh." I nodded at the little phone he still held. "That was Magda. The Seelie Queen asked Sundown to help find him a wife. Because he needs an heir. Because his sister... um."

Another silence.

Tadgh finally moved, blowing out a sigh. "Yeah," he said shortly. "'Um. That's about the size of it."

I chewed my lip. "So, do you... uh... have any ideas?"

"On how to get my extremely gay lover to screw a woman? Nope."

"Shit, Tadgh, I'm sorry. Here I am moaning about the quality of sex I'm getting and you have this on your plate. I'm sorry."

He wiped his hands over his face. "It's not your fault."

"Well, it's not yours either. Tadgh, look, if there's anything I can do... I mean, I'll help you find someone. There must be someone out there."

"A Fae of the High Court. She's not going to accept a Wildfae heir. And none of the Seelie Court are interested. They all have their own affairs."

Silence fell again. For the first time I could remember, I felt really uncomfortable in Tadgh's presence. I dug my nails into my palms, stared out of the window and listened to the clock tick. Finally, when I couldn't stand it any more, I opened my mouth to say something -- without actually deciding on what just yet -- but Tadgh got there before me.

"Aura?"

I formulated my expression into a caring, attentive, supportive one. "Yes?"

"Do you really want to help?"

"Yes," I said without hesitation.

Tadgh and Ell really were dear friends of mine, besides which, I and every other faery had a vested interest in the continued Seelie line. The alternative just didn't bear thinking about. I couldn't believe the Seelie Court were being so selfish and stupid... but then, they were Fae. Selfish and stupid are the order of the day.

"And you really want two men?"

"Uh --" I couldn't help feeling that I'd missed a chunk of conversation. "Well, yes, but we don't have to --"

"Do you mind if one of them is gay?"

I looked at Tadgh. Then because my brain didn't work while I was looking at his handsome, intense expression, I let my eyes slide away and stared blindly at the spider plant on the windowsill.

Then I looked back at him, because the stupid plant wasn't offering me any help. "I'm sorry," I said. "I must have missed something. Run that by me again."

Tadgh drummed his fingers on the desk. "It's a lot to ask," he said. "I know that. Look, forget I --"

"No," I interrupted. "No. Who's the other man? I mean, I'm guessing the gay one is Ell. And if you're asking if I'll be his wife --"

"Not wife, exactly," Tadgh put in hurriedly. "You don't need to actually marry him."

"Well, bear his child," I said. "It's hardly a fleeting fancy." Faeries lived for a long time. A long, long time. I'd be a parent for a good few millennia. "And I'm not sure... that is, I'd have to think about it."

"Sure, sure," Tadgh said. "Think all you want."

I frowned into the middle distance. Sex with Ell was a little too much for my brain to take in right now. Being a parent was a little too much too. So I settled for a nice little side thought instead.

"If..." My voice sounded distant. "If I do this, then I'd be the mother of the second in line to the Seelie throne."

"Yep."

"Who would be raised at Court."

"Well. Partly. You could probably raise him or her in the mortal realms if you wanted. The Seelie Queen is quite keen on mortal relations."

"So I wouldn't have to go to Court?"

"Well. I don't know. Yes, probably, at some point."

My heartbeat quickened. "The Seelie Court."

"It'd probably be quite difficult to avoid it." Tadgh was watching me closely. "Aura? You wouldn't be considering doing this just to get into the Court, would you?"

Just to get into the Court? "No," I said. "Of course not."

A pause.

"Although I do rightfully belong there," I said.

Tadgh sighed.

"No," I repeated. "Of course not. No. I... look. What does Ell think about this?"

He shrugged. "I haven't exactly mentioned it to him."

"But you didn't just come up with it, did you?"

Faeries can't lie. We're great at evading truths, but we can't outright lie.

"No," he said. "I've been thinking about it a while."

"Getting me to have sex with your boyfriend."

"It is what you do."

I raised my eyebrows at him, and he scowled.

"Okay, sorry. Look, do you want to go and get some coffee or something? Go for a walk in the park. I need some nature."

I understood that. Tadgh was Wildfae -- at least half of him was -- so his connection to nature was stronger than mine. Even High Court faeries need to feel the earth beneath their feet every now and then. He'd specifically picked out an office that overlooked the park because the sight of the trees was soothing, even if he was unnaturally high up for a Wildfae, who didn't usually have wings.

We got coffee and set out into the park which was lush with early summer growth. A few feet across the grass and I took off my pretty Choos: partly to save the delicate fabric and partly because it's nice to have grass under my toes.

"I don't want to pressure you," Tadgh said as we walked. "It's just an idea."

I blew on my coffee to cool it and said nothing.

"It's a big commitment," he said. "I understand that. You'd be a parent for the rest of your life." He frowned. "Or not. I mean, you don't have to be involved. You could have the baby and hand it over…"

"What kind of person do you think I am?" I said, outraged.

"Um. Fae," he said.

Okay, good point. We're known for being a little coldhearted. Especially the Unseelie, which is half the blood in my veins. But we're also known for our obsessive love of children. I'd never abandon a child, mine or anyone else's.

"And anyway," I said. "Supposing I did do this. You said something about two men, but only one of them was gay. That's Ell, right?"

"Yeah."

I didn't have a problem with that, objectively speaking at least. Hell, my whole existence has been devoted to having sex with people who'd otherwise be reluctant. "And the other?"

"Well, me, of course."

I stopped dead, nearly spilling my coffee. Tadgh strolled on a few paces before he realized, his broad shoulders moving under the fine cotton of his shirt, his even finer ass flexing as he stopped and turned.

Not for the first time, I had a mental image of those shoulders moving above me, those firm buttocks flexing under my hands. I swallowed.

"Okay, forget all about this," Tadgh said, seeing my face.

"No, no," I said, maybe too quickly. "I'm just -- Tadgh, that makes two gay men."

"No, one gay, one bi."

I blinked.

"You didn't know I was bi?" Tadgh sounded surprised.

"Um. That would be a no."

He looked a little nonplussed. Adorably so. Oh hell, Tadgh was bi? He liked women?

I could have sex with him?

Faeries can't lie. We just can't. If Tadgh said he liked women, then he liked women.

I suddenly felt very warm.

"You've always been with Ell," I said, my brain scrambled for the second time in about an hour. "I never saw you with a woman. And you never said. You love Britney!"

"Because she's hot," Tadgh said.

I stared at him, his big deep brown eyes, his shaggy, shiny mane of hair, his strong face and stronger body, and something went *twing* a few inches south of my bellybutton.

"You like girls?"

"Yes, Aura," Tadgh said patiently. "I like girls. And boys. I'm an equal opportunity lover."

Oh boy. "And... you want to have sex with me. And Ell."

His eyes got a little darker. "I wouldn't entirely object."

My nipples pushed against the fabric of my dress. Toward Tadgh. I guess they knew what they wanted. I licked my lips. "Of course, Ell would have to agree."

"Yes, of course." His gaze was locked on my mouth.

"And I'd have to, you know, think this through. Big decision." My feet moved me forward without my brain telling them to.

"Absolutely. Don't rush into it for the sake of threesome sex."

Next step I took, I felt dampness between my thighs. "Threesome sex," I said breathlessly. "Rushing would be bad."

"Definitely bad," Tadgh agreed.

I was toe to toe with him now. "But, you know, we should…" Hot coffee seeped around my toes as he dropped his cardboard cup. "I mean, we might not be compatible. It might be weird."

"Weird." Tadgh brushed back a strand of my hair. I found myself leaning into his hand.

"With us being friends and all," I said. "And you might not like a threesome."

"I'm willing to try."

"Maybe we should," I began, and ran out of words as Tadgh's breath brushed my mouth.

"Maybe we should," he agreed, and then his lips feathered over mine, and I think I whimpered.

And then he was kissing me. Then my gay best friend was kissing me, cupping my face in his hands and pressing hot, soft lips to my own, and kissing me beautifully.

Chapter Two

He licked along my lower lip and I wound my arms around his neck for support. At some point my coffee had joined his on the grass; I didn't know when and I really didn't care, either. Tadgh nibbled on my lip, and I moaned and opened up and sucked his lip into my mouth.

He tasted of coffee, his mouth hot and delicious. When he slipped one arm around my waist to press my body against his, I felt the bulge of his erection through his jeans. The rough fabric rubbed my bare skin through my thin silk dress and I writhed against it, lifting one leg to wrap around his hip, opening myself to him. The hard denim abraded my clit and I moaned.

"Hey, buddy, get a room!"

The shout pierced the fog I was in and I blinked, looking up at Tadgh.

My *gay* best friend, whose neck my arms were wrapped around, whose cock I was grinding myself against, and whose tongue had just been investigating my teeth.

I couldn't think of a single thing to say.

"Maybe we should take his advice," Tadgh said.

I couldn't think of anything to say to that, either. Except for, "Yes!"

Had we not been in the middle of a very big, busy mortal city in the middle of the day, I would have teleported us to Tadgh and Ell's townhouse, or possibly even sprouted wings and flown us there. But once I put my shoes back on, we walked -- okay, pretty much ran -- across the park instead, across the road -- possibly there was some traffic, that would account for all the horns blaring at us -- and into the sudden quiet of the house.

The lobby was huge, all polished hardwood floors, massive curving staircase and careful, immaculately placed lighting.

Faeries rarely live in hovels. Especially not when they're boinking Seelie princes.

"Are you sure Ell won't mind?" I asked.

"Sure." He grinned and started unbuttoning his shirt.

"I still haven't agreed to anything," I warned.

"Absolutely."

"Strictly condoms only."

Tadgh shrugged the shirt off and I stared, mesmerized, at the glory of his bare chest. He was a big guy, a really big guy. That centaur blood, I guess. Huge, deep chest. Massive shoulders. But it wasn't all muscle -- there was a fair bit of muscle, sure, but it was just decoration on his huge frame.

I went dizzy for a moment, and only came back to myself when I heard Tadgh say something.

"What?"

"I said, we don't need condoms. I can't get you pregnant."

"Let me guess, we're gonna do it standing up?" I said, and lost a few more seconds to crashing waves of lust at such a thought.

"If you want," Tadgh said, "but you know I'm sterile, right?"

I blinked, lust receding for a moment. "You are?"

"Hybrid animals always are," he said. "Half centaur, half high Fae."

"Really?"

"Really really," he said, and unfastened the button on his jeans.

My mouth went dry and I forgot all about hybrids. Shakily, I leaned against a side table to unfasten my shoes.

Tadgh unzipped his jeans halfway. He wasn't wearing anything underneath.

I managed to pull off one shoe and had my hands on the ribbons of the other when Tadgh stepped over and lifted my heel in his hand. "Your hands are shaking," he said softly. "You'll tear them."

I nodded mutely. His fingers caressed my ankles and I shivered.

Tadgh smiled, unfastened my shoe and set it gently down next to the other. His zipper strained under the pressure of his cock, which even constrained looked pretty impressive to me.

A sudden thought popped into my head, and I giggled.

"What?"

I pointed with my toe to the big bulge hiding behind his half-fastened jeans. "Hung like a horse," I snickered.

Tadgh raised his eyebrows at me, and his thumb caressed my ankle bone. The laughter faded as heat spread through my body and I lifted my hands on impulse, took two fistfuls of silk and pulled my dress off over my head.

The silk fluttered to the floor. I stood there with my breasts heaving slightly, nipples rock hard, bare pussy slick with wanting, wearing only a smile.

I don't know what impulse made me leave off my underwear this morning. But for the look on Tadgh's face, I was damn grateful for it.

He yanked down his zipper and tugged his jeans off. I stared, because for all my sniggering about horses, damn, I hadn't been far off. That thing was huge!

My hand strayed toward Tadgh's groin, toward the long, thick, dark, hard cock standing to attention there. A mortal woman might have been afraid of it, but I wasn't. I *wanted* it. I really, badly wanted it.

I licked my lips. He smiled. Then he pulled me into his arms and kissed me, long and hard, his cock pressing hot and urgent against my belly. His mouth was a wonder, so hot and delicious, his tongue sweeping in and taking over. Seducing me.

Oh, yes. Oh, hell yes.

It rose in me again, the dizzying lust I hadn't felt for a long time, if ever, and I clutched at Tadgh's shoulders, desperately clinging on. I had a feeling that if I let go, I'd just collapse in a boneless heap on the floor. I really felt as if my body was filling up with molten lava, boiling and unstable.

Tadgh's hands molded my waist, skimmed down to my buttocks and cupped them, pulling me against him. His fingers stroked the tops of my thighs.

"You're so soft," he murmured against my mouth. "So smooth. I forgot how smooth women are."

"I forgot how big you are," I murmured back, breathless with wanting, and he laughed softly against my mouth and kissed me deeper.

When his hand touched my breast, I stumbled, but he caught me, moving a few steps back and leaning me against the base of the beautiful curving stairway. His eyes were on me as he cupped my breast in his big hand, made my flesh look so delicate and white against him. His thumb brushed my nipple and I caught my breath.

"You're so responsive," he breathed. "It's wonderful."

He bent and ran his tongue over my nipple and I let out a cry.

"How has anyone managed to leave you unsatisfied?" Tadgh marveled, and sucked my nipple into his mouth.

I nearly came from that, clutching at his head, burying my fingers in his thick, dark hair. I thrust my breast into his mouth, lifting one leg to rub against his hip, and promptly lost my balance again.

You see? I'm usually full of grace. It's a Fae thing. But Tadgh had me so brain-dead with lust I couldn't even keep my balance. I felt drunk, really heavily drunk. It was wonderful.

He caught me before I bruised myself on the steps, and I pulled him down to me. "Perhaps we should stay here," I told him. "I can't fall over if I'm already on the ground."

"Good plan," he said, and went back to my breast.

Oh, it was amazing. His hands skimmed my sides, my stomach, my hips. He stroked my thighs, lifted my legs around his waist and settled his big, heavy body against my hips. His cock rested against my slippery wet pussy lips, thick, throbbing, and I rubbed against it, trying to get the friction on my clit that I wanted.

"Tadgh," I begged. "Please."

"Hmm?" His voice vibrated through me, then he lifted his head. "Please what?"

I shifted my hips so his cock lay against my entrance and thrust against him.

"But I'm not done yet," he said, fingering my wet nipple.

"I am," I said. "Get inside me now. You can suck and lick and nibble --" oh, God, "-- all you want, *later*."

"I intend to," he promised solemnly, then he started pushing inside me with that monster cock of his, and my eyes rolled back in my head.

I was sprawled on the staircase, which probably ought to have been uncomfortable but wasn't, in full view of his front door. Ell could walk in any moment. Anyone could walk by and look in through the window.

And see Tadgh stuffing me full of cock, making me shake and moan and writhe. Grasping his buttocks to pull him deeper inside me. Locking my legs high around his waist and begging him to fuck me harder, as hard as he could, and never stop.

The knowledge we could be caught only made me hotter. You don't go long in my line of work without a healthy streak of exhibitionism.

I came after a few thrusts. I was just so hot, and Tadgh was so big, and he kissed me and told me how soft and how beautiful I was, and how tight and wet I felt around him, and how damn good it all felt, and I came, fingers digging in his muscles, my body completely wrung out.

I think he came too. I only really started noticing things again when I realized he'd flashed us to his bed and was holding me close, breathing hard, smelling like sex.

Damn. For a gay man, he sure knew his way around a vagina.

* * *

I woke to find the bed empty but for myself. Tadgh and Ell's room was exquisitely decorated and the bed was freaking huge, more than big enough for two. This thought warmed me as I slunk out and into the bathroom to take a shower.

It was late afternoon. Maybe early evening. I'd slept for a good few hours, cradled in Tadgh's arms, feeling more secure and content than I'd ever expected to. But then, why not? Tadgh was a good friend, a dear, close friend. I knew that pretty much the only reason I'd let myself get so close to him was the sure and certain knowledge that he was gay, and therefore there'd be no sexual tension between us at all.

And then --

And then...

I sighed, switching off the water and stepping out to dry myself. And then Tadgh had dropped the rather huge bombshell that he wasn't gay. Not totally. How could I have just slept with my best friend like that?

What the hell was I going to say to Ell?

I leaned against the towel rail. I'd got so caught up in the prospect of sleeping with a really, really sexy man who'd promised -- and delivered -- a wonderful seduction that I'd forgotten why I was getting into this in the first place.

Did I want to have children? Did I want to get involved in all this?

All my life I'd wanted to be part of the Fae Courts. Even when the stories I heard scared the immortality out of me, I wanted it. Like a kid going to Hollywood: yeah, no one's that stupid, we all know they'll eat an innocent alive. But they still do it.

Well, I'm not so innocent. And I'm a grown up. Maybe it's time...

Although, I kind of thought about children in a different way. I guess if I ever thought about it at all, I thought I'd bring them up in the mortal world. Probably with a mortal husband. I never reconciled my Fae Court dreams with my family dreams. They both seemed unattainable.

But if I could get them both together...

One might have misgivings about bringing up a child in the cutthroat Fae Courts. But if that was the case, then one had never learnt anything about the Fae. They loved children, all children, protected them at a premium. And a royal child would be so adored, so loved, so protected by that most fearsome of entities, the Fae Queen, that I'd never have to fear for its safety.

No. Bringing up a child in the Seelie Court would be far from an ordeal. And Ell would be a wonderful parent.

It's just...

I don't know. Been too long amongst humans. There was a tiny voice inside me that said *A gay prince? That's your happily ever after? Don't you want a little bit... more?*

Dammit.

I trailed downstairs, wearing one of Tadgh's huge bespoke shirts. The soft cotton was wonderful against my skin and it smelled of him. I could hear voices from the kitchen and steeled myself, because one of those voices was Ell's.

"...can tell she's been throwing up three times a day for months anyway, but did she have to decide right *now* that she had a problem? The show is in *two days*! And that was custom *made* for her, darling."

"Well, maybe she can come out of rehab for the show."

"No! The selfish *slobs* are keeping her in. They think a runway show would be too high *pressure* for her. They even blamed *me* for her condition! As if *I* would ever bitch at a woman for her figure!"

Yep, it was Ell. No one else spoke in italics as much as him.

I padded down the hallway and into the kitchen where Tadgh stood at the stove, cooking something delicious, and Ell sprawled at the table with a bottle of wine, looking elegantly distressed.

The two lovers couldn't be more different. Where Tadgh is big and dark, quiet and reserved, Ell is lean, blond -- currently, anyway -- loud and outrageously gay. He calls everyone darling all the time, even people he doesn't like. He's always immaculately dressed, and he has been known to mince quite frequently.

Currently he was slumped over the table, hand curved around his wine, hair disheveled, T-shirt rumpled. It was a designer T-shirt, because everything he wears is couture. It figures: he does design high fashion after all.

"Hi," I said, shyly, twining one leg around the other as I stood in the doorway. I hadn't a clue what to say. Well, what do you say to the boyfriend of the guy you've just shagged?

Ell looked up. "*Darling!*" Lethargy vanished, he leapt up and threw his arms around me. "Baby doll! Come and sit down. Tadgh's been telling me *all* about your idea and, darling, it sounds *fabulous!*"

I glanced at Tadgh, who was leaning against the handmade cabinets, watching us. "Uh, it does? What precisely has he told you?"

"That you're willing to --"

"Think about," Tadgh put in, still watching me.

"-- help me out with my little *problem*."

I frowned. "You make it sound like a medical thing."

"Well, darling, it *is* biology."

He had a point.

"Look," Tadgh said. "I thought that, even if you decide you don't want to be involved in this --"

"Which is fine," Ell assured me, clasping my hand. "It's *totally* your choice."

"-- then at least you might be able to help Ell... uh, become more comfortable with the idea of having sex with a woman."

I shrugged. "Sure, I can do that."

Ell sagged with relief. "Oh, darling, what would I *do* without you!"

I patted his hand. "You'd go on banging your hot centaur boyfriend for another few millennia." Still unsure how much Tadgh had told him -- and, therefore, how I should explain my attire -- I said casually, "I didn't know Tadgh was bi."

"Well, surely it became obvious when you had *sex* with him, darling." At my look, Ell grinned. "We tell each other *everything*, sweets. And of course I was *bound* to ask why there was a frock and a pair of Choos in the hallway. They're *divine*, by the way. *Delicious* color."

"I know, like chocolate and cream," I said.

Tadgh rolled his eyes. "Anyway," he said pointedly. "Neither of us want you to rush into a decision. This is just a casual, friendly thing, right, Ell?"

"Absolutely," Ell beamed at me. "You must *stay* and have dinner with us. And then afterwards you can show me all your," he swallowed, "*girlie* parts so I can get used to them. I guess if anyone can turn me, darling, it's you!"

I think I'm flattered.

I think.

Chapter Three

Tadgh was as good a cook as he was a lover, and Ell kept us both entertained through dinner with anecdotes from his mad fashion world. When I asked if he should be out trying to find a replacement for his bulimic model, he just shrugged and said, "Darling, there will be *thousands* of them queuing up for the chance all *day* tomorrow."

"But will the clothes fit them?" I asked.

"They'll have starved themselves into it," Tadgh said. "Sometimes I think I should run free counseling for Ell's models."

"I don't *ask* them to be thin!" Ell said.

"But you don't hire fat people," Tadgh said.

"Darling, *no one* hires fat people."

Sensing an argument coming on, I created a diversion by taking my shirt off. Well, Tadgh's shirt. The slight temperature drop made my nipples pucker and I shivered, the movement shaking out my hair so it caressed my back.

There was a sudden silence, then the clatter of Ell's knife falling onto his plate.

"You told me to take my clothes off after dinner," I said, leaning back in my chair. They were both staring at me, Ell in slack-jawed amazement, Tadgh with rapidly darkening eyes. His breath came fast.

"Uh," Ell cleared his throat, his eyes darting to his plate, then to the fridge. "Dessert?"

"Yes," I said.

He colored, looking nervous.

"Ell," Tadgh said, moving the plates quickly out of the way, "you see half-naked women every day. Fully naked, a lot of the time."

"Yes," Ell said, twisting his hands, "but they're not really women. I mean, they're not... they're just, like... like mannequins or something."

"Charming," I said. I ran my hands over my breasts. Both men watched the movement.

"They're not... I mean, they're sort of... *asexual*," Ell said.

"That's because they have the figures of small boys," Tadgh said.

He topped up my wineglass, then came to stand behind me. He moved my chair back a little so Ell could get a good view, then he rested his hands on my shoulders. His palms were warm and dry, big hands that felt heavy and good.

"Aura isn't asexual," he said.

Ell swallowed.

"Look," Tadgh said, slipping his hands down to cup my breasts. "Look how soft she is."

"Soft is..." Ell was staring at my breasts, "...soft is weird."

"Why is it weird?" I asked.

"Men aren't soft. Men are hard."

"What about your models?"

"They're all bone," Tadgh said darkly. "How about dressing a real woman, Ell?"

"I don't like real women. They're squidgy, and soft, and --"

"And that's a bad thing?"

Ell looked lost. "It's weird," he said.

I reached out and took his hand. "Am I weird?"

"No," he said, looking torn.

I stroked the back of his hand with my thumb. "Just feel, Ell. You can close your eyes if you want."

His eyelids flickered uncertainly.

"Do you trust me?"

"Yes," he said, although he didn't sound sure of it.

I smiled reassuringly, and put his hand on my breast.

I'm quite proud of my breasts. They're not huge, but they're not tiny, either. Just a nice little handful. Small enough to be firm and big enough to squeeze. They're my best feature.

Well, nearly. But I didn't think Ell was ready for my pussy just yet.

Tadgh cupped my left breast, and Ell, watching, did the same to my right. He weighed it in his hand, stroked the soft skin with his thumb. He avoided the nipple though. Still, I wasn't complaining. Two hot men fondling my breasts, are you kidding?

"And here." Tadgh took Ell's other hand and placed it gently on my shoulder. "Feel her neck."

Ell did, tentatively. "No stubble," he said. "Weird." He stroked some more. "Girl, you must moisturize something fierce."

"I do," I said, pleased he'd noticed. "It's this great stuff I get from a spa on Long Island."

"Yeah?" He ran his hand over my throat. "It's amazing. Do you think I could get some? You think it'd do anything for me?"

I put my own hand out to his jaw. "Oh, come on, Ell, your skin is baby soft."

He grinned, a little smugly. "It is, isn't it?"

Tadgh laughed, moving in a little closer behind me. "This chair is in the way," he said. "How about a change of venue?"

Panic flashed in Ell's eyes, which had been calming down.

"Sofa," I said, and quickly flashed us there, the big sofa in the breakfast area of the huge kitchen. Tadgh pulled me onto his lap and I wriggled, smiling as I felt the not inconsiderable bulge in his jeans.

I crossed my legs, still not wanting to scare Ell, and beckoned him closer. "Have you ever kissed a girl?"

"Uh, once."

Tadgh paused in caressing my breast. "Really?"

"Yeah. But it was..." Ell waved his hand, "...nothing, really. I mean, I didn't feel anything. It was boring."

I put my head to one side. "But when you kiss Tadgh..."

Ell sighed, looking a little dreamy, and I laughed and nudged Tadgh. He needed no further bidding and wrapped his arm around Ell's shoulders, pulling him close. Close to both of us. When their mouths met I had a ringside seat, could smell the clean fresh scent of Ell's skin, the hotter, spicier scent that rose from

Tadgh. Could see the way their lips pressed together, how Ell bit down on Tadgh's lip, and Tadgh slipped his tongue into Ell's mouth.

It was. So. Damn. Hot. My nipples were hard, tingling, aching for contact. My pussy got hotter, wetter, and I shifted on Tadgh's lap as I watched.

Tadgh slipped his hand up the back of Ell's neck, drawing him closer, and Ell sighed, his eyes closing, leaning into Tadgh and kissing him harder.

It was interesting. I'd always expected Tadgh would be more in charge, but Ell took his passion and returned it, even occasionally taking charge. Just because Tadgh was the bigger, manlier man, didn't mean he dominated Ell. They had a partnership. I kind of liked that.

It was only when Ell wrapped his arm around Tadgh's waist and brushed my skin that he remembered I was there, springing back with a look of surprise on his face. "Sorry," he murmured, "I got a little carried away."

He licked his lips. I wanted to lick them too. "Don't apologize," I said. "That was hot."

Ell blushed a little. It was adorable. I leaned forward and dropped a light, closed-mouth kiss on his lips, but as I moved back he caught me by the shoulders, held me there and looked at me speculatively. "Tadgh said you were a great kisser," he said, and before I could so much as raise an eyebrow at that, he'd put his lips back on mine, kissing me tentatively.

I let him control the pace, kissing him back the way he was kissing me. When he licked my lips, I opened my mouth, and when his tongue slipped inside, I stroked it with my own.

He tasted good, traces of wine and pasta sauce, but also a cool taste that was all his own. And he kissed well, sweet and soft, gaining confidence.

I opened my eyes and saw that his were shut. That was kind of sweet, and I smiled against his mouth.

"What?" Ell murmured.

"You're a great kisser, too."

He sat back. "That was... kind of nice," he said, touching his lips. "It's nice kissing someone with really soft lips. And no stubble."

Tadgh manfully refrained from commenting. Judging by the huge hard-on nudging my bottom, he had other things on his mind.

Ooh. Tadgh's hard-on and my bottom. Now there was a thought to keep a girl warm at night.

"Well, there you go," I said, trying to get my thoughts back on track. "You successfully kissed a girl and enjoyed it. It can only get easier from here."

"Speaking of easier," Tadgh said, and shifted under me. "You mind if I take my jeans off? I'm getting a little uncomfortable here."

"Honey, I never mind you taking your jeans off," Ell said.

"Ditto," I added, and we both grinned. Ell clicked his fingers and Tadgh's jeans disappeared, along with his shirt. I squirmed against all his suddenly bare flesh, rubbing my thigh against his hot, stiff cock. "Mmm, damn that's good."

"I can't see," Ell complained.

"Neither can I," Tadgh said, shooting a pointed look at his lover's crotch. Ell waved a hand and his clothes disappeared, and then all three of us were naked on the sofa.

I began to get decidedly hot.

Tadgh rewarded Ell by shifting me on his lap -- as if I weighed about an ounce -- so I was resting higher up, my legs spread wide, his cock rearing up between them so Ell could see it perfectly.

"Oh, lover," Ell sighed, staring.

"I know," I said, and joined in.

For a few seconds there was silence as we gazed at Tadgh's huge, pulsing cock, which was still growing, getting darker and harder and hotter. It nudged the inside of my thigh and I stifled a moan.

"Flattered as I am," Tadgh said from behind me, "we're not accomplishing very much here."

"I don't know," I said. "Ell's getting hard and there's a naked pussy in the room."

"You have a point," he conceded.

"No, you do," Ell said, stroking it. "And it is mostly hiding the pussy."

"Tell you what," I said, as Tadgh's fingers dug in my hips at the contact of Ell's fingers. "How about this? You stroke my breasts for five minutes, then you can stroke Tadgh's cock."

Ell looked up uncertainly at my breasts, which were feeling a mite friendless up there on their own.

"It's a good deal," Tadgh said, one hand moving up to demonstrate breast-stroking for Ell, who reached out tentatively and touched me.

"Both hands," I said, and he stuck his tongue out at me but gamely obliged. He cupped my breasts as Tadgh had shown him earlier, then hesitated.

"Play with the nipples," I said, enjoying the warmth of his palms on my flesh. "Like you would with a guy."

Ell did, and I let out a long breath at the relief of someone finally touching my aching, needy nipples. He stroked them slowly, cautiously, frowning in concentration.

Tadgh's hand smoothed over my side, down my belly, and his fingers feathered over my thigh. He nuzzled my neck, and I wished I could turn around to kiss him -- but if I did, I might disturb Ell's concentration, and I didn't want to do that.

"It's still weird," Ell said, just as Tadgh slipped his fingers between the folds of my pussy.

"What?" I whimpered.

"The squidginess. Not bad weird, just... I'm not used to so much... *give.*"

"Oh," was all I could manage as Tadgh played with my clit.

"Have I been doing this for five minutes yet?" Ell asked.

"No!" I thrust my hips forward, into Tadgh's hand, and Ell finally noticed the movement.

"Hey, that's cheating."

"Nope, we said nothing about my hands and her pussy," Tadgh said, running his finger in little circles around my clit.

"I'm pretty sure it's been five minutes," Ell said. "I want to stroke his cock."

"Okay," I said, "but afterwards you have to use your mouth."

Ell's eyes lit up. "I can suck it?"

"Only after you've sucked these." I patted my breasts. "Deal?"

Ell looked down at Tadgh's cock, which was brushing gently against my labia. Okay, I was brushing my labia against it.

"Deal," he said, and wrapped his hand around Tadgh's cock. Tadgh groaned and thrust up into it, which sent the hot base of his cock rubbing closer against my pussy. I groaned. Tadgh groaned again.

"Ooh, this is fun," Ell said. "I don't even mind the girlie bits."

"Well done," I gasped. Tadgh's hand left my pussy and came up to my breast. Now I had no problem twisting round to kiss him as he fondled my breasts and thrust his cock against my slick pussy lips.

"She's wet," Ell said, sounding surprised.

I broke off kissing long enough to say, "Yes, cuts down on lube," then went back to Tadgh's hot, hot mouth.

I was in heaven. This was actually what dying and going to heaven felt like. Ell hesitantly dipped his fingers into my wetness and I nearly came there and then. He used the moisture to slick his hands over Tadgh's cock, which had Tadgh shuddering and thrusting. And that meant his cock rubbed harder against my labia. Which meant I came.

Loudly.

Happily.

For quite a long time.

When I recovered, Tadgh was nuzzling my neck again and Ell was looking up at me in amazement.

"Don't stop on my account," I panted, and felt Tadgh chuckle.

Then the sound of glass breaking came from upstairs, and all three of us froze.

Chapter Four

"It's probably the cat," Ell said.

"We don't have a cat," Tadgh said.

"Good point." Ell sprang to his feet with a grace I could never replicate. "I'll go."

"Ell." Tadgh lifted me off him and got to his own feet. "Don't be stupid. You're the prince."

"Exactly --" Ell began, but Tadgh had already flashed himself out of the room. "I hate it when he does that."

Feeling slightly self-conscious now that there was no actual sex going on, I picked Tadgh's shirt up off the floor and wrapped it around myself, huddled on the sofa like a spare part. Ell flashed his clothes on with a wave of his hand, then, as an afterthought, materialized a hefty knife in one hand and a gun in the other. Then he gestured at Tadgh's jeans, which disappeared, presumably in Tadgh's direction.

Sometimes I forget Ell is a prince. My powers of telekinesis don't stretch much further than dressing or undressing in a hurry. Ell can move anything, just by thinking about it, and he can rematerialize anywhere he wants. I can only go places I actually know.

Ell twirled the knife in his hand. It was a fancy, twisted blade. Not so much for ornamentation, I was guessing, as to cause the maximum damage when it was used. Right now he didn't look like an effeminate fashionista. He looked like a Fae prince: fast, strong, and deadly. I didn't doubt that he knew how to use that knife. I didn't doubt it at all.

It was actually pretty sexy.

"It's probably just sprites," he said, catching my eye. "Tadgh's being overcautious."

I nodded, unconvinced. My conversation with Magda was replaying in my head. What about Ell's sister? What if she'd sent someone to do away with her brother? I didn't think she was that mean, but you never knew with the High Courts.

"I --" I began, and then there was a thud and a high-pitched yelp from upstairs, and Ell and I both started. A second later Tadgh reappeared in the room, holding a small, skinny, squirming green creature by the scruff of its neck.

"Ew," Ell said, flopping back onto the sofa where I'd been coming my brains out about five minutes earlier. "I hate goblins."

I stared at the little creature as Tadgh shook it, and it dropped a crossbow. It was covered all over in slime and its skin was like that of a fish. Its eyes were big, pale, watery orbs and its mouth was wide and lipless, full of teeth. Several rows of teeth.

Not pretty.

"It's, err, dripping," I said, and we all looked at the slime oozing onto the carpet.

"Goblin blood is, like, so gross," Ell said, and I wondered if I'd imagined the sexy warrior he'd been a second ago. "Is it dead?"

"Nooo," the creature hissed. We all flinched. It sounded like something had crawled down its throat and died.

"I thought you might want to talk to it," Tadgh said, holding it like it was rotten. Well, it smelled rotten.

Since Ell didn't seem to have anything to say to it, I asked the goblin, "Why are you here?"

It waved a froggy finger at Ell. "Kiiill that ooone."

"The feeling's mutual," Ell assured it.

"Who... uh, who sent you?" Looking at the creature, I knew it wasn't of a high goblin caste -- it had four arms, which denoted a worker, a drone -- so it wouldn't have come here of its own accord. Goblins have rules too, you know.

"Massssgaaar," the goblin rattled.

"Masgar?"

"The kiiing."

I glanced at Ell, who nodded. "Goblin bigwig. Revolting little piece of work. Bit of a wuss, too."

"Did you know he wanted you dead?"

"I have to say I didn't. Ask it why."

Evidently, talking to goblins was beneath a Seelie prince. I wished it was beneath me.

"Dooon't have to tell yooouu," the goblin sulked.

Tadgh calmly took a knife from the holster on his belt -- also, I presumed, part of Ell's telekinesis -- and pricked the goblin's neck with it. The slimy little bugger screamed, the sound like nails on a blackboard, and Ell and I flinched again. But not at the sound.

Tadgh's dagger was made of iron. And to a faery, iron really, really hurts.

"Noooo, nooooooo! I tell yooouuu!" The goblin's eyes were fixed on the iron blade Tadgh held just out of reach. "Masssgaaar has a bargaaain. Death to yoooouuu and powerrr for hiim."

"Bargain with who?"

"Unseeeelie."

"Yes, we gathered that."

Tadgh rolled his eyes at me.

"Which Unseelie?" I asked patiently.

"Royaltyyyy," the goblin hissed proudly.

Ell and Tadgh exchanged glances, with each other then with me. There were several Unseelie princes and princesses.

"Which one?" I asked, and Tadgh pressed the knife closer to the goblin, who shrieked and wriggled away.

"Skinny princessss! Eibhlisss!"

Ice ran through my veins. "You lie," I said. "Eibhlis has no powers."

"No liiie! Eibhliiiis!"

I pinched the bridge of my nose. This was all I needed.

"Eibhlis," Ell growled. "She's such a piece of work! Didn't she get into mega trouble for imprisoning a human against its will?"

"Yes," I said, thinking of said human, a feisty pirate queen who'd been set free by a young wizard of my acquaintance.

A wizard who had been taking on my Sundown duties while I was in New York. Duties that had included information for a goblin assassination.

I scrambled to my feet. "Con!"

"What, sweetie?"

"Con! He'll know." I frowned. "And I should warn him, too."

"Who's Con?" Tadgh asked, a touch suspiciously.

"A wizard I know," I said. "He'll know -- I have to go."

"Now?"

Now the idea was in my head, I couldn't shake it. Con had been doing some background work on a goblin assassination: that was all I knew. He might know something that could help us here.

And he might be in danger.

I've spent too long among humans. I shouldn't give a damn about Con and his scary girlfriend. I shouldn't be thinking of them fondly, like friends, because I helped them get together. I'm Fae, and they're mortals. Like cattle.

But I still had to warn him.

"Aura --" Tadgh said, but the sound was lost as I concentrated hard and flashed myself three thousand miles across the Atlantic, across England, to a tiny village by the North Sea.

Con lived in a tiny fisherman's cottage, and by concentrating hard I landed in his bedroom. It was dark, the middle of the night in England, a fact I'd forgotten before I flashed in, and it took me a second to focus my eyes on the tangled heap of limbs in the bed.

They were curled together, Lily looking much smaller and softer than she did when she was awake. I guess with all that ferocity it's hard to tell she's just a girl. Her head rested on Con's chest, her beaded hair very dark against his pale skin. His arms were wrapped tightly around her, very tightly, as if he were afraid someone was going to take her from him.

A pang of jealousy, of wanting someone to hold me like that, ripped through me, and I shook it away. I was being silly, sentimental. Not very Fae at all.

I cleared my throat.

They carried on sleeping.

I coughed.

Nothing.

Rolling my eyes, I reached out and knocked sharply on the bedroom door. Lily's eyes snapped open, and her hand shot out and grabbed the knife on the bedside table. Con, useless sod that he is, came awake with a splutter and stared blearily at me.

"Fae," Lily spat in her guttural accent, "get out of here."

Con squinted at me. "Aura?" He pulled the covers over himself and Lily, and pushed her knife arm down gently. "Don't you knock?"

"I did."

"Traditionally, knocking is done from the outside."

"I was in a hurry. Con, that goblin assassination you did. Who was it on?"

Con blinked at me. Useless humans!

"He doesn't have to tell you anything," Lily said, glaring at me.

Did I say she looked soft and small before? Ha. Eyes open, animated, she looked vicious. She *was* vicious. "No, but if he's of a mind to remember who introduced him to his future wife, he'll be kind and tell me."

Con rubbed at his eyes with the heel of his hand. "I didn't do the assassination. Masika did."

"Right, but you did the background info. Who ordered the assassination?"

"Why do you want to know?" Lily demanded.

"Because a goblin just showed up trying to kill Ell. You know Ell?" I asked Con, who regarded me guardedly. "Seelie prince. The *only* Seelie prince."

"Why would a goblin want to kill the Seelie prince?" Con said. "Surely he'd know what that would mean?"

"He was ordered to do it," I said. "By his king. Masgar."

Con's eyes narrowed. "Masgar? Masgar is the king?"

"He surely is. And how do you know of him?"

"He's kind of a lunatic. He hired Sundown to kill the old king."

"Why can't you faeries ever do your own dirty work?" Lily sneered.

"Politics," I said.

"That and you can't lie when you're asked if you did it," Con said. I shrugged. "Why the feck would Masgar want to kill the Seelie prince?"

"He had a bargain," I said. "With an Unseelie princess."

Con groaned. "Don't tell me they're all insane."

"No. Just the one."

I held his gaze and watched the realization come over his face.

"No," he said. "No."

"Yes," I said wearily, "yes."

"No and yes what?" Lily said. "Sometimes you talk a whole different language."

"It's Eibhlis," I told her. "She's responsible for all this."

"But I thought -- didn't the Unseelie Queen strip her of all her powers?"

"Yes," I said.

"But how --?"

"I don't know," I said, sighing. "I don't know. I just wondered if you could shed any light on it."

Con's head fell back against the pillow. He closed his eyes. "I swear, you Fae are all crazy," he said.

"Yes, we are."

"I have no idea. I'm just... Masgar had the old goblin king killed, and then forged an alliance with Eibhlis?"

"Yep."

"What's he getting from it?"

"Support of the Unseelie Court. Or at least an Unseelie royal."

"And what's in it for her?" Lily asked, having apparently decided I wasn't out to get her or Con.

I raised my palms. "I have no fucking clue. She wants to take over the world."

Con went pale. "Even she's not that crazy."

"History is full of people who want to take over the world," Lily said. She glanced at me and added proudly, "I discovered the Internet."

"Good for you. Check out the porn. Con, you know her better than I do. Do you really think she wants..." I swallowed. It was an awful concept. "Wants Unseelie domination?"

Con pinched the bridge of his nose. "Is it true about the Seelie princess? That she's eloped with an Unseelie?"

"Yes."

"And the only Seelie heir left is your friend Ell?"

"Yes."

"And -- isn't he gay?"

"*Yes.*"

"Then may the gods have mercy on us all, 'cause you lot sure as hell won't."

That seemed like a pretty good précis to me. "Remember I'm trying to stop this," I warned him. "I'm on your side."

"Like we believe you," Lily said.

"She's a Fae, Lil," Con said. "She can't lie."

"Bet she could if she wanted to."

Lily glared at me, and I glared back. She might be a pirate queen, but I'm High Court Fae, and I have the edge.

Usually.

"Okay," I said. "So I need to speak to this Masika. See if she knows anything."

"Well, at least she'll be awake," Con said, and gave me her address. "Oh, and Aura?"

"Yes?"

"Put some clothes on."

I looked down and realized I was only wearing Tadgh's shirt, which wasn't fastened. Crap.

Con laughed, and I flashed myself out.

Masika lived in an ugly, run-down warehouse in a part of London that's usually on fire. I didn't hold out much hope for what I'd find there, but when I flashed myself inside, which took quite an effort of will since I usually have to be able to visualize where I'm going, I was surprised to see it fitted out quite comfortably.

I didn't know anything about Masika except that she'd been with Sundown since forever. All the windows in the warehouse were blacked out and a good portion of the living quarters were underground. Vampire? I could certainly sense one. But it was a male vampire, big and old and powerful.

So I knocked before I flashed in.

Chapter Five

He was lounging on the sofa, watching TV with the sound turned down. *Buffy the Vampire Slayer*. Cute.

"It bothers me," he said without looking round, "that these vampires disintegrate when staked. Vampires don't disintegrate. We lie there and molder just like everyone else."

"Nice," I said. "Thank you so much for sharing."

"What are you doing in my house, Fae?"

I hate vampires. They're so damn cool and smug. Yeah, you've been around forever, you're all strong and butch with the mind-controllingness. Wow. Like I'm so helpless.

And yet...

And yet, they just make me *feel* inadequate. Silly, frivolous, petty. Like they have gravitas and I'm a flighty twit. This particular vampire had only said a couple of dozen words to me and already I felt ridiculous.

"I'm looking for Masika."

"She's not here." He turned up the volume on the TV, and I felt like a schoolchild being dismissed.

I stood my ground though. I'm not silly and flighty. I'm not. Usually.

"I can still smell Fae," the vampire said, boredly. "Why is that?"

"Because I'm still here," I said.

"Yes. Amend that."

"Look, don't you order me around. You've got absolutely no right to --"

"You're in my house, Fae. That means I have every right."

I scowled at the back of his head.

"And don't make that face at me. It really spoils your looks."

Bastard.

"All right," I said. "Would you please tell me where Masika is? Or how I can get hold of her?"

He sighed and turned the TV off, finally turning to face me. The vampire was golden blond; a strong, handsome face with blazing blue eyes. He was shirtless and barefoot, dressed only in worn blue jeans that showed more than they concealed. Broad shoulders. Tight pecs. Hard abs.

Pretty damn lickable. If I wasn't otherwise preoccupied.

"You can't," he said.

"Why not?" Oh fuck, had she been killed and I hadn't heard? I really ought to have gone through Magda to find out, only it was the middle of the night and she'd get pissy with me --

"She's on a plane." He gazed at me boredly. "What do you want with her?"

"Some -- information." I wasn't sure how much he knew about Masika's employment.

"Well, it ain't available." He stared at me some more and I remembered I was only wearing Tadgh's shirt, although it was at least covering the pertinent parts of me now. I knew I smelled of sex too.

Defiantly, I crossed my arms and glared at him.

He laughed. "Nice try, Fae, but I don't swing that way. I prefer my lovers with souls."

I growled low in my throat. "So says the vampire."

"You mustn't believe everything you see on TV. I've a soul as much as the next person." He considered this. "Unless the next person is you."

"I have a soul!"

"But it's a twisted Fae one, and that doesn't count." In one graceful motion almost too fast for me to see, he was on his feet and facing me. "What information do you need from Masika?"

What she sees in you, I thought. "It's about a goblin assassination she did," I said instead.

"Grempiln the goblin king? Cut and dried. One of his generals paid her to do it. Plausible deniability and all that. You can go now."

"I really need to speak to her about it."

He sighed irritably, waving at the door. "Then call her."

"I don't have her number."

"I don't care."

I glared at the vampire. "Fine," I said. I could call Magda for it in the morning. Stupid pissy vampires. I hate vampires. Have I mentioned that?

I started to flash myself out, but nothing happened. I tried again. Still nothing. Like trying to start a car with an empty tank.

Empty -- aw, shit.

"Shouldn't you be gone now?" the vampire said from behind me.

"I'm going," I said, and tried again.

"No, you're not." There was the click of a crossbow behind me, and I turned to see him leveling a bow loaded with a sharpened wooden stake.

"Uh, aren't stakes for vampires?"

"They tend to kill most things."

"It's iron for faeries."

He hefted another bow, this one loaded with the dull gleam of a Fae's greatest enemy. "Thanks for reminding me."

"Look, I'm trying to go," I said, a touch desperately.

"Try harder."

"It'd be a hell of a lot easier without you pointing weapons at me!"

He didn't move.

"Look," I said again. "I just flashed myself all the way over here from New York."

"Well done. I'm very proud of you." He flicked the safety off the iron bow, and I started to panic.

"Okay, all right, I'll go outside. But it has to be below freezing out there."

"It's at least five degrees."

"Oh, right, and to you British that's sunbathing weather."

"Don't be ridiculous. I happen to be Greek."

I stomped over to the heavy, reinforced steel door. It wouldn't budge.

"You want me to leave, you're going to have to open this door," I said, and he kind of waved at it. It opened.

"Very nice," I said, and clomped outside with one final glare at him. Masika could keep him. If she was half as sociopathic as him, they deserved each other.

"Gonna be fun chatting with her tomorrow," I said as the door slammed shut behind me, and I found myself in the chilly London autumn, barefoot and bareassed on the street.

"I hate vampires!" I yelled.

The Buffy theme tune answered me.

Fine. Just fine. I'd make it home... somehow. The problem was that teleporting was like normal traveling in that the greater the distance traveled, the more energy would be needed. I'd just zapped myself five thousand miles across the Atlantic. While that might have tired me a little, it had been a one-way trip. There was no way I'd have enough energy for the return. I might be able to make it as far as Cornwall, or Wales, on the energy I had left, but not much further west. And I'm not much of a swimmer.

"Crap!" I stomped my foot on the freezing pavement. Five degrees my ass.

Conventional transport wasn't an option. Quite apart from the fact that humans set such store by documentation, I was wearing a man's shirt and nothing else. I'd freeze before I even got to an airport. At least I wasn't full Seelie. Ell can't even bear to go outside during the winter in the northern hemisphere. He migrates to Australia, follows the sun.

Follows the sun...

I had an idea. Stonehenge couldn't be more than a couple of hundred miles from here, right? I could get there without a huge effort of will. And even outside the Solstices, those stones held a lot of power. Why do you think they don't let tourists touch them? It's not about preservation. It's about power.

I concentrated hard on the grand circle of stones, well known and beloved to anyone with even a drop of Fae blood in them, and landed in the middle of the henge.

It was even colder here. Fucking freezing, in fact. There were no walls, no buildings to keep the wind from whipping in off the plain, no central heating or traffic to warm the place up.

I spread my feet, raised my arms and drew in the power of these ancient stones. The shape is a focus, like a huge satellite dish for magic. I didn't have a huge amount left in me, drained as I was by the long trip over the sea, and then the shorter one to the stones. But such is the power of the henge that what little I had was amplified hugely, until my skin tingled and glowed and my whole body buzzed.

A magical rush can be quite sexual. The power flowed into me, around me, filling me, and like any power it was hugely enjoyable. I raised my arms, shaking, and bared my breasts to the moonlight. The power caressed me, every nerve highly sensitized, and when I finally gathered enough together and zapped myself into the air, over the stones, across the plains, the villages, the cities, the beaches and the sea, across the harbor and the skyscrapers and the green of the park and the trees and the leaves and the steps of the brownstone, faster than a single thought, an orgasm ripped through me, stealing my borrowed power and combusting it inside me.

I collapsed in a boneless heap on the carpet, incapable of movement.

Footsteps sounded nearby. My eyes were closing.

"Aura?"

Someone knelt beside me. I couldn't stay awake.

"Aura? What the fuck happened?"

"Tired," I mumbled. "Lon' journey."

He pulled me into his lap and I dredged together enough energy to open my eyes. There was Tadgh, so handsome and strong, holding me as if I were breakable. He brushed my hair from my face.

"Where have you been?"

"Enlgl -- Engal -- En -- Lonnon."

"London?"

"Mmm." My eyes slipped closed again.

"All in one night? No wonder you're exhausted. I'll flash you to bed."

"No!" I moaned, my arm flailing wildly as I tried to catch hold of him to stop him. "No flashing."

Tadgh murmured something about me flashing enough for the both of us that I think may have been a reference to what I wasn't wearing.

"You seen it all 'fore," I mumbled, head lolling. Tadgh gathered me into his arms and I snuggled against him, comfortable and warm as he carried me through the house and up to bed. "'Night."

He laid me in sweet-scented sheets. "Goodnight, darling," he said, and just as I slipped into unconsciousness I felt his lips brush my forehead.

* * *

I didn't wake fully until late the next morning, but I floated near the surface once or twice. The first time I was brought there by a surge of magic that made me feel vaguely nauseous, like the scent of booze when you're hungover. Usually magic makes me feel shiny. But not right now.

I heard Tadgh's soft voice from very close by. He was holding me, I realized, cradling me as I slept. A wave of affection swamped me, and I missed what he actually said.

Ell answered, and I guessed he'd just flashed in. "I hate the Court. It's all so political and full of bullshit. And my mother is impossible."

"Did you find anything out?"

The mattress tipped as Ell flopped onto it. "Nah. But everyone's very angry about it. Except the ones that aren't."

"You suspect any of them?"

"Not really. They're just the shitstirrers. Mother's sent some spies over to Unseelie to see if she can find anything out."

There was a pause, and I started to drift back under. Then Tadgh said softly, "What about Niamh?"

Niamh was familiar, but I couldn't remember where from. I was so tired.

Ell didn't reply directly to that. Instead he said, "Tadgh?"

"Mmm?"

"There's a girl in our bed."

"Yes. It's Aura."

"Oh. Well, that's okay, then."

I smiled, and drifted off again.

* * *

I floated near the surface when Ell and Tadgh got up for work. Okay, that's a lie. I actually did wake up. But that's not something I'd ever admit to in front of Ell and Tadgh. They thought I was asleep when they started kissing.

I didn't mind, not in the least. After all, I was the one in their bed. But I thought it was sweet of Ell to move away, so as not to wake me up.

But I was awake, and I heard them go on kissing over by the cashmere rug, and then one of them gasped and moaned quietly. Wet sucking sounds ensued. Someone's getting a blow-job, I thought, and smiled into the pillow. Then the bedside drawer slid open -- by itself, or rather, I suspected, by Ell's telekinesis -- and he moaned again.

I amused myself trying to work out which one was moaning. I figured Tadgh for the strong silent type, but would he be the one sucking off Ell? Or would it be Tadgh's cock in Ell's mouth?

The thought made me wet. Hearing his -- whichever one he was -- moans of pleasure made me wetter. I wanted to see, but at the same time, listening was even hotter.

Then I heard a voice breathe, "Ell," and I knew it was Tadgh getting sucked. Oh boy. I wanted to wrap my own lips around that thick cock of his. I wondered if they'd fit. Surely Ell was having to do one of those snake-dislocating-jaw things?

I thought about the heavy, meaty weight of it in my mouth, the taste, the texture, and I started breathing faster. I wanted to touch myself but I didn't want to give myself away. They might stop, and I didn't want that.

Then Tadgh moaned again, his breathing coming heavy, and the wet sucking stopped. Then there was a lot of panting. A lot.

I couldn't bear it any longer. I peeked out through one eyelid, and saw Ell on his knees, his face hidden by Tadgh's huge cock. His hand was buried between Tadgh's buttocks, working in the lube he'd magicked from the bedside drawer. Tadgh stood there with his legs apart, his eyes closed and his hands on Ell's head.

"In me," he whispered, "I want you in me."

Ell grinned up at him, and then all of a sudden Tadgh was on all fours, his ass in the air, and Ell was sinking his cock into it.

Both of them groaned. I don't know how they thought I was still asleep. I closed my eyes again, the image of it imprinted on my brain as wet sliding sounds began, soft moans and heavy panting. Gasps and sighs, making me hotter just to hear them as I pictured them moving together, Ell's long cock sliding between Tadgh's beautiful buttocks, Tadgh's heavy cock pulsing and straining. Ell's elegant fingers stroking, pulling, smoothing the hard flesh until Tadgh came -- I heard his muffled groan, his gasp -- his ass tightening around Ell's cock. Ell came too, letting out a quiet shout. Well, not that quiet. You can't shout quietly.

I didn't blame him. Not for shouting, not for fucking. I'd fuck either one of them on a moment's notice.

As soon as I heard them both leave the house, I buried my hand between my legs and gave myself a small orgasm, just to round things off.

Then I fell back asleep again.

Chapter Six

I woke up late, rolling over in the huge bed that smelled of big sexy men, and smiled. I still felt pretty lazy, but not exhausted and not sick any more. A quiet day at home was called for, I figured, and with that in mind did very little for several hours. I took a long hot bath, washed my hair in shampoo that reminded me of Tadgh, and got dressed in shorts and a sweater of Ell's. It wouldn't have taken much energy to zap my own clothes across town and onto my body, but I was experiencing a mild "never again" feeling, like you get after a night of heavy drinking.

The deli a few blocks over sent up breakfast for me, and then lunch. The most effort I expended all day was making a pot of coffee and carrying it up to the roof garden to look out over the park with the windows open. The trees lifted my spirits, made me feel a hell of a lot better, and the sun warming my skin soothed away the last traces of my magic hangover.

By the time the vampire turned up, I was feeling like myself again.

Someone hammered on the door, and I frowned, confused, because I felt a vampire close by, and yet it was still sunny outside. Something didn't compute. The terrace didn't have a view of the front door, so I set down my newspaper and trailed lazily down the stairs to see what was going on.

I wasn't scared. I knew so long as I stayed inside I was safe: the vampire couldn't enter without an invite.

Downstairs, a shadow was cast over the gleaming hardwood of the lobby floor. The fanlights in the big door were blocked out by whoever was standing on the other side. Someone powerful. Someone old.

Someone fucking scary.

I took a breath as the vampire pounded the door again, reminded myself about the invite thing, then went over and opened the door.

The person standing there was dressed in one of those full-body veils that women wear in strict Arabic countries. Only a mesh panel over the eyes gave him or her any vision of the outside world.

Which accounted for the sunlight thing.

"Vampire," I said.

"Fae," said the vampire. A female voice, although a million miles away from the sweet, pretty voices of the Fae. This woman had a low, husky voice, a whisky-and-cigarettes voice, a voice that made certain girlie parts of mine perk up interestedly and remind me I wasn't one hundred percent straight.

But she's a *vampire*, I reminded them, and they quieted down again.

"What do you want?"

"Can I come in?"

"No."

"Oh, come on. It's fucking roasting out here. And this veil thing is just sadistic."

"It suits you."

"Look, I'm not here to hurt you," the vampire said, but something in the way she stressed the "you" gave me pause.

"Who are you here to hurt?"

The vampire sighed. "If I tell you Johann sent me, will that make any difference?"

I frowned. Johann was the Sundown, Inc. boss in London. Why was he sending a vampire here?

I leaned against the door, thinking about it, and the vampire just walked straight past me, into the house.

I spun around in amazement. "You can't do that!"

"Just did, honey."

The vampire pulled off the veil. Underneath it she had straight black hair and gleaming bronze skin that was rather exposed by the supple leather outfit she wore. A cropped top and pants that were open laced at the sides, letting me know she wasn't wearing a thing beneath them. The leather molded a whipcrack body, hard and toned but for the perfect high breasts revealed by the tiny top.

My girlie parts started getting interested again.

But my eyes were drawn to the scars that spattered her face, her neck, her shoulder and her arm. Like someone had thrown boiling oil at her. The skin was pink, puckered, irredeemable.

By those scars, I knew her.

"You're Sundown's assassin," I said.

She smiled, showing fangs. "Masika."

Masika was a vampire. Of course. God, I'm so stupid.

"I heard you were looking for me."

"You came all the way here because you heard?"

"No."

I narrowed my eyes at her. Standing here in my shorts and sweater, I felt very vulnerable, very lightweight, very... Fae.

Bloody vampires.

"Johann told you?"

"Dare told me."

"Dare is your..." I looked her over again. Vampires were animals. Nothing more. "Mate?"

Her lip curled. "Yes," she said. "He's also the oldest vampire in the world."

"I find that surprising."

"Oh?"

"I thought you looked older."

She bared her fangs at me. "Don't piss me off, Fae," she said. "Or I might just do what I was paid to."

A tremor of fear ran through me. "And that is?"

"Kill the Seelie prince."

I found myself sitting on the bottom step in the lobby, my head between my knees, the vampire patting my back rather ineffectually. "Breathe," she said, "don't pass out on me. I don't want to get the smell of faery all over my clothes."

I raised my head sharply, fighting dizziness. "I don't want to smell of vampire," I said. "You're the one who's touching me."

She raised her hand, sitting back on her haunches. "You're welcome." She ran a hand through her gleaming hair. "No wonder Dare hates Fae."

I took a deep breath and sat up straight, regarding her. She sat watching me, like a cat would, her body still but her eyes always moving, never missing anything. I don't like predators. They make me feel like food.

"Are you really here to kill Ell?"

She inclined her head. "That's what I was paid for."

"Paid for? By who?"

"Unseelie," she said, glancing around the lobby, then standing up in one effortlessly graceful movement. I hauled myself to my feet by the banister, still feeling weak.

"Wouldn't be Eibhlis, would it?" I asked.

She shrugged. "I dunno. Johann didn't pass on the details."

"Why didn't Magda tell me?" I meant to ask myself, but clearly my internal monologue wasn't working.

"Probably figured it'd become clear when I told you."

I squared my shoulders, and tried to look threatening. "I won't let you do it."

Masika burst out laughing. "Little girl," she said, shaking her head, "I'd like to see you try."

"I'm Fae," I said, irritated. "I have magic. Big, protective magic."

"You're a sex faery," Masika said. "You have the power to get people off. Unlike you, I actually read employee files."

I felt my face heat. "I'm not an employee. I'm a consultant."

"Whatever. You couldn't stop me from killing the Seelie."

"I'd damn well try."

She cocked her head and regarded me. "Well, then, there might be some hope for you."

I frowned, but she didn't elaborate. Instead, she wandered off into the house, her heels tapping sharply as she strode around like she owned the place.

Have I mentioned I hate vampires?

"Pretty nice place," she said.

"Nicer than yours." I couldn't resist.

She shrugged. "I'm not into ostentation."

"Which explains your outfit."

Masika ignored me, loping through the living room to the kitchen. She didn't venture far in, though, what with all the sunlight flooding in through the skylights. Seelie Fae like lots of light. It's their element.

Which made me wonder if reasoning might work with the vampire.

"You know what Ell represents?" I asked as Masika made her way up the stairs, her butt swinging sexily in front of me.

"The face of haute couture, last fashion mag I read."

I beamed on his behalf, before sobering. "I meant in Fae terms."

She ran her hand over the wooden paneling in the upstairs parlor. "He's the sole Seelie heir. Unless his sister comes back."

"They wouldn't take her," I said. "It's too risky. She's clearly gone over to the dark side."

Masika raised an eyebrow. "Literally."

So she did know.

The thing about the Fae is that while we spend our very, very long lives squabbling and bickering over the most trivial matters, we're actually the most important creatures in the whole universe.

The Seelie Court doesn't just represent summer, sunlight and warmth. It *is* those things.

"If the Unseelie Court gains control of the Seelie…" I trailed off. The thought really was too horrible.

"Summer will diminish," Masika said.

I made my way over to the sofa and sat down carefully. "No," I said slowly. "Summer won't diminish. There are no half measures in the High Courts. It's a constant power struggle. Absolutely constant. But there has to be a balance of power, because if one side falls, then the other takes over. Rules.

Supreme. Last time the Seelie had a weak ruler, Earth went through an ice age that lasted fifty thousand years."

"There's still ice at the polar caps."

"And there's drought at the equator. I didn't say the balance was nice. But the Earth moves through cycles of summer and winter, warm and cold, light and dark. I know the idea of permanent darkness probably sounds great to a vampire --"

"Yeah, sunburn is really a bitch."

"But if there's no Seelie Court, there will be no summer, no light, no warmth." I swallowed, because it was such a hideous concept. "Without sunlight there will be no plant life. The herbivores will starve. The carnivores will starve. The planet will die."

Masika was silent a second. "I guess Seelie is the side to root for, then?"

I shrugged. "If the Seelie Court was in charge then the Earth would just burn up. We'd all fry. Nothing would grow -- and we're back to the planet dying."

"If you know all this, if the Fae all know this, then why do you carry on fighting?"

I blinked at her.

"Do you want the Earth to die?" Masika pressed.

"We *are* the Earth."

"Then -- why fight?"

Still nonplussed, I said, "Because that's what we do."

She stared at me a second, then sighed. "Right. Of course it is."

"It's just part of who we are."

She rolled her eyes. "I hate faeries."

"Feeling's mutual."

She sauntered to the sofa opposite me. "So we're both agreed, killing the Seelie prince would be of the bad."

"Yes," I said gratefully.

"But you know, he's going to die one day."

"Is that a threat?"

"Merely an observation. And when he does die, there will be no Seelie heir."

"He could have children."

She gave me a look. "Even I know he's as gay as they come," she said. "His mother's hired Sundown to find a walking womb for him, but I can't see it happening."

"You can't?"

"No. Would you shag a gay man?"

I nearly laughed at that. "Have and would," I said.

"Well, I suppose you will shag anything."

I didn't rise to that. I was thinking.

Masika stood up. "How good are you?" she asked.

"I can get an orgasm out of a stone," I said absently.

She laughed. "No, I mean in terms of defense. If I tried to kill him, could you stop me?"

I looked her over. She was tall, toned, and had that hard look in her eyes that said she'd kill anything if she was getting paid enough. "Honestly?"

"Yes."

"No. I couldn't stop you. Especially since it turns out that whole invitation thing is a myth."

She raised her eyebrows.

"I didn't invite you but you still came in."

"Oh. Well, that's because I'm older than Rome," she said. "There's not much I can't do."

I stood up glumly. "So I can take down the garlic and holy water?"

She touched the scars on her face. "Holy water won't stop me," she said distantly, but I figured from the scars that it might slow her down.

"Tadgh might," I said.

"Who?"

"Ell's lover. He's part centaur. Big guy. Lots of muscle."

She shrugged. "I'm still not very intimidated. But then I'm not the one who's going to try and kill him."

My skin prickled. "Johann's sending someone else?"

"No. I'm the best."

She said it simply, a statement of fact.

"But if someone wants your friend dead, then dead he'll be. My advice is to find out who that person is, and nullify them."

"Nullify?"

She started down the stairs. "That sort of person won't stop until they're dead. And even then it's not guaranteed."

After Masika had left, I sat thinking for a while. She was right, much as I hated to admit it. Someone -- probably Eibhlis -- wanted Ell dead, and wasn't likely to stop until it had happened.

That meant two things. One, that Ell needed a constant bodyguard, and two, that he really, really needed this heir. Once a child was on the way, it might stop the plotting. No Fae would ever intentionally harm a child, and that by extension made Ell safe, because there'd be no point in killing him if he already had an heir and the Seelie throne was safe.

Really, he needed several heirs, to be completely safe.

I flashed myself home and got out my spell books.

It was turning dark when Tadgh came home and found me cooking up potions in the kitchen.

"Mmm," he said, chucking his jacket on the kitchen chair, "something smells disgusting." He wandered over and dipped his finger in.

"And yet still you want to taste it," I said in wonder, shooing him away. "It's not for you."

"Who's it for?"

"Ell. Fertility spell. And protection, too."

"Protection? We dealt with the goblin menace."

"That sounds like a bad B movie." Tadgh grinned at me, looking disheveled and gorgeous in his shirtsleeves. "I think Ell needs more constant protection."

"From?"

"Well, the vampire assassin I met today, for one."

Tadgh's grin vanished, and I filled him in on Masika's visit as I stirred the potion. "He needs one of us with him, Tadgh. All the time. As soon as I finish this I'm going over there." I bit my lip. "Is he still down a model?"

Tadgh shrugged, still frowning. "Yes, but I thought you didn't want to do it."

"Well, not particularly. But I don't want to leave him alone. Once Masika goes back to Sundown and refuses the job, it's pretty much open season on Ell."

Something flashed across Tadgh's face. A mixture of anger, fear, and guilt, I think, with a healthy dose of determination. "You finish this," he said. "I'm going to Ell."

He flashed out before I could say anything. I finished up the potion, stuck it in a bottle, and checked my reflection in the kitchen mirror. An upside of being in a Fae house: we're so vain, there are mirrors everywhere.

Fae are naturally tall and slender, and our average looks are considered amazingly attractive by mortals. Even so, I wasn't sure I was quite skinny enough for Ell's catwalk show. Well, anyway, I'd just glamour the audience into thinking I was.

I flashed myself to his studio in a Tribeca loft, and found myself in an orgy of silks and satins and gorgeous girls trying desperately to look as if they weren't flirting with Tadgh, who was standing off to one side with his arms folded over his massive chest, frowning.

No one noticed me arrive, but they sure as hell noticed when I went over to Tadgh, wrapped my arms around his waist, and kissed him.

"Enjoying the view?" I asked against his mouth as his hand trailed through my hair.

"I am now," he said, grinning, and I kissed him again.

"*Aura!*" Ell's shriek echoed across the studio. "*Gorgeous* girl! What are you doing here?"

"Do you still need a spare body?" I asked, posing with one hand on my hip.

"Oh, darling, are you volunteering? Of course I do! I *love* you!"

He threw his arms around me and kissed me on the lips, and I swear the whole room went silent as the other girls tried to digest the sight of the very gay Ell and his boyfriend both kissing the same woman within a matter of minutes. And it wasn't a friendly kiss, either. It was a proper, deep kiss. Ell sure was grateful.

"Mmm," I said when he let me go. "That ought to keep the gossips busy."

After a frantic hour of fitting and pinning and crying and begging, pretty much all of it on Ell's part, Tadgh excused himself and went home to make supper. Ell continued wedging me into his creations, which were admittedly gorgeous, and it was after midnight when we finally flashed home, exhausted.

Tadgh was reclining on the sofa in the upstairs parlor, reading the business section of the paper. He'd showered and changed and looked twice as sexy as ever with his silky hair falling in his eyes and the warm scent of soap rising from his skin. From the kitchen, yummy cooking smells were drifting.

"Something smells delicious," Ell said, eyeing him.

"Yeah, and there's food, too," I said.

Tadgh sat up, smiling. "How'd it go?"

"Manic," I said, "and now I'm starving." I allowed myself a wicked grin. "And unlike the other girls in the show, I'm allowed to eat tonight. Whatcha got for us?"

"Roast beef, Yorkshire pudding, potatoes, the works," Tadgh said, leading us downstairs. "I figured you'd be late, and it all keeps well in the oven."

I threw my arms around him in a hug that was part gratitude and partly because I wanted to feel all that muscle and smell all that skin.

"How come you're such a good cook?" I asked as we sat down, and Tadgh served huge platefuls of gorgeous food.

"I figure it's my latent homosexual tendencies," he said, straightfaced, ladling gravy onto my plate.

Ell gabbled nonstop about the show and his creations and his nerves, adrenaline fuelling him on and on. He ate three platefuls of food while he described to Tadgh, in minute detail, everything about the outfits he had for me to wear. Tadgh gave every appearance of listening patiently, and carried on pouring wine. By the time the food had run out it was early morning, and I decided Ell needed a diversion.

I took my clothes off again.

Then I vanished Ell and Tadgh's clothes, too.

"Oh, honey," Tadgh grinned, "you brought dessert."

Ell swallowed.

"No goblin attacks this time," I said.

"There better not be," Tadgh said darkly.

"And I think we should all get ourselves to bed," I said.

"All of us?" Ell looked between us nervously.

"Relax, Ell, I don't have anything you haven't seen before," I said.

"Well, not before yesterday, at any rate," Tadgh said.

"But... you have *squishy* bits," Ell said.

"And very nice squishy bits they are, too," Tadgh said, and then the three of us were sprawled naked on the huge bed upstairs. "Now. Plan, Aura?"

I smiled encouragingly at Ell. "Since you were making such wonderful progress yesterday --"

"I was?"

"I had an orgasm and everything."

Tadgh muttered something about me being able to orgasm at the idea of new shoes, which I ignored.

"I think it's time to move on to the next step," I said. When Ell looked panicked, I put my hand on his arm to reassure him. "A step which I'm pretty sure you won't have any qualms about, since it's already something you're used to."

Ell opened his mouth to protest, then closed it, looking confused.

"Uh, remember he's never fucked a girl before, Aura," Tadgh said, taking Ell's hand. Ell clutched nervously at him. "Ever."

"Yes, but what's the one thing you can do with girls that you can also do with guys?" I asked. "Apart from kissing."

"We did the nipple thing yesterday," Ell said.

"Okay, apart from that."

"Are you going to suck him off?" Tadgh asked.

"Okay, there are plenty of things you can do with both," I said, rolling my eyes. "But I was talking about anal."

Ell blinked. "But -- what's the point of that?"

"It's supposed to be fun," I said, getting a little annoyed.

"Well, of course it is. But it can't get anyone pregnant," Ell said, "and isn't that supposed to be what I'm doing?"

"We're working up to that," I said. "Besides, I haven't had a good ass-fucking in ages. But if you don't want to do it --"

"Oh, no, I want," Ell said quickly.

"And I sure as hell want to watch," Tadgh said, running his hand over my breast. I shivered.

"You can help him, if you want," I said.

"I thought you'd never ask."

The bedside drawer shot open and the lube smacked into Tadgh's palm.

"Now," I said. "Where do you want me?"

Chapter Seven

Tadgh dipped his head and licked my nipple. "Take your time deciding," he told Ell over his shoulder. "You should make sure you're comfortable with your decision."

"Yes," I said, gasping as he sucked my nipple into his mouth. "Comfort is important."

Ell looked at the bed consideringly. "I don't want to, um, offend you, darling," he said, "but I, er. Your squishy bits…"

"Off-putting?" I asked.

"Um. Little bit."

"Facedown, then," I said. "I don't mind." A little thrill ran through me at the thought. "In fact, I'm not sure if I mentioned that I do love it from behind."

"That makes two of us," Tadgh murmured, his hand slipping between my legs. His fingers found my clit and I moaned softly. Behind me, Ell was piling up pillows, and then Tadgh, without removing his hand, turned me over and laid me down so my breasts were flat against the mattress and my ass was up in the air.

"Beautiful," he said. He parted my legs from behind, ran his hand from my wet pussy lips to my asshole. I shivered in expectation.

A second hand touched my buttocks, a smaller, defter hand. Ell.

"You do have a beautiful ass, Aura," he said.

"Why, thank you. I've always admired yours through your clothes. You'll have to show it to me properly some time."

"Oh, sure." His finger stroked my asshole. "I'd love to."

"Can I compare them?" Tadgh asked.

"That way madness lies," I said. "But I'm sure Ell will agree if I say we're both perfectly happy for you to play with both of them."

"Oh, yes," Ell said. "More than happy."

It was oddly comforting to chat to them like this, and at the same time it was incredibly hot. Here I was with my ass in the air, totally unable to see what they were doing, working things out by touch. The hand that consistently delved down to my pussy, stroking my clit and sliding a finger or two inside was Tadgh's, I was reasonably sure. He stroked my thigh as well, the soft bit of skin where leg turns into buttock. He seemed particularly enamored of that bit.

Whereas Ell stuck with the safe bits. Men have buttocks, and men have assholes. He was in familiar territory there, and he seemed much more comfortable with it. Which was what I'd figured. We'd start slowly, and work our way up. He'd be diving for treasure in my cunt before long.

When a tongue touched my asshole I wasn't sure whose it was. Wasn't sure I cared. It was wonderful, all soft wet licks and gentle probing. Someone spread my ass cheeks far apart and drizzled lube between them, and he carried on licking, stroking with his finger, seeking entrance.

When Tadgh stroked my back, turned my head and kissed me, lying beside me, I knew it was Ell at my asshole. Doing, I guess, what he does best. I slipped one arm around Tadgh, careful not to move my hips, and kissed him sweetly while his boyfriend rimmed my ass.

"He's good," I gasped as his finger slipped inside me.

"Oh yes," Tadgh agreed, stroking my cheek. "He's very good."

I ran my hand down his back, shuddering as Ell probed with his tongue. Tadgh's cock bumped against my knee, hard and hot and slippery with moisture. "What are you going to do?" I asked.

"What?" Tadgh was licking my fingers.

"With this," I nudged his cock. "Are you going to put it in Ell, or me?"

Tadgh shook a little. "Oh God," he moaned. "How am I supposed to decide that?"

I laughed, and then I gulped because Ell had removed the two fingers he'd been dipping into my ass, stretching and lubricating it, and I felt the head of his cock there.

"Is that all right, Aura?" he asked me, before he entered. "Is this okay? Are you ready?"

I pushed my ass back to feel his hot cock against it, once again touched at his concern. "Oh yes," I said, and tried not to moan. "I'm ready."

He pushed inside me, hot and hard, and I panted against the mattress. Tadgh stroked my face reassuringly.

"He feels so good," I whispered, and he whispered back, "I know."

Ell had his hands on my hips as he sank into me, then back out. Next stroke, he went in deeper, and then the one after that deeper still, until he was all the way in and his balls brushed my wet, swollen pussy lips.

"Ew, squishy bits," he said, but he was laughing as he did, and I could feel by the way his cock pulsed inside me that he clearly wasn't finding it a turn-off. "You have a *gorgeous* ass, darling. It's so tight!"

"Think I can try it later?" Tadgh asked.

"Sweetheart, you can put that cock of yours absolutely anywhere you want," I told him, and he grinned.

"I intend to."

I moved gently with Ell's thrusts. He didn't pound into me but fucked me gently, carefully. Tenderly. I felt the pressure building inside me, my clit aching for attention, my pussy a desperate void. If only Ell would touch me there, I'd come really hard.

But he didn't. Not that I expected him to. He was fucking a girl, and that in itself was pretty impressive. When he came inside me, he shouted out, the same way he had this morning when he'd fucked Tadgh, and then he sank down over me, his warm body covering mine, his skin damp against my back.

He pressed a kiss to the back of my neck. "That was glorious, darling."

"It was," Tadgh agreed. He'd stayed beside me the whole time, kissing my mouth, my face, my neck. His cock was a huge, pulsing hot brand against my thigh.

"But you didn't come, did you?" Ell asked anxiously.

"No, but it's all right," I said.

"I'll take care of that," Tadgh said, and as Ell moved off me, carefully withdrawing, Tadgh pulled me into his arms and kissed me thoroughly. He moved down my body, sucking my nipples, and then he parted my legs and wrapped his tongue around my clit.

My whole body bucked in sudden release and I cried out, shuddering and shaking as he licked me.

"Oh God, I needed that," I said.

Tadgh looked up, his eyes very dark, and said, "I know." He moved back up my body then, and slid his cock into my dripping wet pussy.

"Thought you fancied the back way," I said, closing my eyes at the feel of him filling me.

"Maybe later," he said, and sat up with me in his lap, impaled upon his huge cock.

After staying so still for Ell, it was a wonderful release to be able to move on Tadgh. His hands on my hips, he held me as I rode him, fast and hard, sucking my nipples into his mouth as I arched my back and ground down on him. His fingers stole round my back, between my buttocks, and found my asshole wide and empty, still slippery with lube and come.

He slid two fingers inside, and I came again, shuddering and clutching at his shoulders. Tadgh kissed me, thrusting deep into my pussy as his fingers reamed my back passage, three and four fingers filling me up.

"Oh God, oh *God*," I cried, and came again, just as he did, his thick cock filling me with hot come. My body spasmed for what felt like hours, waves of wonderful pleasure crashing over me, wiping me out.

I barely felt Tadgh lay me down on the bed in Ell's arms, snuggling up so I was wrapped warm between both of them. But I did feel Ell's lips brushing my temple.

"Three orgasms all in a row," he marveled. "Sometimes I wish I was a woman."

I nestled against his hard chest, tucking my head into the curve of his warm neck as Tadgh pressed his softening cock against my butt.

"I'm glad you're not," I murmured, and drifted into sleep.

* * *

I spent the whole of the next day with Ell, being fitted for clothes and rehearsing the show, which was at some huge swanky hotel that had only opened a few weeks before. He was so busy with nerves he forgot to be embarrassed around me, unlike when he first woke in the morning to find me sleeping on his chest. Ell's so adorable.

Tadgh came by on his lunch hour, but got so uncomfortable with the amount of stares he received that he didn't stay long. I mean, hell. This is fashion: all the girls and most of the boys like men, and Tadgh is a pretty prime specimen.

When he came back after he'd finished work, I took matters into my own hands and dragged him round to be introduced to everyone. I did this with my hand in his back pocket and my breasts rubbing up against him at every available opportunity. He put his arm around my shoulders and broke off conversations to kiss me. Much confusion was to be seen on everyone's faces because of course they all knew he was Ell's boyfriend. A few of the nastier ones smirked knowingly at the prospect of Ell finding out.

Then Ell came bounding over, threw his arms around us both and gave us big smacking kisses.

"Darlings!" he cried manically. "Everything's going so well!"

The show was a wonderful success. Ell is a very talented designer and his clothes made the models look fabulous. At the end, he dressed me as his bride and walked me down the catwalk to take his bow. The irony wasn't lost on me, nor on Tadgh, who sat next to the editor of *Vogue*, laughing into his hand.

Then it was over, and as Ell bounced out into the crowd to be adored, I wove my way backstage to take off the heavy makeup and change into ordinary clothes.

Although the wedding dress did feel pretty cool.

I took off the veil and was turning to put it back on its stand when an image in the mirror caught my eye. A very tall, very beautiful woman with bronzed skin and a gorgeous mane of golden hair. She wore a floating silk dress in a perfect shade of green that skimmed her delicious curves. She smelled like a summer meadow, like warmth and sunshine and long hot days of glory.

She was so immaculately perfect in every respect that I'd have known she was Fae even without the huge waves of power emanating from her.

"He's a talented designer," she said, her voice like a choir of angels.

"Yes," I said, carefully rearranging the veil before turning to face her and curtseying, "he is, your majesty."

The Seelie Queen smiled. "You look much finer than these wretched skinny humans."

"Thank you, your majesty. You look very well, if I may say so."

Her smile deepened. "You may, Aura of the Wildfae."

I felt a pang at her words. My father was High Court Unseelie and my mother was High Court Seelie. I'm not Wildfae. But since they eloped, leaving both Courts behind, I have no ties to either. Therefore, both Courts consider me Wildfae. When they consider me at all.

"You have never tried to seek allegiance to either Court," she said, running her fingers over the fine silk satin of one of my earlier gowns.

"No, your majesty."

"Do you not care for Court life?"

I chose my words carefully. "I have very little knowledge of it, your majesty."

"Did your parents never speak of it to you?"

I closed my eyes at the old pain. "My parents died when I was very young, your majesty. If they spoke of it, I don't remember."

When I opened my eyes, the queen was stroking the bridal veil, her lovely face sad. "Your mother and I were friends in our youth," she said. "I cried for a year after her death."

I blinked. I'd had no idea. My parents were killed when a goblin crew, searching for one of my father's Unseelie brothers, ransacked our house in the Faerie realm. I was in the mortal world, and have pretty much stayed here since.

"I didn't know that," I said.

"No. Well, you wouldn't. Your parents were very careful not to take sides, I understand. Fraternization between the Courts can be..." she blinked moist eyes, "difficult."

I said nothing.

"My son has told me much about you," she said, bringing her head up, her face brighter. "About what you're doing for him."

"He has?"

"Yes. It isn't easy to find a suitable mate for a prince," she said, and added wryly, "especially one who's as gay as a mintball. I appreciate you... helping him to be more comfortable with a woman."

"Oh," I said. "Well, no problem. I mean, thank you."

The queen nodded. She turned to go. Then she said, as if it were an afterthought, "You will be welcome in my Court, Aura. You will always be welcome."

I stood frozen, staring after her as she wove elegantly through the chaotic, messy dressing room.

Welcome in her Court?

I stood there for about five minutes, completely frozen. Welcome. In. Her. Court.

When Parker, Ell's very harried assistant, bustled over and told me Ell and Tadgh were waiting for me in the lobby, I darted out there so fast I think I might have actually flown a little while. Ell was leaning against the reception counter, giggling animatedly with the receptionist, and Tadgh stood checking something on his PDA. So big and tall and broad and male, both of them, not just Tadgh. Ell's immaculately cut sweater and slacks showed off his tight, toned body, and Tadgh in his suit looked like a tamed brute.

I raced over to them both, breathless with excitement and heat, and grabbed them both.

"Aura?" Tadgh sounded surprised as he caught me around the waist. "Are you ok -- mmph!"

I shut him up by plugging his mouth with mine. I was going to Court! The Seelie Court! I was *welcome* there! I seriously don't think I've been this excited since I discovered multiple orgasms.

I left Tadgh's mouth and turned to Ell, kissing him just as hard.

"Home," I said when I came up for air. "Now. Home."

"Uh, actually, we just got a suite here." Tadgh shifted at my side and I felt the slight bulge that told me what my kiss had done to him. "To celebrate Ell's --"

"Suite!" I shrieked. "Yes! Where? Now! Go now!"

The receptionist stared, wild-eyed, as I tugged them toward the elevators. Well, you would, I suppose: crazy girl in a wedding dress jumping all over two guys and snogging them both madly. It's not something you see every day. Ell darted back for a key, and then we were in the elevator, just the three of us, out of anyone else's sight, and he teleported us to the suite.

It was big, grand, beautiful, and I wasn't remotely interested. I grabbed Ell with both hands and swung him round in a circle like a giddy child.

"Guess what?" I yelped, beaming so wide I thought the top of my head might fall off.

"What?"

I grabbed Tadgh and pulled him into our mad whirl. "I'm going to Court!"

Tadgh stared at me. "Faerie Court?"

"Yes! Faerie Court! Seelie Court! Ell's mother came to see me, she *came* to see *me*," I cried, breathless, and come to think of it rather dizzy from all that spinning. I let go of them both and plopped down on the thick fluffy rug in the middle of the room.

"She came to see me," I gabbled. "She said she used to be friends with my mother, which is mad 'cos no one ever told me, and then she said she really appreciated me helping Ell out, and that I was welcome at her Court any time! She told me I was *welcome*!"

Ell and Tadgh exchanged a smile. Ell sat down next to me and pulled me into a hug. "Of course you are, sweetie. I told her how wonderful you'd been to me, to us. She said any friend of mine was welcome in the Court, but when I told her what you were doing to help me out she insisted on meeting you so she could thank you." He brushed a strand of hair out of my eyes. "I was going to tell you, but I thought it would make a better surprise."

"It did! It's amazing! God, Ell," I crushed him to me, "you have no idea what this means to me. I can finally go to *Court*."

Tadgh sat down on my other side. "Congratulations, sweetheart." He hugged me, and I kissed him, and then I kissed him harder, because I was madly keyed up and when I get really excited there's only one kind of release that can help me.

"I think it's time," I said to Ell.

"Time?"

"For you to have sex with a girl. I mean, we wouldn't want to disappoint your mother, now would we?"

Ell swallowed.

"It won't hurt a bit," I said, and then I kissed him, and, comfortable with that at least, he kissed me back while I vanished all our clothes. I felt Tadgh's hands on my back, stroking and soothing, and then his lips were tracing my spine and I shivered in delight.

I pushed Ell down onto his back and straddled him, still kissing him while Tadgh licked and stroked my back. My God, that man has magic hands.

I decided to pass on the favor, moving down to Ell's throat and kissing the rough skin there, licking his Adam's apple, biting into his collarbone. Ell gasped at the assault. Straight or gay, I don't think anyone would be capable of saying no to me tonight.

I sucked on his nipples, scraping gently with my teeth, licking it better, and Ell moaned slightly, catching my head in his hands, burying his fingers in my hair. My head moved down his wonderful flat stomach, nipping and tasting, and as I got to the line of hair that ran down like an arrow pointing toward his cock, I felt Tadgh's hands and mouth move lower on my back, lower and lower, until he was licking my asshole.

I whimpered. I actually whimpered. And then I took Ell's long slim cock into my mouth and sucked it deep.

"Holy *fuck*," Ell cried as I squashed my gag reflex and took him all the way in. I'm not a sex faery for nothing. And it kept me from crying out as Tadgh ran his tongue along my throbbing pussy lips and darted it inside.

I squirmed. I wriggled. And then I nearly choked, because Tadgh knelt up behind me and fed his big fat cock into my aching, dripping cunt.

God, it was wonderful. I can't tell you how much I love this, love being full of hard, throbbing cocks.

Tadgh stroked my ass as he thrust into me from behind, probing with a finger made slippery from my own juices. As Tadgh plunged into me, Ell thrust his hips upwards, fucking my mouth, filling me with his taste and his hot flesh. I stroked his balls, looked up at his face and saw his head thrown back, his eyes closed and his mouth open. His cock throbbed in my throat. It wouldn't be long now.

As Tadgh stuck his finger into my ass, I came, ripping my head away from Ell's cock to gulp in huge amounts of air, dizzy and boneless and screaming for more.

And more was right at hand. There in front of me was Ell's cock, dark red and shiny, bobbing around all lonely by itself. I pulled forward away from Tadgh's still hard cock and impaled myself on Ell, whose eyes slammed open in shock.

"Ah, God, you feel good," I moaned. His penis was thinner than Tadgh's, but then that's not saying much. He was still big and stiff, filling me up nicely, his balls soft against my ass as I bounced up and down on them. I squeezed his cock with my pussy muscles, and Ell's eyes rolled back in his head.

"You feel pretty good too," he managed, gasping. "Hooray for squishy bits!"

"Hooray," I yelped, working my hips back and forth, up and down, moving with manic energy. "Oh, oh, oh!"

Ell's cock was pulsing inside me now, jerking with the need to come, and then he did come, inside me, squirting his seed inside my cunt, and I, delirious, came too, crying out madly.

But I hadn't even had chance to get my brain back in order before Tadgh was grabbing me and rolling me onto my back and sliding himself back inside me again. My orgasm just went on and on. My whole body pulsing and thrashing, incoherent cries flying from my mouth as Tadgh surged into me again and again, filling me up inside. His lips were on my neck and his hands on my breasts, and then he came too, and we lay there in a boneless heap. Sweaty and exhausted, and in my case at least, pretty indescribably happy.

For about five minutes the only sound was the three of us breathing hard. Tadgh rolled off me, onto his back, then gathered me and Ell on either side. We snuggled up, and I draped one leg over Tadgh's hip. My cunt was still soaked and dripping with come, my nipples swollen where they grazed his chest. I felt magnificently sated and at the same time desperate for more. As soon as I could move again.

Which might be some time.

Then Ell said, "I just had sex with a girl."

I laughed, reaching over Tadgh to pat Ell's shoulder. "You did," I said, "and you made her come, too." I felt really lightheaded at my next thought. "You know, people used to believe a woman was more likely to conceive if she came."

"Did they?" Ell asked sleepily. "Then I'm glad it's a skill I possess."

Tadgh ruffled my hair and I kissed his chest. Then Ell's voice came again, all traces of sleepiness gone now. "Aura?"

"Mmm?"

"We didn't -- I wasn't wearing a condom. Did you do a spell?"

"No," I said, smiling drowsily.

"Oh, crap. I'll just --"

"No," I said, squeezing his shoulder. He lifted his head and regarded me over Tadgh's chest.

"No?" he said.

Tadgh looked at me too. "*No?*"

"No spell," I said. "Well. Not that kind of spell anyway. Some kind of fertility or protection thing might be nice."

Ell sat up, staring at me. Tadgh's eyes searched my face.

"Unless you don't want me to have your baby," I said.

"Don't want... Aura, are you crazy?" Ell reached over and grabbed me by the shoulders, shaking me upright. Tadgh slipped his arm around my waist, holding me up. "I never wanted anyone else but you! Ever since this whole crazy thing started, I've been desperate to think of ways to persuade you!"

I blinked. "Really?"

"Yes, really!" Ell looked at Tadgh, who nodded.

"We both really wanted you," Tadgh said.

I brushed my hand over his groin. His cock stirred. "Well, you did at least."

"Aura, are you serious?" Ell cried. "You'll do it?"

"I might already be doing it," I said, lying back and snuggling into Tadgh's warm embrace. Ell scrambled over the two of us and grabbed me from behind, kissing any part of me he could reach.

"Aura, I *love* you!"

I smiled, and thought about how he'd told the queen I was helping him, and got me an invitation to Court without me even asking, and all the other lovely things he'd done for me.

And then I thought about bringing up a baby with these two wonderful men, and said, "I love you too."

Chapter Eight

I kissed Tadgh, and then turned and kissed Ell, who flashed us to the gigantic bed in the master bedroom of the suite and magicked some champagne for us all.

"Not for me." I fluttered my eyelashes. "I might be in a delicate condition."

"Sweetheart, you've never been delicate." Tadgh poured champagne all over my breasts and started licking it off.

"I object! I'm Fae. Of course I'm delicate."

"Oh, you were at least a dress size bigger than the other girls tonight." Ell dipped his head and started licking my other breast. I stroked his head proudly.

"Not that it's a bad thing," Tadgh mumbled around a mouthful of nipple.

"Absolutely. I meant it as a compliment. Hey, Aura! I could design a new range of maternity wear! Want to model it for me?"

"Sure," I said, curving a leg around each of their waists. "Ell, you know you're going to have to have lots more sex with me, just to make sure."

"I know," he said. "You know, it's not that bad."

"Oh, cheers."

"I mean --"

"How about baby wear?" Tadgh interrupted, his hand sliding down to caress my pussy.

"Ooh!" Ell's eyes widened and he gave up licking. "A whole new line of children's wear!" He jumped out of bed, grabbed a sketchbook, and started drawing things.

Tadgh rolled his eyes at me, and poured champagne all over my stomach and thighs. Then he bent to lick it off, spending far more time than was strictly necessary, champagne-wise, on my clit. He stuck his tongue right in my pussy, and I saw stars.

"No champagne there," I managed, and he laughed against me, the vibrations making my eyes cross.

"Tastes pretty good to me though," he said, and then he started stroking my ass again. I guess he can't help it. Having spent so long sleeping with a gay man he's bound to be a little anal-fixated.

Not that I'm complaining. Hell, just the thought of that gigantic cock of his filling me up, stretching me out, made me pretty dizzy.

"Ell," I called hoarsely as Tadgh started sliding his fingers into my ass and his tongue into my pussy. "Come over here."

Ell glanced over and saw me writhing on the bed. "I don't think there's any room for me down there, sweetie."

Tadgh lifted his head. "There's plenty," he said with a wicked smile, and then he sat up against the headboard and spread his legs. His cock stood up proud, big and thick and dark and hard. I licked my lips. Then I licked his penis.

"Aura," he moaned, clutching my hair, and I swallowed him down. It took quite some effort, but I managed it. Tadgh thrust into my mouth once, twice, then he stopped and said, "No, I want to be in your ass."

"Isn't that usually my line?" said Ell, climbing onto the bed and fondling my pussy from behind. I was so proud of him right then that I nearly came. But instead I scrambled round so I was sitting between Tadgh's legs, my back to his chest. His cock pressed hotly against my back.

"I want both of you," I said, reaching down and spreading my pussy lips apart. "Ell, you're gonna have to go in the front way again."

He nodded manfully. "I think I'm getting the hang of it now."

"I'm so proud," I told Tadgh, "aren't you?"

"Proud and horny," he said, and I laughed, shaky with expectation.

I moved myself up and back until the head of his cock was resting between my buttocks. He'd already stretched me out and lubed me with his fingers, and the very tip of him slid in easily. I felt his size, thought about how good he was going to feel, and slid down onto him.

Tadgh groaned as I took him as far as I could. Not quite to the balls, because no one has that much room inside them. Ell reached down between us and stroked the root of Tadgh's cock where it didn't quite fit in. He stroked Tadgh's balls, and I watched, transfixed, his hand disappearing under my butt.

"Your turn now," I told him, and he looked up, swallowed, nodded, and knelt in front of me.

When Ell pushed his cock inside me, I thought I might faint with delight. I've always, always loved being taken this way. My body full of hot, pulsing male flesh. God, it's wonderful.

They started moving, gently at first, finding a rhythm. Ell moaned as his balls brushed against Tadgh's. I whimpered when Tadgh stroked my clit. And then again when Ell dipped his head and suckled one of my nipples.

"He's really getting the hang of this," I panted to Tadgh, who turned my head and kissed me. I reached down and grasped Ell's butt, pushing him deeper inside me, slipping my fingers between his buttocks and stroking his asshole.

He shivered, his whole body shuddering, his cock quivering inside me.

"Oh," I moaned, and then Ell started pounding into me, and I pushed him on, harder and deeper, using my own wetness to push my finger inside his ass. His head fell to my shoulder, his teeth biting into me, and as Tadgh picked up his pace and started thrusting harder, I felt myself starting to spin away into orgasm, bucking and screaming, on and on, over and over as they thrust so deep inside me they filled me up completely, coming too, the three of us at the same time.

It went on and on, fireworks and shooting stars, my body in ecstasy, and when I finally came back down to earth they were with me, holding me tight, my family.

My family.

* * *

A couple of months later, I sat sunning myself on the roof terrace of Ell and Tadgh's townhouse. Every Fae has green fingers, and the terrace was a riot of lush greenness, bright blooms and dense, glossy leaves. The early evening sun warmed my skin, the last of the Seelie influence before Ell started packing his bags to move to the Southern hemisphere.

I lazed like a big cat, fighting down the constant urge to smile, until I remembered I was alone and beamed at the foliage.

"You look pretty happy," came a warm voice from my left. My head snapped in that direction, and I saw a beautiful girl with golden tresses flowing to her knees. She was dressed in silky, diaphanous green that matched her eyes, and she regarded me with her head tilted to one side.

I felt the same energy from her I felt from Ell. "Niamh?"

She smiled, a gentle, pretty smile. "Yes, Aura of the Seelie."

I just -- just -- bit down a big smile at that. The Seelie Queen had welcomed me into her Court, given me a favored position at her table, and showered me with gifts. No doubt if I schlepped up and told her I wasn't going to have Ell's baby any more, she'd throw me to her hellhounds, but I didn't figure I was in much danger for the time being.

I eyed Niamh. Well, no danger from the Seelie Court, anyway.

Ell's sister arranged herself prettily on a stone bench. "Aren't you going to congratulate me on my marriage?"

"Congratulations. You nearly upset the balance of the seasons."

One delicate eyebrow arched. "Did I?"

I narrowed my eyes at her. "A Seelie princess marrying into the Unseelie? Are you mad?"

"No," she sighed. "I'm in love. You of all people should know it's got nothing to do with rationality."

"Me?"

"Yes. You're in love with a gay man. Well, he can't be that gay, since he's in love with you too."

I opened my mouth, then shut it again.

"You've pledged your child to the Seelie Court, haven't you?" Niamh said.

I nodded, warily. "It's Ell's child. The heir. The second in line," my stomach constricted, "now that you've defected."

She gave a slight smile. "I threw the whole Court into a tizzy, didn't I?"

"Little bit."

"Blood is blood, after all. If I had a child and Ell never did, well..."

"'Well' doesn't come into it," I said.

"No, I suppose not. But the problem has been resolved," Niamh said, looking right at me. "Seven -- what, seven and a half months? -- Mother will have her heir."

I crossed my arms protectively over my stomach. "How did you know?" Tadgh and Ell didn't even know yet. *I* only just knew.

She shrugged. "Fae."

"Uh, me too."

She grinned. "Fae *royalty*. That kid of yours is going to have some impressive powers." Her smile faded. "I came here to tell you something. I know about the problems of succession. And I didn't go to the Unseelie just to cause problems. I love Nihandrias. He loves me. We're like Rommel and Julius."

I thought quickly. "Romeo and Juliet?"

"Yes. Except without the bloody ending, hopefully. I've no wish to upset the balance of the seasons. Nihandrias and I agreed we would never have a child until after Ell did."

I blinked at her. "Even knowing Ell might never have a child?"

"Even knowing." Her fingers clutched the fabric of her dress. "There's something else, though. Eibhlis -- Unseelie princess --"

"I've heard of her," I said flatly.

"She seems to have some mad ambition to see the world ended. She's gone completely Angelus and Drusilla. I intend to speak to the Unseelie Queen about her."

"I thought someone already had."

Her lip curled. "A human? She's not going to do anything on the say-so of a *human*. Even a wizardly one. No." She sighed. "Eibhlis needs to be stopped. If the queen calls on you for testimonial, will you speak to her?"

I considered my newbie position within the Seelie Court. "Yes, but I want Ell or another high-ranking Seelie with me. Not you," I added. "Sorry."

She sighed again. "I understand. Well, goodbye, and congratulations."

She gave me a smile, and was gone.

About ten minutes after his sister had vanished, Ell popped onto the terrace. I guess Niamh used some sort of female intuition to discover I was pregnant, because Ell seemed to have no idea.

"Hello, darling." He kissed my cheek. "Good day?"

"I've read fourteen magazines. Apparently stripes will be in next season."

"Oh, rubbish, darling. *I'm* not doing them."

I smiled. Tadgh flashed onto the terrace, and with only a warm smile in my direction he had my insides melting. Maybe Niamh was right. Ell is a darling and I adore him, but he doesn't make my heart beat faster like Tadgh does.

"Hello, gorgeous." He slid onto the chaise beside me and kissed my mouth.

"Back atcha." I felt my smile bubbling to the surface again, and held out my hand to Ell. He took my place on the chaise and arranged me over his and Tadgh's laps. "Hmm, cozy."

"Sure is." Ell grinned down at me and stroked my stomach.

Then he paused.

"Aura?" he said, his voice trembling just a little.

"Hmm?"

"Are you --?"

I let my smile creep up another notch. Ell stopped breathing for a second, clutching me tight.

"Aura, are you?" Tadgh touched my leg, and I beamed at him.

"I am," I said, excitement swelling in me.

"Oh my God." Ell whooped suddenly, springing into the air -- and I mean right up into the air, magnificent pink and purple wings unfurling and swooping us around in a loop. I laughed, clutching him giddily. "Aura, Aura!"

He flew me back down to the chaise and kissed my face all over. My clothes vanished. Tadgh's dark green wings surrounded us both, and then he was kissing me, murmuring, "Congratulations. Oh, sweetheart..."

Ell threw his arms around Tadgh and they kissed, and I fluttered into the sky on my own crimson wings, swirling in giddy loops before zooming back down into their arms, laughing and purring with delight, warm and secure and happier than I've ever been.

Then a bright flash split the warm air, coldness flowed in, and before I could even lift my head, Ell swept me behind him and Tadgh reared on his hind legs -- *hind legs,* in centaur form. He was magnificent, huge and gleaming in the slanting sunlight, his wings even bigger than before.

A prickle of cold energy scratched my spine. Ell's eyes met mine. "Eibhlis," he said, "you'd better get off my roof terrace before I call in my mother's hounds."

I peeked around Tadgh's wings for a second before Ell tugged me back. What I saw was a mad creature with purple teeth and flaming red eyes snarling at Tadgh. She was naked and pale, her spiky wings beating the air.

"She's let herself go," I muttered to Ell, who gave me a quick smile before touching Tadgh's back between his wings, making them vanish. No longer protected, he stood beside Tadgh, in front of me, and raised his chin.

"I heard that!" Eibhlis shrilled.

"Well, it's true," Niamh's voice sounded, and then she flashed in.

I tried to magic up some clothes, but with all the royalty hanging around my magic had just fled. Even my wings had vanished. "What is this, a free show?" I grumbled, hiding behind Tadgh's glossy flank.

"You!" Eibhlis shrieked, pointing at Niamh. "Turncoat!"

"I've explained all this," Niamh said calmly. "I pledged my loyalty to the Unseelie Court and gave up all ties to the Seelie. But," she met her brother's eyes, "I've also pledged to birth no heir until my brother has secured his own line."

Ell stared at her, and then he gave a tiny nod. Niamh returned it.

"Well, you're mad!" Eibhlis cried.

"Hello, kettle? This is the pot. You're looking scruffy," I said, and she turned those mad red eyes on me.

"You! You -- you -- *sex faery*!"

"Yes?" I said with as much dignity as I could, standing there stark naked.

"Mother!" Eibhlis wailed, and Ell instantly wrapped his arms and his wings around me. Good job, because the arrival of the Unseelie Queen brought with it a swirl of freezing air that made the glossy plants wilt. Ell turned me so I was back behind him and Tadgh again. Protected. Safe.

My lovely boys.

The Unseelie Queen looked at the three of us in disdain, then at her daughter. "Eibhlis," she said, "once more you disappoint me. The Unseelie Niamh tells of your treachery. Again."

"Are you going to believe her over me?" Eibhlis stared at her mother in disbelief. "She's not even Unseelie!"

"She has pledged her loyalty, and proven it, too," the Unseelie Queen said. "Wildfae Aura," she began, and then paused. "No. You are Wildfae no more. Seelie Aura." I prickled with pride. "You bear a Seelie child."

"Yes." I beamed, peeking out between Tadgh and Ell, who was still holding me tight. "I do."

"No, it's all ruined," Eibhlis wailed.

"Do you testify that my daughter," she sneered the word, "has plotted against you?"

"No," I said, and Eibhlis's head snapped up. "But I do swear she tried to have Ell killed."

"Daughter," the queen said. "Is this true?"

Sulkily, Eibhlis nodded.

"Plotting to destroy the balance of the Courts," the Unseelie Queen said. She closed her eyes a moment, her lovely, terrible face pained. "Eibhlis, no longer of the Unseelie, I banish you from my Court, from the realm of Faerie, and strip you of your powers. Henceforth, you shall be mortal."

We all stared. Eibhlis let out a dreadful, keening cry. Thunder clapped.

Then they were gone.

Tadgh turned himself human again, and the three of us rubbed warmth back into each other. Niamh's quiet voice spoke up. "Congratulations, brother."

Ell paused, and looked over at where she stood. "Thank you. You'll understand if I don't ask you to be godmother?"

She gave a small smile. "I understand. Goodbye."

She vanished, and it was just the three of us. Ell rubbed my arms. Tadgh stroked my back. My hands were on his butt.

"Well," I said into the silence, "where were we?"

Epilogue

It's a boy. Or, actually, it's two boys. And a girl. I may have gone slightly overboard with the fertility spell.

Cat Marsters

Cat lives in a village in southeast England, which, while not quite a fairytale setting, is nonetheless very pretty and was mentioned in the Domesday Book of AD 1087. She shares a house with only slightly batty parents who hardly ever tell her to get a real job, and a musician brother who knows there's no chance she'll ever get one if he doesn't. Life is kept from being boring by the often hilarious antics of three geriatric cats and a dog who thinks she's Marilyn Monroe.

Cat has been writing all her life, but in order to keep herself rich in shoes and chocolate, she's also worked as an airline check-in agent, video rental clerk, stationery shop assistant, and laboratory technician. She's aiming for a fairytale cottage, and asks all potential Prince Charmings to apply in writing with pictures of themselves and their Aston Martins.

Visit's Cat's web site at www.catmarsters.com.

Changeling Press E-Books
Quality Erotic Adventures Designed For Today's Media

More Sci-Fi, Fantasy, Paranormal, and BDSM adventures available in E-Book format for immediate download at www.ChangelingPress.com -- Werewolves, Vampires, Dragons, Shapeshifters and more -- Erotic Tales from the edge of your imagination.

What are E-Books?

E-Books, or Electronic Books, are books designed to be read in digital format -- on your computer or PDA device.

What do I need to read an E-Book?

If you've got a computer and Internet access, you've got it already!

Your web browser, such as Internet Explorer or Netscape, will read any HTML E-Book. You can also read E-Books in Adobe Acrobat format and Microsoft Reader, either on your computer or on most PDAs. Visit our Web site to learn about other options.

What reviewers are saying about Changeling Press E-Books

Ann Vremont -- Wyvern Heat

"4 Stars! The love scenes are darkly erotic, deeply moving and completely beyond anything simply vanilla. Ms. Vremont takes you to the very psyche of characters and immerses you in decadent need and dark longing."

-- Keely Skillman, eCataRomance Sensual Reviews

Beverly Havlir -- Bandar: License to Pleasure

"5 Angels! With its strong characters, the intricate story and the sensational sexual encounters, you'll have difficulty putting this one down."

-- Trang, Fallen Angel Reviews

Dakota Cassidy -- Ex-Files 1: Mayhem and Maddie

"This very sexy story will have you laughing, frowning and most of all thinking. Well done, Dakota Cassidy."

-- Anita, Enchanted in Romance

Elisa Adams -- Immortal Games: Betrayal

"4.5 Blue Ribbons! Love scenes are romantic with an erotic edge that will have readers breathless. Elisa Adams knows how to weave a tale of darkness and light that readers won't soon forget."

-- Angel, Romance Junkies

Lexxie Couper -- Shifting Lust 1: The Chamelyon's Curse

"Shifting Lust 1: The Chamelyon's Curse will grab your attention, draw you in, and keep you hooked!"

-- Trang Black, Just Erotic Romance Reviews

Willa Okati -- Lust Magick

"Willa Okati spices things up and shines in her latest erotic M/M story... HOO-BOY, she writes some H-O-T stuff! Erotic imagery abounds, and her descriptions of all things sensual and sultry will have your pulse pounding and your mind whirling with possibilities and positions. Prepare to be entertained, transported and aroused by the mouth-watering men of Lust Magick."

-- Michelle, Fallen Angel Reviews

Reneé George -- Black Thunder

"Miss George draws you in and doesn't let go until the very end. Black Thunder is a story about love and honor, death and retribution, forgiveness and release. It's a story with a message most of us long for in everyday life... that in the end, love really does conquer all."

-- Diva Minx, Literary Nymphs

Michele Bardsley – Tucker's Paradise

"4 Angels! Tucker's Paradise is a charming book that will have the reader wanting more. The two romances -- Gil and Riley and Gilmore and Paradise -- are both heartwarming as each couple is unwilling to let society dictate who they will and will not love. While the physical side of each relationship is explosive, the deep emotional bond balances the relationship. I enjoyed that Ms. Bardsley took a very honest look at how some looked at and still look at interracial relationships."

-- Tewanda, Fallen Angel Reviews

Anisa Damien -- Scarlet Ties: Taste

"5 Angels, Recommended Read! Ms. Damien weaves a terrific story that will enchant the reader from the beginning."

-- Tewanda, Fallen Angel Reviews

www.ChangelingPress.com

Printed in the United States
77981LV00002BA/20

9 781595 964854